# FRANK'S WORLD

# FRANK'S WORLD

## George Mangels

St. Martin's Press × New York

*To YOU* . . .

This is a work of fiction. All the characters and events portrayed in this book are fictitious, and any resemblance to real people or events is purely coincidental.

FRANK'S WORLD. Copyright © 1995 by George Mangels. All rights reserved. Printed in the United States of America. No part of this book may be used or reproduced in any manner whatsoever without written permission except in the case of brief quotations embodied in critical articles or reviews. For information, address St. Martin's Press, 175 Fifth Avenue, New York, N.Y. 10010.

Design by Sara Stemen

Library of Congress Cataloging-in-Publication Data

Mangels, George.
    Frank's world : the odyssey of a fleshy lump / George Mangels.
        p.  cm.
    ISBN 0-312-11791-4
    I. Title.
PS3563.A4696F73      1995
813'.54—dc20                                    94-44487
                                                    CIP

First Edition: April 1995

10 9 8 7 6 5 4 3 2 1

contents

When Confucius was asked what would be the first thing he would do if he were to lead the state, he said "rectify the language" . . . as societies grow decadent, the language grows decadent. Words are used to disguise, not to illuminate, action: You liberate a city by destroying it. Words are used to confuse, so at election time people will solemnly vote against their own interests. Finally, words must be so twisted as to justify an empire that has now ceased to exist, much less make sense . . .

—Lewis Lapham, *Harper's Magazine*

*Everything that is expected of an ordinary weapon is expected from a silent weapon by its creators, but only in its own manner of functioning: it shoots situations instead of bullets; it is propelled by data processing instead of chemical reactions; it originates from bits of data instead of grains of gunpowder, from a computer instead of a gun; it is operated by a computer programmer instead of a marksman, under the orders of a banking magnate instead of a military general . . .*

—*Silent Weapons for Quiet Wars*

*Why are there people like Frank? . . .*

—*Jeffrey Beaumont,* Blue Velvet

# FRANK'S WORLD

# I.

*TIME would heal the wound that was Frank; the*
*world would continue to spin, to wobble, its axis only*
*slightly skewed, momentarily displaced, by the brief,*
*shuddering existence of one man—one THING—a*
*post-human mutant, a blurred Xerox copy of a*
*human being, the offspring of the waste of technology,*
*the bent shadow of a fallen angel; Frank was all of*
*these things . . . he was the sum of everything dark*
*and sticky, the congealment of all things wrong and*
*dark and foul in this world and every other seedy rat-*
*hole world in every back-alley universe throughout the*
*vast garbage dump of creation; God rolled the dice*
*and Frank lost . . . he was a spiritual flunkie, a univer-*
*sal pain-in-the-ass, a joy-riding, soul-sucking cosmic*
*punk rolling through time and space and piling up a*
*karmic debt of such immense magnitude so as to in-*
*variably glue the particular vehicle of the immediate*
*moment to the basement of possibility—planet*
*earth—and force Frank to RE-ENLIST, endlessly, to*
*return, over and over, to a flawed world somewhere*
*to spend the Warhol-film-loop nights of eternity serv-*
*ing concurrent life sentences roaming the dimly lit hall-*

*ways of always, stuck in the dense overshoes of physi-
cality, forever, until finally—one would hope there is
always a FINALLY—eventually, anyway—God would
step in and say ENOUGH ALREADY and grab Frank
by the collar of one of his thrift-shop polyester flower-
print shirts and hurl him out the back door of the cosmos, expelling the rotten orb into the great wide
nothingness and out of our lives—sure, that would be
nice—but so would a new Cadillac—quit dreaming—
it just doesn't work that way . . .*

*God knows that in some cases spiritual rehabili-
tation is not possible; God knows that ultimately there
can be no death penalty for matter: once created, a
Frank cannot be destroyed; God has no choice, really,
other than to give Frank and those like him Free Will
as he does all other beings here in the depraved playpen of the spiritual bowery; Frank had simply chosen
NOT to evolve, to move directly from death into a
new life without the usual between-life instructional
festivities; and so there was no waiting period between
lives, no period of reflection and evaluation, no period
of rest, no moment of respite, no eternal reward, no
otherworldly layover, no angelic conference with the
higher tribunal, no review by the council of three, no
stroll through the library of lives, no glance at the
master plan, no heavenly reunion with long-lost family
members . . . none of that shit; Frank's case file was
promptly dealt with upon the instant of death—and
he died so many times, so many ways: chained to a
tree and eaten by a tyrannosaur in Lemuria; vapo-
rized attempting to detonate a primitive nuclear de-
vice in Atlantis; hurled into a pit of snakes in Egypt;
stoned to death by his wife and children in Babylon;
thrown to the lions in Rome; catapulted into the Atlan-
tic Ocean in the Middle Ages; burned at the stake by
his own troops in the Crusades; personally drawn and
quartered by Attila the Hun; hurled out of a Vatican*

2

*window by the Pope himself; tied to a stake and used
as buffalo bait by the Navajo Indians; killed by his
own troops in the Civil War; brutally stabbed and
butchered by Florence Nightingale; run over intention-
ally by Henry Ford in the first car ever built; tied to a
hot-air balloon by the Wright Brothers and left to float
away—and his paperwork was expedited—calls were
made, exemptions granted, strings pulled—and he
was quickly processed—PUSHED, really—into a new
life, hurled directly from one pathetic existence
straight into another; God had, in effect, thrown in the
All-Encompassing Towel . . . and so, upon the occasion
of Frank's latest demise, God felt more than a bit
queasy when handed the papers verifying, officially,
that Frank was, once again, DEAD—shot in the face
by Himmler himself after one too many Hitler lingerie
jokes—and He lost it, really, and began ranting at His
angels in that booming, pissed-off Wrathful Deity
voice of His—"NO WAY, not THAT asshole again, I
WILL NOT have HIM coming back here soiling up my
clouds and fucking with the minds of my angels . . .
GET HIM out of here . . . get him out of my sight . . .
get that man a BODY . . . I don't want to see his ugly
face again for fifty years . . . I COMMAND you to
watch over this thug . . . I tell you I don't want to see
his face again for half a century or I swear I'll QUIT
and if you don't believe me then you just try it, you
just go ahead and TRY IT . . . you think I LIKE this
job? . . . you think I don't have BETTER things to
do?"—and the angels scampered and Frank was dispatched immediately to the first earthly vacancy . . .
to his parents—the LOSERS in this particular lot-
tery—who realized something was wrong—very
wrong—the moment Frank was born; their initial
pride wore off seconds after their son's grand and
lewd entrance: he came into this world looking like a
bookie and smelling like a stale, cheap cigar; his fa-*

ther swore on his last breath that Frank had whisky on his first; Frank didn't cry as he entered this world: he belched; Frank wasn't born: he escaped from somewhere else . . .

But what were they to do? . . . when a child is born, the parents are stuck with their love-bundle: they cannot RETURN it to Sears the way they return a BLENDER and complain that the fifth speed—PUREE—works more like they expected MASH to work, and that they are therefore dissatisfied with the product and would like to trade it in for one of those free-standing neo-Bauhaus lamps made of metal but with plastic washers that look sturdy but break precisely the fourth time one attempts to adjust the "adjustable" extend-o-arm: the washer CRACKS—can you believe that?—well, the engineer who designed that part was given a nice raise: you can believe THAT—planned obsolescence cannot be OBVIOUS: one must not TEST the stupidity of the sheep—merely EXPLOIT it—and that washer—a well-made time bomb, sitting there quietly, waiting to self-destruct—cracks—like a heart—precisely the fourth time it is stressed, and so the customer once again trudges down to the Family Store, where America Shops, to dutifully complain—they know exactly where to go after all these years, after all these PRODUCTS: they know the floor number; they know the room number; there is no waiting in line or looking bewildered or dazed or embarrassed for these people; the number-crunching clerks in RETURNS have become their FRIENDS, shallow friends, disposable friends, in the tradition of the land of paint-by-number friendships and planned obsolescence, but friends nevertheless—and their complaints of course go nowhere, or, more precisely, are redirected directly back at them—that is the PURPOSE of a RETURNS department—as the clerk points out defensively that, after all, it's YOUR fault . . . if YOU had spent the

4

*extra twenty-four dollars and gotten the EXTENDED
two-year four-color limited-edition one-time-only Faus-
tian-bargain black-hole small-print left-hand-path war-
ranty—if YOU hadn't been so CHEAP—then the
product in question, the extend-o-lamp, would have
been happily covered for another full year and you
could have shipped it back to Chicago, 60609, where
paperwork would sit collecting dust while cigarettes
were smoked, bets were placed, cards were dealt,
and, in certain departments, young clerks mounted
and cross-threaded by eager junior technicians from
the shipping and handling departments; eventually, a
marginally competent employee might actually perhaps come across the needlessly complex, soiled repair invoice—form J6X stroke 624 597 mark 3YW
substroke 4 stroke 9—and forward the expanding
pile of paperwork to PARTS, where the cycle would repeat at least twice before a new washer—cost: four
cents—would be wedged in and the lamp forwarded
to SHIPPING, where, after additional weeks of neglect
and abuse, it would be shipped, thrown fatalistically
into the hands of the Postal Surface and eventually,
hurled from a speeding postal truck onto the front
porch of YOU, the happy consumer, who, rather than
resenting this mail-order mauling, "understands these
things," having been anticipating an even longer delay,
having been conditioned to anticipate being
SCREWED OVER, equipped only to lash out in SELF-
DEFENSE, befuddled by KINDNESS, and you could
have removed the lamp from its box, plugged in,
juiced up, turned on, bombs away, and there you
WOULD HAVE gone, off on yet another year-long
odyssey of light-giving, adjustable service—no, one
cannot return CHILDREN—God does not give
RECEIPTS . . .*

*They certainly would have returned FRANK if
that had been possible—he was clearly defective—*

5

but, sadly, they took the unexpected arrival of this strange parcel of flesh as some sort of cosmic omen from God, their close personal friend, who was communicating to them in his typically subtle way—he really could be a jerk sometimes—and based on this leap of faith they elected to keep their child, their wonder, their sperm and egg, their Sturm und Drang, their time bomb, their monument to themselves, their mistake, their fruit, their vegetable, their fetus, their future thug, their worst nightmare, their unborn dreams—which would remain unborn—their vague memories of the future—their OWN planned obsolescence—their FRANK—yes, they would have returned him, had they known—but how could they?—and so they kept him—or, rather, HE kept THEM—and within days they realized what they had on their hands: a bad apple, a creep, a monster, a deviant super-tot, a defective waddling mutant; and the months went by and he grew and he learned and he ate and he took over their lives and he mushed their thoughts and he soiled their carpets and soon HE was calling the shots and THEY cowered and quivered . . . his guttural hoots and groans became LANGUAGE—his first words were "What's a horse to do?"—and the words became COMMANDS . . . and soon he was soiling their minds and fouling their souls, spinning abstract webs of mind-carving non-local anti-logic and hurling small, hostile hurricanes of thought into the air; he spent his days waddling about the house like a toy Schwartzkopf and his nights like a compact William Blake, hearing sounds that were not there, chained to an earthly prison with a tear rolling down his cheek; dinner, where he reigned like a Hitler Junior Action Figure, was a living portrait, a ghastly Munch, a rasping Goya: two screaming souls and the product of their misguided union; his parents crouched in fear, terror in their hearts, lumps in their throats, deathly

6

still, looking like furniture—he a frail chair crumbling under the weight of 300-pound squatting twins, she a frail vase held aloft by a raving madman—and their fears that he would suck the oxygen out of the night and replace it with psychic smog were eternal, immortal, and very real; the memories are NOW and make their throats tighten and cause doors to open and close inside their minds . . . , mother broke the lead-pipe silence in a twitching, tenative, air-raid soprano—she birthed this unholy whatever, after all—and the words staggered out, reluctantly, as if forced at gunpoint;

"Frank . . . would-would you like some ham . . . I-I-I . . . made it with b-bacon strips? . . ."

Frank looked at his mother—more precisely, he looked THROUGH her—he looked behind her mind and inside her soul, in the basement of her dreams, in the closet of her desires, in the trunk of her memories, and he rummaged around, picked out a particularly bad one out and brought it back out with him into reality—and, reaching up with his coarse, cigar-shaped fingers, gently, and yet with a suggestion of etheric violence, a hint of violence not yet committed—a seep of mayhem leaking in from the future—he moved his hands through her metallic silver-gray Barbara Billingsley hair with a gently shaking motion, like an engine idling; he rumbled; he eyed her as a cat would a trapped bird—with a curious, unnatural alliance of love, curiosity, and twisted, demonic lust: an onlooker might have thought that he wanted to EAT his mother—perhaps he did—and he spoke:

". . . WHAT IF THERE IS NO LOVE? WHAT IF EVEN THAT IS AN ILLUSION? WHAT IF IT ONLY RAINS? WHO THEN WILL TEND TO THE CROPS OF OUR SOULS? WHAT IF ENNUI IS NOT ENOUGH? WHAT EXISTS BEYOND BOREDOM? WHO ARE WE TO SAY THAT THE EYEBALL OF A

7

SPARROW IS NOT FIT TO WEAR AS A NECKLACE?
CAN FINE LACE BE SMOKED? CAN A SALMON
SKIN BE SPREAD OVER A TABLE IN A DECORATIVE
MANNER? WHY DO I SWEAT? WILL GOD STOP AT
A RED LIGHT? DOES GOD SWEAT? . . .

Mother's and father's overloaded nervous systems simply were not engineered to deal with such a
torrent of preschool postgraduate thought; nerve endings collapsed and fused; synapses broke rank and
dove for cover; father spoke:

"Ya bastard runt . . . ya talk like a MANIAC . . .
SHADDUP! . . . what are ya, crazy! . . . SHADD-
UP! . . ."

Frank didn't think highly of his father; his father
usually paid dearly for such outbursts; father adjusted
his tone and continued . . .

". . . Well, well, well . . ."—father paused, composed himself, and took a reflective suck on his pipe,
pondering the strange questions that young Frank had
posed while at the same time trying to inhale enough
carcinogens to cause himself to keel over and drop
dead instantly, legs and arms sticking straight up like
a cartoon dog; at least that way he wouldn't have to
play this stupid GAME anymore, wouldn't have to deal
with this monstrous LIFE—". . . and I bet the fish are
biting at the big lake this weekend, yessir, I bet they
are, big fat trout with silver streaks and tails a
flappin' . . . I can almost see 'em . . . I really can . . .
yessir, I sure do love weekends, yes I do . . . a man
works hard all week at a job he is proud to have, he
earns his pay to support his family, which he loves
more than anything in this world, he enjoys himself
with a beer or two on his day of rest . . . and he does
not concern himself with the ALMIGHTY SWEAT
GLANDS . . . pass the butter, son . . ."

Frank's eyes probed the table like a drunken
gargoyle: he found his father's frightened orbs the way

8

light finds dark and he absorbed them completely; he sucked the light from his father's eyes until they became his own . . . he spoke:

"... DOES BUTTER HAVE CONSCIOUSNESS? DOES BUTTER FEEL? DOES A COW KNOW THAT IT BIRTHS BUTTER AND THAT ITS SACRED JUICES WILL BE SPREAD UPON SLICES OF SCORCHED, COMPRESSED GRAIN? WHAT SENSATIONS DOES THE TOAST EXPERIENCE? IS IT A SEXUAL EXPERIENCE FOR THE TWO SUBSTANCES? IS THE BUTTER DEAD? . . ."

Silence—well, near silence—enveloped the room; the butter gurgled, attempting to answer; father smiled bravely and started speaking in a strange low voice, apparently hoping to somehow resume control of the situation by making his voice deeper; too bad it doesn't work that way; the words emerged in a low rumble and immediately scattered:

"... A man works, a man plays, a man eats, a man sleeps . . . a man looks after his family . . . a man's family does not discuss the metaphysical life of butter . . ."—father was staring into space; his forehead was crinkled, inverted almost; it was as if his pineal gland was digging in, trying to hide itself . . .

"... A MAN DIES, A MAN ROTS . . . A MAN'S BODY IS SUCKED INTO UNDERGROUND TUNNELS BENEATH THE SEWERS UNDER THE MANHOLE AT THE SHOPPING MALL . . . A MAN IS SLICED AND DICED AND CURED AND DROOLED UPON BY THE UNDEAD LIZARD PEOPLE . . . THE LIZARD PEOPLE DO THEIR UNHOLY DANCE IN UNDERGROUND CAVERNS COUNTING THE EONS SINCE THEY'VE BEEN TRAPPED BENEATH THEIR VANQUISHED AND NOW ROTTING WORLD, COUNTING THE MOMENTS UNTIL THEY STORM THE SURFACE IN SILK LACE STOCKINGS AND TRAINING BRAS SMOKING CIGARS TO RETAKE WITH RIDICU-

9

LOUS EASE THE PLANET EARTH FROM THE BAS-
TARD HUMANOIDS, THEIR OWN DECAYING CHIL-
DREN FROM A MILLION YEARS PAST WHOSE DNA
HAS GONE STALE AND BAD AND IS NOW SPIRAL-
ING DOWN INTO THE FUTURE . . . A MAN BE-
COMES BUTTER . . ."

The fluid Goya froze and hung there like a slab
of meat on a hook: the family had been sucker-
punched by Frank's LIZARD STORY, a sort of hellish
world creation anti-fable he had been composing, an
oral myth of reptilian proportions, updated daily and
embellished shamelessly, a psychic beastiality bondage
hardware assault weapon that he wielded like an astral chainsaw . . . no one ate butter on that particular
evening; no one spoke; only Frank moved, his little
mouth slowly twisting and working pieces of gener-
ously chewed ham back and forth, as if attempting to
massage them back to life: his eyes moved from face
to blank face; his vision bored into the souls of his
parents, who were virtually paralyzed with dripping
forks frozen in place; he slipped right down through
their eyeballs and lurked momentarily in the waiting
room outside the pineal gland, loitering like a depraved unshaven janitor leaning on his mop handle
and smoking with relish a foul, tainted cigarette, the
sick smell of sweet cheap whisky soiling the air as he
exhales in a raspy blast of oily smoke; Frank had yet
to become Frank Booth, film creep or he just might
have said: ". . . Don't YOU LOOK AT ME . . . DON'T
YOU FUCKIN' LOOK AT ME . . ."

10

## 2.

# the forest of no return

Frank spent most of his childhood in front of the TV,
ignoring his parents almost from birth: initially fascinated by their grotesque features and bizarrely predictable habits, he soon found them irritating and
boring and instead focused upon their captor, their religion, their shrink, their visionary, their leader, their
guru . . . their ZENITH; he longed to squat and learn
at the four feet of the great master, to absorb the secrets of the all-knowing glowing one, to be initiated
into the secret mysteries of electric soul-gobbling, and
so he spent his toddling years squatting in front of the
box, inches away, sucking up images and bathing in
the warm pink radioactive glow—it was the closest
thing to LOVE he knew or wanted to know: one-way,
unconditional, undemanding, a mechanical, techno-
substitute for the love of God—who may or may not
have existed, anyway—and he just sat there, ignoring
humanity as he ignored his own bodily functions; he
defecated whimsically, he pissed triumphantly, he
scratched, he belched, he croaked, he drooled, free
from any self-conscious delusions about the noises and
waste of his body-machine-vehicle; he just sat there,

sucking up the answers to questions he didn't ask, sucking up worlds, sucking up the soul of all and everything—and shitting it all back out again . . .

Television dominated his thoughts as it dominated his life and his culture; it was at once a friend, a teacher, a mentor, a companion, a prison guard, a warden, a public defender, a judge, a jury, a bailiff—relationships are complicated—a sibling, a poet, and a traveling salesman . . . it was more than just a box in the living room; it was a member of the family, a household pet: he petted and groomed his box-friend; he twirled the sensual plastic knobs; he rubbed the natural grain wood finish; he painstakingly adjusted the whirling colors; he fondled the antenna; he stuck a fork in the wall outlet and felt the electric current jolt through his body, tasting the very blood that flowed through the veins of the great machine; he knew its flaws, he knew its quirks; he knew its vertical, he knew its horizontal . . . and IT knew HIM . . . the television was another BEING, really, and he stared at the creature day and night, absorbing the supra-real glowing worlds, the trans-real matrix, without pausing to consider whether what he was watching was REAL or not, not caring, really, passively soaking up knowledge, allegory, illusion, and advertising—the four horsemen of television—until his eyes became red and swollen, nearly popping out of his head, and his mind oscillated at precisely sixty hertz and swam with repeating visions of Cadillacs, cigarettes, and sexy women . . . the box was more than an appliance, more than just a collection of tubes and wires and resistors and capacitors: it wielded power and majesty; it was ALIVE, with a consciousness, a soul, a mind, a WILL; it ACTED, we REACTED: it cried, we cried; it killed, we killed; it loved, we loved; it smoked, we smoked . . . we laughed, we chortled, we loved, we danced, we jazzercised, we shopped, we drugged ourselves silly, we voted, we allowed ourselves to be brainwashed into accepting mindless game shows and boring lives, we plugged our arteries with doughy processed food substitutes, we fried our brains with sugar and caffeine, we mistrusted anyone different from the implanted archetypal box-gods, we based our lives and dreams on the advice and examples of two-dimensional fictional images, we filled the empty spaces in our hearts with cheese puffs and dip, we stepped on our fellow humans, we consumed, we obeyed, we reproduced madly like flies, we swallowed lies like candy . . . we did all these things; we did what the box TOLD US to do, no questions asked— that was part of the magic of the relationship; no questions COULD be asked; no questions were RE- QUIRED; one could not and did not have to respond to the television; one could not and did not have to question the wisdom of something that was NOT RE- ALLY THERE; one could not and did not have to ques- tion the motives of an APPLIANCE; one could not and did not have to question television just as one could not and did not have to question GOD . . . oh yeah . . . He made the birds . . . SO WHAT? . . . TV told us where the birds live and what their mating patterns were and what color their wings were when they flew south in mid-March awaiting the spring sol- stice to lay their powder blue eggs in the cracks be- tween certain rock formations which heat to a comforting and steady seventy-three degrees during the nine-week gestation period while the mother leaves the nest on alternate Tuesdays at nine-thirty to fly six-foot circles around a moldy cereal box with a decaying picture of Joe Montana's arm and one third of his million-dollar smile saying EAT ME, a box stolen from Idi Amin's private garbage dump by the domi- nant bird-king and dropped here in the desert and buried in the sand a quarter of a mile from the pa-

*tiently waiting egg, and she flies round and round in a ritual dance presenting her ceremonial offering to the great ghost-bird of the Kalahari, the great winged-god leader-spirit that had deposited this magic box here in the middle of a sensible bird's worst nightmare . . . TV EXPLAINED things; God left us to think most of life out for ourselves, and guys like Kant and Nietzsche thought and thought until their ears bled and their eyes popped out and their brains started oozing out of their noses; God left us a legacy of questions and no answers . . . TV provided ANSWERS—many of them WRONG, of course, made up by some rat-faced fact-bending idiot with a bow tie cramped into a folding chair in a studio office somewhere, staring at his potted plant and dreaming about his lunch of irradiated Kraft Macaroni and Cheese, picturing the little cheese things bubbling away seductively in the microwavable foil compartment with the peel-back cover, providing wrong answers for the Western world—but that was somehow beside the point—that was the beauty of it—because all that mattered was that they were ANSWERS, answers from HIS small world, which is smaller than the world of anyone who has a LIFE—he doesn't—certainly no bigger than each of our worlds—more likely smaller, weirder—but they become OUR answers, answers that God could not or would not give us, answers radiating through space, amber waves of situation comedy rippling outward in every direction, three-camera universes weaving through the etheric electromagnetic mind-web of the great god TELEVISION and into boxes around the world, leaking out of the many lips of the One Great Mouth and into the eyes and ears and minds and hearts and souls of the viewers at home, where not enough of it is properly digested and shitted out, where too much of it STICKS . . .*

*Frank watched anything, everything, anytime, all*

the time; he watched at all hours, all channels; when his parents were out he would stack the family's four sets on top of each other, sometimes facing screens upside down or sideways . . . it didn't really matter HOW he arranged them: it was context and contra- diction that amused him as seemingly incompatible worlds seeped out, side by side, and collided, some ex- isting vertically, others horizontally, all sharing the time and space between his ears: war footage—exploding napalm-doused villages, children screaming in terror— general splattering—spilled out of Vietnam and rubbed up against the telepathy-coated and trans- dimensionally remolecularized world of *My Favorite Martian,* a next-door kind of place where a grizzled alien lived rent free and manipulated reality and thought with his extendable frontal-lobe antennae; two quick flips of the dial and reason, order, and social programming oozed from the groomed plastic world of *Leave It To Beaver,* a black-and-white place where any vague attempts at original thought by young Theodore were promptly squelched by big bad Ward's incessant conformist rhetoric and dogmatic lectures and replaced with the accepted socio-generic corporate-matrix belief system, and this world slammed violently into the concrete wall of abstract symbolism and apocalyptic horse sense that radiated from the brilliant neo-Blakean utopia of *Mister Ed,* the talking, rapping horse . . . how would WARD have explained Mister Ed to the little wide-eyed Beaver and his "big brother," the embryonic corporate pig Wally? how would Ward have explained genital herpes, for that matter? or Ornette Coleman? or the Village Peo- ple? or Kennedy's missing brain? or VIETNAM? . . . Frank didn't trust this being, this GOD of hardware and electricity—just as he didn't trust WARD—and yet he was hooked, fascinated, riveted, reeled in, im- prisoned, entrained, derailed: he kept one eye perma-

nently fixed on this know-it-all, this busybody, this tat-
tletale, this babbling one-eyed owl, sucking up wrong
answers and parallel worlds with the obsessive, insa-
tiable enthusiasm of a twisted prodigy . . . initially, television made no SENSE to Frank, appearing before
him as living collages of random images that bounced
about before his blank, raw mind; his first, instinctive
response was fundamentally correct—they WERE just
random images—and should have been properly catalogued and filed before the paper pushers over in reason wedged their heads into the picture and
misinterpreted and distorted the raw data with their
madness and downwardly spiraling DNA nightmare-
from-the-id self-important ego-puffing; and so he kept
watching, learning to vibrate in harmony with the radiating electric waves and sensing—incorrectly—a primal, surrational importance in the dance of images
that tripped out of the box and flooded the empty
pages of his thoughts . . . soon his brain adapted fully
to the new environment and the images became
MORE than images; soon they were REAL; soon they
were friends, strange friends, weird friends, appearing
day after day, hour after hour, leading their lives in
front of him, FOR him, molding him, shaping him,
BEING him; eventually, the TWO became ONE: the
small rectangular void from which all beings two-
dimensional arrived and the small vehicle with yellowed diapers that was FRANK . . .

Some images were more formative than others—some were merely spaces between the AN-
SWERS, lifeless particles between the little wedges of
supra-reality that slipped through the cracks between
the bubbles of color and worked their way deep into
Frank's mind, beneath the thoughts, into the master
control room, into the house of levers and knobs,
where the volume could be turned down or up, where
the color could be adjusted, where dreams simmered,

*where death waited patiently in the outer office read-
ing* Life *magazine, where life PIVOTED, where memory and thought blurred, where serial killers and saints
were created and launched out into the plastic semi-
real world—some of these images STUCK, others
didn't . . .* Mister Ed *was an early formative influence: who could not be moved by a talking horse that
dated Mae West? who could not be moved by a
thinking horse that threw existential tantrums and
made long distance phone calls, a horse with taste
that donned sunglasses at night and played the bon-
gos with his tail while shouting "GO, DADDY-O, GO!"?
who would not prefer the company of such a glamor-
ous, worldly creature—two dimensions or three . . .
did it matter?—to the company of a woman who
dressed like a color-blind mute, who fluffed her
freeze-dried hair incessantly, who smelled like a discount perfume factory, who had eyes the color of
poached eggs and the charisma of an aging, malfunctioning Hoover vacuum cleaner, his mother? who
among us would not have chosen to follow the PY-
THAGORAS of horses, a wizened, grizzled, shamanis-
tic, artistic, sensitive, neo-romantic retro-bohemian
pothead hermetic philosopher, a sophisticated, downtown horse with a great jazz record collection and
true fashion INTEGRITY, rather than fill the small
shoes of a man who lived only to work and worked
only to survive, a man so dimwittedly single-pointed as
to be defined by nothing more than his mere existence as a low-level office cog and by his dimly lit,
fading dreams of staggering into a Holiday Inn lobby
on some nameless broken-down blurry Sunday and
spotting either ill-tempered golf hack Hale Irwin or
nattering phlegmobile Keith Jackson, disconnected 40-
watt sports announcer, reduced to venting the freeze-
dried corners of his seedy imagination into the dusty
polyester world of professional bowling, the last stop*

*before death, where balls roll, pins fall, and no one*
*cares, where the excitement never ceases because it*
*never BEGINS, his father, the sum of whose vague*
*ambitions consisted of working until he fell over on his*
*broom handle and perhaps experiencing a chance*
*meeting with one of two truly sorry slices of vegetative*
*celebrity half-life that existed only in a false imagined*
*semi-reality through the benevolence of the great god*
*TV—these were the HOPES that filled the void in his*
*life like the imitation fruit-substitute filler that cements*
*the empty spaces of a Hostess Fruit Pie; these were*
*his sad, sad DREAMS—it was an easy choice for*
*Frank: Mister Ed in a landslide . . .*

*While people like Ed—TV entities are PEOPLE,*
*really, points of consciousness that exist and influence*
*thought and hence MATTER, as real or unreal as any*
*human that waddles about in a semi-functional vehicle*
*of flaccid flesh; Mister Ed is as real as Richard Nixon,*
*for example, except that Ed—as defined by the fringe*
*thoughts and composite personalities of a panel of six*
*semi-funny chain-smoking Milton Berle wannabes that*
*meet twice a week to debate what IS and what IS*
*NOT funny in this world and stuff that creature, that*
*essence, that sum of funniness, into the two-*
*dimensional vehicle that is Mister Ed, the vehicle that*
*transcends three dimensions and sails beyond space,*
*existing and living forever, teaching through millions of*
*box-lips at once, transcending time, living the hipster-*
*sunglasses-at-night horse good life throughout time,*
*throughout space, roaming the eternity that is syndica-*
*tion, a transdimensional consciousness wedging its way*
*outwards through the spaces between worlds and into*
*eternity . . . hell, Mister Ed is ALWAYS and EVERY-*
*WHERE: his molecules of hay and hair and shit and*
*his Billie Holiday records and his phone bills and his*
*neo-expressionist masterpieces are beamed through-*
*out the galaxy, riding the waves of sound and light,*

riding the smelly wind, enveloping the Crab Nebula, parting the foul skies of Orion, riding the crystalline winds of Sirius, sailing past Alpha Centauri and around the North Star and enveloping every red giant and descending every black hole and coming out the other end of every dimension, smelling the cracks between dimensions, crashing every hipster party on every world and anti-world, seeping into every breath of every living thing, puddling between the sheets of every bed in the universe . . . so goes Mister Ed: surfing the waves of time, shouting for all eternity to hear: "GO DADDY-O, GO!"—except that Ed is much funnier than Richard Nixon . . .

One of the great tragedies of Frank's early life was the sad decline and fall of Mister Ed—proud, hip, all-knowing, all-seeing—who, despite his brilliance, never made it past his half-hour stereotyped sitcom hell: he was forced to carry—in every sense—Wilbur and Carol, a couple of pathetic washed-up comedic losers, for years; Ed truly carried the whole cast, including writers—whom he rescued more than once with his subtle shadings of delivery and cosmic nuances—and wasted his prime years propping up stupid humans who actually believed that THEY were more than stiff comedic props for the great ED, when the only thing FUNNY about them was their sad little lives, their twisted ambitions, their sick, perverted dreams, their very EXISTENCE; Ed knew that the washed-up comedian who played Wilbur thought it was HIS show because the producers HUMORED him and told him that . . . but was it called *Mister WIL-BUR?*; Ed knew that this Wilbur creature WAS funny, but not because his JOKES were funny, but rather because the IDEA of a man playing a pathetic comedic foil to a HORSE was funny—or at least Ed thought so as he tumbled through space—and Frank agreed, sitting on earth, sucking it all up and picking his ass . . .

**19**

sadly, Ed never shook the ball and chain that was Wilbur; he died and went to rerun heaven, doomed to repeat the same lines throughout eternity, unlike his confidante and drinking buddy, Francis the Talking Mule, who started the whole talking, thinking existentialist equine film movement: Francis was no intellectual match for the great ED—Ed had a grasp of the arts and an intuitive understanding of the fundamental futility of life that was beyond Francis—but Francis was FIRST, and, more importantly, Francis made FILMS: he did the big-screen dance, looming larger than life above small children; a fifty-foot mule in a three-foot world, he walked the walk, talked the talk, went for the fuckin' joyride that was Hollywood in all its slippery, fungal glory; Francis was the STAR that Ed should have been, and it sickened Frank to think of what Ed COULD have been if only he had dumped Wilbur and made that first FILM . . . television wedged itself between the cracks and tickled the soul, but the Big Screen was like an electroshock cattle prod hammered down the earthquake faults of human identity which ripple and shudder at magnitude ten and slip and slide and pulverize and resettle into new and rarely improved and NEVER stable identities and wait for the next inevitable twitch and shudder that will send reality sprawling once again like pieces of ice flying around a high-speed blender and create a new and even more unstable formation and reinforce the creeping paranoia that has flooded the dazed soul that WAS you but has become something else, something different: THAT was what FILM could do . . .

Frank first sensed the power of film upon viewing his first and hence most formative film: at the tender in most cases but in his case hardened and greased age of five, he slipped in the side door of a crumbling downtown art-deco theater and wedged

*himself into an imitation red velvet seat that was*
*twice his size and creaked in defiance as he slowly,*
*methodically rocked back and forth and sucked on the*
*stale butt of a half-spent Old Gold Filter that he had*
*found on the floor, the sticky world that is the theater*
*floor, the sticky reality beneath the screen where*
*dreams are created and shattered; he sat there with*
*big eyes and tobacco-stained lips and watched MAGIC*
*unfold before him, larger than life, larger than televi-*
*sion: he watched* Babes in Toyland, *one of those Ca-*
*praesque Reaganesque Hitleresque grotesque*
*right-wing flying-carpet whirling-dervish CIA think-tank*
*mind-control reality-frying sticky-sweet baby-food ap-*
*plesauce sugar-and-spice whips-and-chains come-here-*
*little-girl robotic Hoover Institute Langley computer-*
*generated hologram disinformation-type films, a Walt*
*Disney JOINT: Frank would come to see Walt, Uncle*
*Walt, for what he REALLY was—or at least what*
*Frank perceived him to be, as only Frank, alone in the*
*solitary world inferred and defined by his misinterpre-*
*tation of the data fed to him by his senses, COULD*
*perceive him to be—the way his collected impressions*
*of Walt fit into the empty spaces, the floor plan, the*
*under-the-floor plan, of his world, Frank's world—*
*which was the only world he knew—what else could*
*he know?—and which, unfortunately, was a world, a*
*very real place, where others might without choice or*
*notice become drawn into and pinned and trapped on*
*occasion the way a passenger can be trapped in a*
*bright yellow taxicab driven by a homicidal, tweaking*
*low life with cold black eyes, a swirling tornado frag-*
*ment of a brain stem wired on speed, bad rock 'n'*
*roll, and endless uncaring asphalt: Frank came to see*
*Uncle Walt as a master—an unwitting master, per-*
*haps, but that was really beside the point—of propa-*
*ganda, a tool of the unseen hand in the velvet glove;*
*Walt was a sly dog with an evil eye and a wagging*

tail: he never said what he meant, he never meant what he said; he said what your dreams wanted to hear, and what he really meant was layered deep below the surface, wrapped in barbed wire, laced in a not-quite-there montage of myth, symbol, ritual, and good old American pinko Nazi Fourth Reich spin-control brainwashing; Uncle Walt was a smiling mo-therfucker handing out psychic candy bars laced with illusion to the Babes in Toyland . . . Walt, like Capra and Hitler before him, manipulated mobs with illusion, and he duplicated the collective illusion that is Amer-ica in theme-park form and accessorized the place with subtle references to nonexistent rewards offered to little people who make big sacrifices in their small worlds with their small houses and large mortgages and small children and big dreams and small cars; Walt prayed on their laziness, on their SMALLNESS, on their HUMANITY, sucking the humanity right out of them, spray painting their illusions blue and pink and parading these two-legged cattle around The Happiest Place in the World, a trashed orange grove in the heart of the smog belt, Disneyland, the pre-approved funnel for their all-American dreams; Walt prepared them for a life of decaying hopes, factory to-morrows, and a utopian, mythic future that would never arrive . . . Walt PRIMED the PUMP . . .

As interpreted by Frank's twisted one-eyed one-way wrong-way tunnel vision—the sensory labyrinth that filtered information into Frank's World—*Babes* was a fascistic, Faustian black comedy social manipu-lation training tool in which gypsy kids (DREAMS) ran away from their families (TRADITION) only to find they had taken an existential wrong turn into The For-est Of No Return where they were molested by a bunch of surly, thuggish trees (NATURE) before finally escaping and finding the paradise lost that is Toyland (CAPITALISM) where after hours of (NON-UNION) factory labor they find themselves with all the (WOODEN) toys that they can possibly consume, dismembered trees ritually refigured into playthings to feed the neurotic fantasies of the modern, disconnected youth; the materialist steamroller triumphs again, and the spiritual world, eternal and unseen, is once again trampled; nature is properly mauled, and, in the face of this insanity, driven to violence, which triggers more tree mauling and feeds industry growth, leading to more toymakers and more toys, which are consumed as candy, fueling the addictive cycle to repeat again; lather-rinse-repeat (APOCALYPSE) . . . *Babes* was a film about CAPITALISM and the orgasmic satisfaction of demented, unlimited consumption, it was a training film for the nation that would develop the largest drug habit in the history of Western civilization: the Babes in Toyland matured into the Babes in Cokeland, and as they sucked up episodic two-dimensional illusory reality and priced juicers, mobile phones, and half grams, their Constitution was discreetly abridged and their rights severely muffled by smiling motherfuckers in black suits with frontal-lobe implants and large prisons started dotting the landscape; while they were playing with their toys the DREAM was sucked dry by the long sticky tentacles of the invisible hand . . . Frank emerged from *Babes* into a different world: colors were WETTER; sounds were OILIER: Frank looked around him at the shopping centers and the toy stores and the Sears auto repair shops and the endless main-street movie houses and the lingerie display mannequins and the tie racks and the donut shops and the blockhead architecture and the six-foot plastic neon french fries; he looked about him at The Forest Of No Return and realized the trees had been RIGHT: we had stumbled in, we had bumbled in . . . NOW WE CAN'T GET OUT . . .

Frank loved the trees: he loved their knots, their scabs, their hideously disfigured trunks and limbs; these trees were not just NATURE, but nature MAULED and MUGGED; these were not trees that one HUGGED; these were trees that dressed in black leather and smoked non-filter cigarettes and put the butts out on their trunks and had Harley tattoos and sold drugs to teenage girls with short skirts and festering hearts; these trees were not majestic redwoods, stately miniature cherry trees, or merry fucking Christmas pine trees: these were twisted, gnarled OAKS, mutant oaks with ATTITUDES . . . The Forest Of No Return was Hiroshima; the trees were the Undead . . . Frank there after BECAME an undead tree from The Forest Of No Return: he would stand in the yard, always on the same spot, precisely three feet from the rusting mailbox near the corner of the decaying picket fence which enveloped the lawn that contained a world of small bugs with foul thoughts and small diseases and bordered the gently sloping asphalt of the one-car, one-life driveway, always striking the same lurid pose, one leg awkwardly stretched out behind him, mimicking the disfigured majesty of a mangled tree limb, bent in a twisted, gnarled curl, arms frozen in mid-flail, poised in a state of suspended, animated attack; his face always appeared shriveled, his gaze thoughfully demented, as if he was preparing prophetically, to vomit; people passed by the house and WONDERED about young Frank: they wondered about Frank as they wondered about old men who came out of their houses only to buy quarts of Early Times; as they wondered about women who wandered onto the interstate at night singing blissfully; as they wondered about dogs with cloudy eyes that attempted to air-fuck small children; as they wondered about small children that stuck their index fingers up their mysterious butts in the bathtub and removed small, smelly turds, which they sniffed . . . Frank reigned for hours at a time in this cigarette-smoking, thuggish tree pose, looking out through the vehicle of his flesh with wild eyes and haunting the people that passed in pale silence and pretended not to look back: no one invited Frank to have a nice day; no one commented on the weather; no one inquired about Frank's health; no one asked about school or apples or apple pie or trees or mom or Mother Mary or hell or Hell's Angels or Satan or Kenneth Anger or Walther P-38s . . . they just WALKED: briskly, stiffly, eyes locked ahead, avoiding the present, frozen somewhere off in the distant anywhere future, auras reeled in tightly in protective, defensive stances of glazed fear, walls of disdain protecting them—they hoped—from the influence of Frank's twisted psychic hurricane; sometimes they walked, sometimes they ran; sometimes they sprinted; sometimes they stumbled and crawled on bloodied knees; cars sped up; children on bikes pumped their legs furiously to increase speed . . . Frank didn't care: he knew it didn't matter; he knew that nothing could protect them from the rippling wave of his being; to be exposed was to be fouled; Frank knew that we do not live in a multiple-choice universe: Frank knew that one could NOT choose NOT to participate in the apocalypse; Frank knew that in real life, one could not CHANGE CHANNELS . . . and so, for several years he roamed The Forest Of No Return that grew invisibly in the yard, scaring people, and no matter how many times they crossed his path, he remained a truly frightening experience, standing in the small yard next to the rusting mailbox grinning like a stiff, sculpted corpse, looking like a sick monument to some rotting piece of prized roadkill . . .

As he grew older, Frank developed—cultivated, rather, the way one might cultivate a garden of poisonous herbs—a special hobby: ruining people's days,

*if not their lives; as he grew older and started to com-
prehend the depth of the potential intensity of human
interaction, the potential for the exchange of emotion
and feeling, he grew to understand how wide open
and vulnerable the human heart was, how a few
crafted, chiseled words could simultaneously puree
and mash a heart with a sterility and precision un-
matched by any scalpel; he cultivated this skill with
the obsessive passion of a defective, thuggish Mozart;
he knew that the damage inflicted by WORDS did
not heal easily; a well-placed wordwound remained
twisting and thrusting for years upon sad years; the
process of healing was not natural, automatic; if one
did not confront the creature wrapped around one's
soul while sitting stiffly on a couch Tuesdays at eleven
for years at a cost of thousands of dollars in a most-
likely doomed effort to heal the wordwound, then one
would bleed continually, massively, all over the carpet
of life for one or a thousand lifetimes, until the soul
became weary and withered and found a way to put
itself out of its misery . . . Frank's earliest targets were
the unfortunate residents of the neighborhood; one
day, one moment, he cornered and hemmed in young
Lizzie Goose-Hall, a neighbor, who happened to be
passing by—and that moment will never be forgotten:
it is etched on the inside of her eyelids in wide-screen
high-resolution technicolor glory, gleaming like a
Costco discount emporium warehouse bathed in a
dazzling spotlight, surrounded by hundreds of uncoor-
dinated dancing girls from the great state of Iowa
where the corn grows tall and the cattle fat and the
wind blows free and so does the dust, unburdened by
nutrients due to overplanting, dancing girls high-kicking
to Beethoven's Ninth—it was one of those moments
that transform a lifetime—an INTERSECTION, a
shared moment, a fragmentary moment—a karmic
sucker-punch for little LIzzie, whose family had the*

*grave misfortune of living three doors down from*
*Frank, three small well-maintained all-American happy*
*lawns away from the boogie man of their entire his-*
*torical gene pool's collective memory, three doors*
*down from the evil and fear and horror that over-*
*whelms the majestic, illusory, fucked, total beauty of*
*Lizzie's home planet, the green brown and blue play-*
*pen known as earth; for Lizzie it was the last moment*
*of the first day of the rest of her sad life, and with a*
*pure mind and a quiet heart she moved out into the*
*bright NEIGHBORHOOD; she had blue eyes and a*
*red bike, and she loved to ride her little bike in big*
*circles, occasionally drifting three doors down in her*
*concentrically expanding outward meanderings despite*
*the firm and sincere warnings of her loving and pro-*
*tective parents, their eyes bulging in suspended terror*
*as they warned her gently to STAY AWAY from that*
*thing, that post-human, prelizard mutant interplane-*
*tary botched biochemical meltdown disaster clone . . .*
*STAY AWAY FROM FRANK, they would say . . . but*
*of course such a warning pushes a small button near*
*the doorway to the command center of a child's mind*
*and the child proceeds directly to the area that they*
*have been warned to avoid; this glandular urge can be*
*overridden, to some extent, by the WILL, but the will*
*in a five-year-old is not strong; a five-year-old WILL in-*
*variably be drawn to that which is forbidden; and*
*each week, circling about on her small red bike, her*
*big blue eyes fixed on Frank's house, she drifted a lit-*
*tle bit closer to big trouble, maybe an inch, maybe*
*two: but closer . . . and as the days and weeks*
*passed, as she grew slightly in stature and courage,*
*she moved past one, two, and finally three doors, until*
*one day, one damned and yet glorious afternoon, as*
*the sun shown high and proud and kids throughout*
*the great midrift bulge of the earth, tropics Capricorn*
*to Cancer, drifted in and out of hazy summer dreams*

*and wandered gracefully through shifting sands on beaches white to black, exuding summer beauty and slipping their toes into the gentle salt water wash of the waves of the great oceans of mother earth, into the other world, the hidden world of dolphins that look down upon humans and pity the spiraling decay of their DNA and also mammoth beasts without names that live shapeless black lives without eyes in the evil black depths and sharks, great sharks that eat human beings whole and watch with eyes that never sleep, one day the concentric circle of her little red bike's well-worn, slowly extending route collided with the force that was Frank . . . her blue eyes locked onto Frank, wedged uncomfortably in his front yard, the THING that her parents had pleaded with her to avoid: she looked upon The Forest Of No Return and entered; she stuck her feet out, as kids do, using the expensive imported leather of her nice little suburban shoes to skid her little red bike to a jagged halt; feet planted on the ground, she looked with big open eyes at the vehicle of her OWN demise; she looked at Frank, lurking in The Position, his mouth twisted, deformed, curdled into an impossible arch as if forty years of howling winds had carved barnacles in his seemingly wooden features; he quivered slightly, rustling the implied branches that hovered like gray ghosts around his wiry, gnarled frame; he looked at Lizzie—looked through her—and belched, loudly: Lizzie stepped back, almost falling off her bike; she could SEE the SMELL coming at her like a wave of mustard gas and she wrinkled her cute nose reflexively; the wave passed, searing her hair and leaving a putrid green tint on the edge of her aura, which should have been promptly dusted, as one dusts lint off a coat, but there was no angel present peering over Lizzie's shoulder, no one to protect her, no one to care, no one to cry, and so it was not dusted—and she would*

*never understand that little green voice that would
from that moment on until the day she died at age
fifty-four from a corroded liver which gave out suddenly under the chronic assault of tequila as she forever spent the Friday nights of her five marriages
dancing like a depraved madonna on wobbly tables in
sleazy flesh emporiums up and down the once great
state of California searching for the final solution to a
problem that she did not know existed but that would
drive her to a toxic and painful death—the voice that
forever screamed "Fuck Me" . . . Lizzie squinted
slightly, her eyes burning momentarily; she looked at
Frank in wonderment, as one looks at a man being
handcuffed and shoved face first into the ground that
holds so many secrets by six uniformed policemen
with pressed hats and puffed out chests and faggy,
pleated mustaches and stupid, glazed looks of lizard-
like satisfaction on their robotic pizza-grease faces;
Lizzie cocked her head slightly, as if trying to nudge
the world, her world, back onto its proper axis . . .*

"What are you . . . what are you DOING? . . ."

*Frank turned, like the craggy tree in* Babes *had
turned, oak tough and bark hardened, a piece of bad-
ass timber that had seen too many axes, too many
oversized flannel shirts, too many matches, too many
long hot summers and too many Marlboro reds flung
too close to tree flesh that was nearly singed too
damn many times; even trees have their limits . . .*

"WHAT AM I? . . . I AM THE BIG BANG, LIT-
TLE ONE . . . I AM THE PROLOGUE TO YOUR
CONCLUSION . . . I AM THE LEAK THAT PUDDLES
DEEP WITHIN YOUR MIND, THE MIND THAT YOU
DO NOT KNOW, THE MIND THAT WATCHES
AND DOES NOT SLEEP . . . I AM THE THOUGHTS
THAT SIMMER, THE DREAMS THAT PUDDLE, THE
MOMENT—THIS MOMENT—THAT EXTENDS
INTO ETERNITY . . . I AM THE NIGHTMARES THAT

*RISE UNSEEN, WEBBED BY INFINITY AND
CHAINED BY DESIRE . . . I AM THE FUNHOUSE
MIRROR, LITTLE PIECE OF RAW MEAT . . . I AM A
TREE, CAN'T YOU SEE? . . ."*

Lizzie looked at this tree-thing and did not
know what to think; her little synapses flailed about,
searching for a cross-reference that was simply not
there . . .

*"WHAT AM I DOING? . . . I AM YOUR FU-
TURE, LITTLE PASTURE . . . I AM THE NINE-TO-
FIVE LIES, THE SMOOTHNESS OF A PROMISE, THE
COARSE MEMORY OF A WET TONGUE, THE
CHEAP WHISKY SMILES, THE CRUEL GENE POOL,
THE NAKED GREED, THE STENCH OF A MILLION
NIGHTMARES, THE DEAD AIR OF THE ASPHALT
SKY, THE WRECKED DREAMS OF THE CRIPPLED
TREES, THE GLASS TOUPEES, THE CHEAP STARES,
THE ROLEX WATCHES, THE NAGGING
THOUGHTS OF DEATH, THE VAGUE MEMORIES
OF THE GRAVE, THE BELCHING, THE COLOGNE,
THE LAWYERS, THE GREASY WAX BUILDUP, THE
BILLIONS AND BILLIONS OF CLIPPED NOSE HAIRS,
THE WASHER-DRYERS, THE DEATHBURGERS, THE
RULES, THE SIGNS, THE PRESS CONFERENCES,
THE PRESSED FLESH, THE SPIN DOCTORS, THE
CRACKS BETWEEN THE SMILES, THE FUNGUS IN
THE SOULS . . . I AM YOUR FUTURE, LITTLE PAS-
TURE . . ."*—he shivered emphatically at this point,
angrily rustling the invisible dead leaves of his wrinkled
appendages . . . he smiled and released his pose; he
bent down into a crouch, smiling, his hands folded
neatly and resting on his thighs . . .

*"I AM THE EYES THAT SEE TOO MUCH AND
SHATTER LIKE THIN GLASS . . . I AM THE TRAC-
TOR TRAILER THAT WILL BEHEAD THE CHILD . . .
I AM THE END OF THE WORLD . . ."*

Lizzie's world—or, more correctly, Frank's World,

into which she had stumbled and from which she could not get out of—was moving in blurred slow motion, like a fluid abstract photograph of a naked fat woman taken by some perverted Frenchman in the twenties, his mind bent by absinthe as he sat wringing out damp thoughts in a hot café where the tables were too small—the kind of photograph that LOOKED BACK—and as Lizzie flapped her arms they leafed through the air like a series of drawings, like a primitive cartoon, and she felt her eyes lock, unable to rotate or recalibrate, and she fought to twist her torso back toward the safety of the inner circles of her wandering concentric expansions that had—until this fateful day—defined what had been her small, concentrically evolving life; her bike fell between her card-flapping thighs and shattered into a fractal Busby Berkeley dance, a million licorice twists of color and sound, and she ran, weeping, home to the arms of her mom, her womb, who was watching *The Young and the Restless* but would soon be holding in her arms a child who would never again be young and would always be restless, even after death, lying in her grave next to some mindless, smiling idiot in a polyester suit; Lizzie would not close her eyes for three days . . .

Frank slowly lifted himself out of his crouch and watched innocence defined, manifested, corrupted, maligned, and totaled stagger down the street; he watched the frail knees wobble that would become scarred and creak on unsteady tables; he watched the small hands quiver that would become tense and arthritic and spout liver spots; he watched the hair fly gently in the wind that would later fall out in clumps and hang limply; he watched the eyes that would see but not feel as men of a thousand smells grimaced in dwarfed, compartmentalized relief and released their small oily loads into her lonely patch . . . he watched little Lizzie go home . . .

# 3.

the ubiquitous "they"

*When Frank reached the proper age, the process of EDUCATION was undertaken; he subverted the process almost immediately, however, and used the opportunity, the exposure to large groups of vulnerable minds over a span of years, to extend the range of his influence, to recalibrate his psychic weaponry, to move beyond the battered family core and leak out into the community at large; Frank's plan was to suck up the souls of his classmates . . . Frank didn't like school and school didn't like Frank; he was popular, but in a Lee Harvey Oswald, magic-bullet kind of way; the other kids never took their eyes off of him; he was THEIR God; they lived in fear of Frank pelting them with large rocks or pissing on their textbooks or dropping dog shit in their coat pockets or slipping lizards into their backpacks; the faculty stayed clear of IT and suggested to each other in grave whispers over hushed coffee that perhaps he was the Anti-Christ. Frank attended school because his parents' small nightmares were no longer enough to sustain him; school offered a bigger game, a larger board, a living field of dreams where the opportunities for psychic*

*mayhem were nearly infinite, a theoretically happy*
*place festooned with joy and laughter where, tragi-*
*cally, Frank would have hundreds of minds—a verita-*
*ble banquet—laid before him, and he could distort*
*the souls of his new friends and malign their little*
*world views over the months and years like some sick*
*junkie sculptor with cramped hands disfiguring the*
*limbs and torsos of an army of grotesque living works-*
*in-progress . . . intellectually, he was worlds beyond*
*the miniature normals, the young lumps of mediocrity,*
*and he reigned, Hitler-bright, with a switchblade imag-*
*ination and a dry, bacterial wit; he frequently quoted*
*dark philosophers and writers like Crowley, Burroughs,*
*and Lovecraft, pummeling the other kids with remarks*
*such as "ONE MUST ALWAYS ASSUME THAT THE*
*ORACLE IS NOT OMNISCIENT" or "IMAGES, MIL-*
*LIONS OF IMAGES; THAT'S WHAT I EAT" or "I BE-*
*CAME AWARE THAT I LOOKED UPON A DYING*
*RACE WHICH MUST ESCAPE ITS PLANET OR PER-*
*ISH" . . . in the classroom, he always sat in the back,*
*next to the big picture windows, looking out and*
*down—not UP, like the other kids, not UP into the*
*clouds and beyond where dreams and hopes and am-*
*bitions floated about like so many cheery white angels,*
*but rather DOWN, into the ground, where the earth-*
*worms sludged without remorse through the world of*
*dirt and fungus and slime and decaying plant mold,*
*eating and shitting, eating and shitting—not UP but*
*DOWN; he beamed strange thoughts into the backs*
*of the other kids' heads and spent many hours hap-*
*pily knotting the cords that raised and lowered the*
*huge razor-edged window blinds that let in or shut out*
*the sunlight into exquisite, functional hangman's*
*nooses that he occasionally slipped around the neck of*
*the girl who happened to be sitting in front of him,*
*which for three consecutive years had been young*
*Nancy Glassberg, whose bright blue eyes turned glassy*

like cracked marbles and who remained traumatized and squirrellike until her twenty-seventh birthday when she took a hard right turn on a long straightaway in the fog on picturesque Highway 1 and landed with a majestic splat several hundred feet below on a lovely expanse of rock jutting out of the Pacific Ocean, the great ocean that holds our dreams and our remains along with varieties of fish that we cannot imagine, creatures in bad moods that will eat us whole or in parts, at their discretion . . .

Frank had an intuitive understanding of the "educational system"; he realized that it was, in fact, nothing more than a large corporation; the "teachers" were merely pedantic burger-flippers, assembly-line hacks mass-producing new parts for THE MACHINE, living parts, molded, shaped, predictable, orchestrated, choreographed, templated; the "students" were nothing more than the base materials of capitalism, malleable blobs of cosmic putty to be shaped and pounded into "productive members of society," accepting social slavery as a computer accepts programming, "for the greater good" (of the few and their advancing fortunes), COGS, fitting snugly in the gearbox of the American Dream, wedged into a plodding destiny, conditioned, confused, content, preoccupied, competitive, ambitious, isolated, stressed, arrogant, docile, virtually incapable of generating original thought, reduced to quoting obscure poetry from the Middle Ages, aimlessly "busy," without any "spare time," not even for a passing thought about the welfare of their fellow man or even their OWN personal evolution—they have "things to do"—and so they WILL remain, PARTS of the larger machine, willing to defend to the death their right to remain dim-witted and sheeplike . . . the COGS, thus "educated," remained devoted to their assigned cog-tasks, which they performed vigorously during work hours, while after work they patiently waited *for the NEXT day's work, in a stupor, docile, passive, sluggish, punch-drunk, shanghaied, mei-li'd, mai-tai'd, hog-tied, dislocated, isolated, subdued, submerged, drugged, numb, tranced, sedated, distracted, blissfully ignorant—except for a few of the stubborn rabble on the fringes of culture—the drop-outs—who form sleazy rock bands with names like The Smokers— they chain smoke throughout their performances, blue lights drifting slowly through the smoky blur of feed- back and drums, twenty minutes of "All In Your Mind," which it is, of course—or The Electric Toilet or The Seamy Underbelly or The Ill Wind or The Devil's Anvil or The Leathercoated Minds or The Ugly Janitors or Forensic Snowball or The Half Lives or The Rippling Fleshpockets or The Great Gobs Of Spit or Lick the Fat Elvis or Love Snot or Not Your Mother's Tampon or Celebrity Sex or The Peeling Limbs or The Explod- ing White Mice or The Smiling Mindfuckers or Pieces of Lisa or The Crumbsuckers or Die Cheerleader or Disco Inferno or Throbbing Gristle or The Mutants or The Cows or The Holy Shits or Crispy Ambulance or The Great Unwashed—while the sheep cling tightly to the pre-approved official social happy normal matrix and form bands like The Monkees or The Bee Gees or Dick and Dee Dee or Dickey Do and the Don'ts or The Ding Dongs or Don and the Good Times or Don, Dick and Jimmy or Jan and Dean or Johnnie and Jack or Honey and the Bees . . . that's how imaginative they are, lining up at the slop trough every night at six, not realizing—until it's too late and they're are halfway up the ramp—that THEY'RE the slop, their lives an ENTREE to be gobbled up by the few, the proud, the self-chosen, the inbred, the rich, the ubiqui- tous "THEY" . . . there is no "they," of course, no master list of names and addresses, no faces; that's part of the JOKE: there is no "they" to be hunted down when the "revolution" begins, which is why there will BE no "revolution" . . . "they" EXISTS only as an abstraction exerting influence in the real world, a force acting upon imagination, a psychosocial web of hidden WILLS, a summation of biological, genetic, electromagnetic, microbiotic, social, pedagogic, psychological, karmic, cosmic, mythic, internal and external FORCES, a living IDEA, a socially engineered MOONCHILD, lurking around corners, creeping out of shadows, spilling from dreams, a macro-cabal whose roster includes not only the obvious—Richard Nixon, the Vatican, ITT—but also others preferring to remain silent and unseen . . . "the System," "the Masons," "the Commies," "the Nazis," "the Right," "the Left," "the Middle," "the Rich," "the Poor," "the Welfare Cheats," "the Criminals," "the Politicians," "the Brotherhood," "the Sisterhood," "the Media," "Television," "Hollywood," "Langley," "the Voices," "the Dolphins," "the Dracos," "the Pleiadians," "the Bankers," "the Mafia," "the Vatican," "the White House," "the Black Lodge," "the Military-Industrial Complex," "Big Brother," "Little Sister," "Mom," "Dad," "Walter Cronkite," "God," "Satan," "Mister Ed" . . . WHOEVER, WHATEVER—"IT" is probably all of these things, thrown together in varying proportions into a sticky, random recipe, like one that might be found in a Martha Stewart cookbook (SHE'S ONE OF THEM) . . .*

*The education process consisted of the sheer dumping of facts, the layering of a thick, false history over the natural world of the senses: the blank slates of the young minds were filled with rules and laws and information and bullshit and overload and inference and suggestion and instructions and belief systems and limitations and pressure and coercion and brainwashing and extortion and spin-control doubletalk new speak buzz phrases like "democratic system" and "checks and balances"—Frank always suspected that there was a great deal of cash involved in addition to the checks—and nationalistic rhetoric and pedantic mythology—Frank's favorite educational myth being the one about Columbus, the malodorous sailor who "discovered" America in what Frank mused was about the same way a thief might "discover" your wallet: aiming for India, he and his crew of convicted felons landed in the West Indies, partyed with the indigenous locals, who had happily looked after the property for 250,000 years, and then began a tidy program of mass genocide in the name of Christianity; Frank didn't believe in the American Dream or the Pilgrim Dream or the Dreamtime or the French Dream or the Canadian Dream or the Catholic Dream or the Protestant Dream or the Jewish Dream or the Muslim Dream or the Multinational Corporate Boards of Directors' Dream or the Bilderbergers' Dream or the Industrialists' Dream or the Bankers' Dream or the Masonic Dream or the Draco Dream or ANY system of mass regimented thought control; he didn't BELIEVE anything, except perhaps that human beings were bred from PIGS and were growing more and more piggish as their genes floundered and history frantically staggered backwards, rewinding itself, their DNA plummeting, their accumulated will surging toward global self-annihilation, individual cells of the larger being offing themselves in a thoughtful attempt at self-medication by the collective greater being—and all-encompassing jingoism and embellished puffery and tall tales glorifying and romanticizing the thuglike efforts of the "public servants" who—in cahoots with the president and his staff of felonious thugs, err, "cabinet officials"—after consulting with the oil barons and banking czars—script, debate superficially and legislate the "will of the people," and the dream rumbles forward, except it is THEIR dream, not yours, and soon it's ALIVE, oozing through backyards and barbecue pits, moving across the land like a large red, white and blue virus; frisbees and footballs fill the gray air; cowboy boots are polished; guns are cleaned; warehouses with cold, cement aisles sell everything imaginable and many things unimaginable; toys are purchased and discarded; chickens, turkeys, cows, pigs and trout are preserved and hormoned, raised in death camps, slaughtered, roasted, broiled, baked, pan-fried, grilled in fecal matter, barbecued, eaten raw, boiled and stewed, and while the public is kept distracted by the flag-waving politicians and the allure of television and trinkets, unelected officials lobby for tobacco and guns and oil and spit and mucous and vomit and nuclear power and nuclear waste and nu-clear families and radioactive families and munitions and arms and broken legs and broken promises and cement overshoes and biochemicals and bioengineering and bioweaponry and biobullshitgrantgettersuckasses and H-bombs and neutron bombs and smart bombs and dumb bombs and drugs and booze and transvestites and three-headed dogs and junk food and television and gas-hogs and toys and Barbie and Ken and Lassie and Lockheed and Barney and Beavis and Butt-head, and on behalf of these interests sena-tors and congressmen are bought like Singapore whores, while O, meanwhile, back at the Fed, the ubiquitous bankers control the flow of "money" by raising and lowering interest rates and creating paper fortunes through stock market manipulation, currency devaluation, hyper-inflation, deflation, whimsy, high loan rates, low prime rates, flat rates, curved rates, fixed rates, cement overshoes, assisted suicides, depressions, recessions, power lunches, bank failures, S&L failures, corporate failures, liver failures, failures to communicate, skullduggery, fraud, greed, waste and larceny, ripping off YOUR money year after year after year, increasing the "national" debt as they go—your* debt, their dream . . . getting the picture?—until the debt hits such monstrous heights that the treasury topples over, crushing a great many dreams on the way down . . . but by this time the bankers and their entourage will be long gone, seated comfortably on their private jets, bound for greener pastures and fresh blood, leaving behind a cardboard illusion, a rusty shell of a country, America the Billboard, the broken streets a war zone, the bent dream a genetic memory, but THEY won't care, stretched out on mattresses in pools drinking vodka and orange juice from inflatable plastic floating cups that say Novus Ordo Seclorum on them, working on their tans, and manipulating global exchange rates from their mobile phones, surrounded by Secret Service types in sunglasses, listening to old Benny Goodman records, floating, somewhere, inside the exclusive electrified barbed-wire-enclosed by-invitation-only vacation retreat mecca of Pine Gap, Australia . . .

Frank knew the gam: REALITY CHESS; were the aggressors in the greatest of all wars—the battle for reality—the clash of the belief systems—the war waged for the space between our ears as we fight off the attacking waves of information and illusion and programming and brainwashing and mind-fucking in an attempt to decide what—if anything—is REAL and who—if anyone—we should TRUST and what—if anything—we should BELIEVE; the reality with the most believers would win by CONSENSUS; the battlefield of this great thought war is the sum of our combined imaginations, the matrix of our intertwined WORLDS; their greatest weapon is THE MACHINE, their army, the "teachers" and "students": by controlling what is "learned," THEY control what is BELIEVED; by controlling what is "known," THEY determine REALITY; by controlling "history," THEY shape the FUTURE . . . Frank knew that THEIR version of "history" was merely that—their version of history—mere propaganda—and so he focused instead upon the several million topics they DID NOT address, subjects that apparently were off-limits, such as, for example, oh . . . let's see . . . pit bulls and dime bags and marshall stacks and high magic and low magic and black magic and magic fingers and bedroom magic and bedroom eyes and vagina dentate and Goethe's suppressed color theories and Tesla's venusian contacts and the rising tantric serpent and spiritual evolution and divine enlightenment and the law of one and vedic philosophy and transmogrification and isotropic teleportation and the best time to see a UFO—Wednesday at 10:00 P.M.—and lacunal amnesia and hypnopompic parapsychology and antinomianism and Zandark, "Commander in Chief of Directing Technical Transmissions Via Mental Telepathy and the Combination of Mediumistic Telepathy Under the Direction of the Confederation of Cosmic Space Beings and the United Cosmic Council" and geomancy and neomancy and somamancy and Nancy with the laughing face and feng shui and lung mei and wu chi and om and mu and pan and the wang chung and the ouroborus and the doors of perception and the song of creation and the guardian snake of the north and the spear of destiny and the holy grail and the thule society and the skull and bones society and the theosophical society and the sword-swallowing society and the illuminati and the council of thirteen and the knights of malta and the lemurians and the hyperboreans and the akashic record and the sephirothic tree of the kabala and the great pyramid of shensi and the cave of brahma and the yellow cloud people and pythagorean cosmic morphology and mayan stone yokes and alchemical philosophy and left-handed bengali tantrics and vegetotherapy and cherubins and phrenology and prognometers and gri-

*moires and prophetic ecstasy and void beingness and*
*kundabuffer and the osirion and the integretron and*
*the emerald tablets and the rainbow city and the holy*
*songs of bacchus and resonant liquid crystal-colloidal*
*membranes and enochian verb construction and intel-*
*lectual hieraticism and shamanic healing and*
*prediluvian tunnel networks and interdimensional por-*
*tals and asymmetric harmonic pulsations and cosmic*
*dust and crystalline biology and prima materia and*
*the left eye of horus and the nine lords of time and*
*the feast of the hive and all souls night and babylon*
*working and novus ordo seclorum and masonic mind*
*control and mediums and the massage and aching*
*glands and the incredible decade and the rapture and*
*the harvest and the apocalypse and the octopus and*
*the rothschilds and the rockefellers and the philadel-*
*phians and the hoover institute and the bilderbergers*
*and the jason scholars and the order of the rosy cross*
*and the order of the brotherhood of death and the*
*order of the sacred word and the order of the dragon*
*and the order of bees and rand and lockheed and*
*general dynamics and holmes and narver and heckler*
*and koch and smith and wesson and general foods*
*and du pont and nugan-hand and wackenhut and ge-*
*nentec and raytheon and bechtel and langley and*
*bethesda and los alamos and dreamland and mon-*
*tauk and fort carson and fort dietrich and fort meade*
*and white sands and pine gap and edwards and*
*groom lake and dulce and cabazon and project sigma*
*and project alpha and project delta and project*
*pounce and project plato and project snowbird and*
*project grudge and project gray van and project invisi-*
*bility and project rainbow and project phoenix and*
*project aurora and project artichoke and project pan-*
*dora and project bizarre and project monarch and op-*
*eration yellow fruit and operation moon blink and*
*operation blue fly and operation dead end and opera-*

tion firm hand and MK-ULTRA and executive order #11490 and alternative three and MJ-12 and alien genetic projects and alien social manipulation and implants and unusually stiff network anchorpeople and implanted screen memories and holographic reality inserts and thought scanners and deep freeze and clones and abductee monitoring and replicative failure and radiohypnotic intracerebral control and electronic memory dissolution and reverse vector radionics and economic inductance and low-level bio-medical telemetry and covert funds acquisition and black budgets and alien craft back-engineering and martian colonies and x-drones and amplitrons and thought chairs and time rifts and reverse time waves and population acclimation and free energy and bioweaponry and sonic weaponry and scalar wave weaponry and ELF grid wars and confusion weaponry and tactical microwaves and sound curdlers and remote thought control and telepathic lobotomies and antimatter reactors and zero-spin energy transfer and party levitation and diamagnetism and implosion theory and hyperoxidation and polarity therapy and reverse speech analysis and ozone therapy and fourth density polarization and projected thought forms and monsters from the id and relativistic psychoactive wave equations and lozenge-shaped anomalies of electromagnetic aberration and unified vector geometry and walk-in babies and inslaw and ouija boards and the gulf breeze six and world bankruptcy and the mark of the beast and the sound and genetic databases and scientology crypts and nanotechnology and purity of essence and lenticular disks and meandering lights and the space confederation and the galactic tribunal and the cosmic brotherhood and geomagnetic dimensional windows and confinement camps and genetic organism population control and invisible life forms and archetypes and astral beings and elementals and binah and

*a'ashliah and kerubim and anaxephhydrias and
garodiel and zathanat and zazur and the barbarous
names of evocation and the wand posture and the
formula of the watcher and the woodpecker signal
and the buzzsaw signal and nihlism and death and
tax fraud and objectivism and expressionism and dada
and the cabaret voltaire and survival research labs
and the temple of psychick youth and the people's
temple black light discipline room and the church of
the flowing morath and the assemblage of concerned
visigoths and the divine society of poddill and the sacred society of fingerpointers and the divinely sordid
imperium of the enchanted colon and the church of
the exalted stoolism and the sect of the spinning spas-
tics and the church of the cosmic chuckle and the
church of the auntie christ of the lather-stained panties and the exalted order of the whirling dervishes
and antoni gaudí and nicholas roerich and luis buñuel
and hieronymus bosch and indrid cold and paracel-
sus and apollonius and john dee and helena blavatsky and
dennis hopper and fatty arbuckle and betty page and
rudolph steiner and marie laveau and charles manson
and charles whitman and john wayne gacy and john
wayne and wayne county and jayne county and wil-
helm reich and wernher von braun and jack whiteside
parsons and robert oppenheimer and king fahd and
prescott bush and joe kennedy and omnipotent high-
ness krill and m. k. jessup and james forrestal and
gary stollman and george van tassel and danny
casalaro's wrists and kennedy's brain and einstein's
brain and stalin's brain and exploding brains and
UFOs and EBEs and ELFs and ICBMs and LSD and
DNA and DMT and NBC and UPI and SDI and TBC
and TLC and the FBI and the CIA and the BBC and
the FDA and the CDC and the NSA and the CFR and
the BLM and the EWL and the HEL and the NSC
and the AEC and the KGB and the OPC and the DOE*

and the DIA and the DOD and the NIH and the
WHO and the OTO and the CSS and the ONI and
the OSS, RIP, and the NIMH and GLADS and FEMA
and DUMB and MAJIC and DARPA and DEFCON and
SALT and AIDS and DMAE and NAMBLA and CREEP
and the repository for germinal choice and snuff tv
and snuff films and snuffed politicians and elvis's pill
problem and hitler's lingerie and hoover's lingerie and
cross-dressing power dressing and power plays and
power trips and the roots of power and the invisible
hands of power and the sucker-punching fists of
power and the giant fungus under minnesota and lo-
phophora williamsii and banisteriopsis and trichocerus
pachanoi and mandrake and hyocyamus niger and the
forty-nine planes of existence and the music of the
spheres and octave shocks and devil's snuff and be-
together powder and graveyard dust and two jack's
extract and the master musicians of joujouka and the
sex pistols and john coltrane and sun ra and cecil tay-
lor and karlheinz stockhausen and harry partch and
moondog and wynonie harris and barbeque bob and
hazil adkins and the trashmen and throbbing gristle
and the fugs and the chocolate watchband and the
slits and glenn branca's guitar army and "Straight, No
Chaser" and "All the Things You Could Be By Now If
Sigmund Freud's Wife Was Your Mother" and "Medi-
tations on a Pair of Wire Cutters" and "Whoop and
Hollar Stomp" and "Tight Like That" and "Grandma
Plays the Numbers" and "Wine, Women, Whiskey"
and "God Save the Queen" and "Two-Headed Dog"
and "President Ford Is a Square Queer" and "I Love
the Sound of a Severed Head Bouncing Down the
Stairs" and "Chop Chop Lizzie Borden" and "The
Singing Grandfather (Will Kill You Dead)" and "I Had
Too Much to Dream Last Night" and "Love Comes in
Spurts" and "I Don't Want to Go Down to the Base-
ment" and "Now I Wanna Sniff Some Glue" and

*"Now I Wanna Be Sedated"* and *"You Should Never Have Opened That Door"* and *"Personality Crisis"* and *"Pretty Vacant"* and *"I Walked with a Zombie"* and *"Slug Bait"* and *"Nag Nag Nag"* and *The Incredibly Strange Creatures Who Stopped Living and Became Mixed-Up Zombies* and *Even Dwarves Started Small* and *Nosferatu* and *That Obscure Object Of Desire* and *Eraserhead* and *Doctor Strangelove: Or How I Learned to Stop Worrying and Love the Bomb* and *The Subterraneans* and *Say It With Bullets* and *It Won't Rub Off, Baby* and *How to Blow Your Mind and Have a Freakout Party* and *The Prisoner* and *Videodrome* and *They Live* and *Invaders From Mars* and *The Long Knives* and *Panic in Needle Park* and *Nightmare In a Damaged Brain* and *Überfall* and *Night and Fog* and *The Trip* and *Faster Pussycat! Kill! Kill!* and *Meet Mr. Lucifer* and *Love and Bullets* and *A Clockwork Orange* and *Thirsty Animal* and *Satyricon* and *Cul-de-sac* and *Repulsion* and *The Accidental Death of an Anarchist* and *Pierrot-le-fou* and *Hangmen Also Die* and *Shivers* and *Scum* and *Bad* and *Edward Penishands* and *The Hindlick Maneuver* and *Little Miss Curious* and *This Dick For Hire* and *Twin Cheeks* and *In Search of the Wild Beaver* and *Island of Mutations* and *Valley of the Dragons* and *Creatures the World Forgot* and *Nymphoid Barbarian in Dinosaur Hell* and *Empire of the Senses* and *I Spit On Your Grave* and *Astro-Zombies* and *Worm-Eaters* and *Mr. Smother* and *The Unpublished Facts of Life* and *The Invisible College* and *The Illuminoids* and *Dead Men Tell Tales* and *Disneyland of the Gods* and *Cosmic Trigger* and *Naked Lunch* and *Naked City* and *Concerning A Certain One's Sphere, Which, From Confirmed Habit, Poured Forth Venomous Sarcasms Against Others* and *The Sex Life of the*

*Foot and Shoe* and *Magick in Theory and Practice*
and *At the Mountains of Madness* and *120 Days of
Sodom* and *House of Dolls* and *Requiem for a
Dream* and *Heaven and Hell* and *The Third Eye*
and *Life Between Death and Rebirth* and *Concen-
tration and the Acquirement of Personal Magnet-
ism* and *The Book Sealed with Seven Seals* and *A
Wanderer in the Spirit Lands* and *The Night Side
of Nature* and *The Debatable Land Between This
One and the Next* and *The Book of Enoch* and *The
Book of Lies* and *Growing Up Absurd* and *King
Mob* and *Extraordinary Popular Delusions and the
Madness of Crowds* and *Searching for Hidden Ani-
mals* and *Lost World* and *Arizona Cavalcade* and
*Psychic Archaeology* and *No Longer on the Map*
and *Host with the Big Hat* and *Strange World* and
*Hiroshima* and *Secrets of Masonic Mind Control,
the Alchemical Psychodrama and the Processing of
Humanity* and *The History of the Angels and
Their Gallantry with the Daughters of Men* and
*The Life of Merlin Ambrosius, His Prophecies and
Predictions Interpreted and Their Truth Made
Good* and *Les Paradises Artificiels* and *Cosmic
Pulse of Life* and *Other Tongues, Other Flesh* and
*The Monks of War* and *Uninvited Visitors* and *The
Book of the Damned* and *Road in the Sky* and *The
Kybalion* and *Message from the Pleiades* and *Nine
Chains to the Moon* and *The Council of Seven
Lights* and *The New England Airship Wave of
1909* and *The Case of the Flying Christmas Tree*
and *Flying Saucers Have Landed* and *Operation
Trojan Horse* and *Somebody Else Is on the Moon*
and *Matrix III: The Psycho-Social, Biological and
Electronic Manipulation of Human Consciousness*
and *Cosmic Puppets* and *Inside the Flying Saucers*
and *A Search in Secret India* and *A Journey to the
Earth's Interior* and *The Hollow Globe* and *Mes-*

*sengers of Deception* and *The Choppers* and *They
Knew Too Much About Flying Saucers* and *Mind-
fuckers* and *Secrets of the Vatican* and *Junkies For
Satan* and *The Eclectic Taxidermist* and *Holy
Spear, Holy Blood* and *The Druidic Times* and
*Flying Serpents and Dragons* and *The Fate of the
Lizard People* and *Manson in His Own Words* and
*The Wars of Gods and Men* and *The Divine Py-
mander of Hermes Mercurius Trismegistus* and
*Libellus De Alchymia* and *Corpus Hermeticum* and
*Eirenaeus Orandus* and *De Occulta Philosophia*
and *Hermippus Redivivus* and *The Key of Solomon*
and *The Will, The Arcanum of Magical Initiation*
and *Janua Magiae Referata* and *De Anima* and
*The Squeezing of Parson Foster's Sponge, Wherein
the Spongebearer's Immodest Carriage and Behav-
ior Towards His Brethren is Detected, The Bitter
Flames of His Slandering Reports Are by the
Sharp Vinegar of Truth Corrected and Quite Ex-
tinguished, and, Lastly, the Virtuous Validity of his
Sponge in Wiping Away the Weapon-Slave is
Made Clear, Crushed Out and Clean Abolished*
and *Influence of Politics and Religion Upon the
Hair and Beard* and *The Temporal Mirror of Eter-
nity* and *The Key of the Cabinet* and *Mother Brid-
git's Dream-Book and Oracle of Fate* and *The
Apology for the Great Men Who Have Been
Falsely Suspected of Magic* and *Turbo Philo-
sophorum* and *The Frightful Compacts Entered
into Between the Devil and the Pretended Invisibles
with Their Damnable Instructions, the Deplorable
Ruin of the Disciples, and Their Miserable End*
and *Diddling Considered As One of the Exact
Sciences* and *Pandora's Box* and *The Marriage of
Heaven and Hell* and *Listen Little Man* and *Monkey* and *The Secrets of the Veda* and *Words of Ec-
stacy in Sufism* and *The Invisible Helpers* and *The*

**47**

*Mind Benders* and *The Play of the Infinite* and
*Games of the Gods* and *Dolphin Dreamtime* and
*The Serpent in Paradise* and *Anti-Gravity and the
World Grid* and *The Hills Have Eyes* and *Enigma
Fantastique* and *The Clock People of Mount
Shasta* and *Voodoo in New Orleans* and *The Wild
Duck* and *The Inferno* and *Les Chants de Maldo-
ror* and *The Nether World* and *Don't Look in the
Basement* and *The Dark Side of History* and *Heart
of Glass* and *The Mass Psychology of Fascism* and
*Mysterium Conjunctionis* and *We Talk, You Listen*
and *Juliette* and *Junkie* and *The Encyclopedia of
Barbie Dolls* and *From A to B and Back Again*
and *The American Jitters* and *Pasteurized Milk: A
National Menace* and *Murder Can Be Fun* and
*Hollywood Babylon* and *Hitler's Secret Life* and
*Fetish Times* and *Memoires Illustrating The His-
tory of Jacobitism* and *Excalibur Briefing* and *The
Secret World Government* and *Witchcraft and the
Illuminati* and *The Fourth Reich of the Rich* and
*The Occult Technology of Power* and *GRUNCH
of Giants* and *The Trillion Dollar Lie* and *Above
Top Secret* and *Rush To Judgment* and *Man the
Puppet* and *Report From Iron Mountain* and
*Sleepwalking Through History* and *Silent Weapons
for Quiet Wars* and *Behold a Pale Horse* and God
knows what else . . .

Frank was not interested in dulling his wits by
answering the moronic questions that his teachers
posed, questions for which there were always "right"
or "wrong" answers—he knew that it just didn't work
that way—and so he spent his time gazing out the
window and down, pondering lizards and tying hangman's knots, until one day, one fragmentary moment,
when Mrs. Hildegaard Dieseldorfer, teacher, regretta-
bly posed a question to the class about LIZARDS;
Frank's back stiffened, his thoughts congealed, and his

*hand shot up; grudgingly, Mrs. Dieseldorfer scowled
and acknowledged him . . .*

*". . . Err, Frank . . . a lizard's diet . . . consists
primarily of . . . what? . . ."*

*Frank sat very still, exuding frozen calm and sa-
voring the sweet odor of fear as it filled the classroom; some students began choking without knowing
why; others stifled gags or felt queerly uneasy; some
wanted to throw up; one had strange, leathery
thoughts about Mrs. Dieseldorfer; one thought of pigs
and studded body corsets; Frank spoke:*

*". . . WHERE DO I BEGIN? . . . PERHAPS IN
THE CLOSETS IN THE BACK OF YOUR MINDS? . . .
PERHAPS WITH THE CREATURES LURKING IN THE
CRACKS IN THE CAVES OF MYTHOLOGY? . . . PER-
HAPS WITH THE BEINGS CONCEALED IN THE
HISTORY THAT REMAINS UNTOLD? . . . PERHAPS
WITH THE MONSTERS THAT INHABIT THE DARK-
EST OF THE DARK MYTHS AND FILL THE LEG-
ENDS AND POPULATE THE SHADOW WORLDS,
EXISTING IN THE DREAMS OF EVERY CULTURE,
DIFFERENT AND YET THE SAME, THE VENGEFUL
DRAGONS AND WINGED FLYING GILA MONSTERS
AND HUNGRY DINOSAURS AND OMNIPOTENT
DEMONS AND FLESH-EATING REPTILES AND DI-
VINE SERPENTS AND SCALY DEVILS AND SLIMY
CREATURES FROM BLACK LAGOONS AND PTERO-
DACTYLS AND VAMPIRES AND WEREWOLVES AND
BLOODY THINGS WITHOUT NAMES AND ABOMI-
NABLE SNOWMEN AND MOTHMEN AND POLY-
MORPHS AND BETA-F WINGED HUMANOIDS
AND DELTA-FORM HUMANOIDS AND DRACOS
AND REPTILIANS AND IKALS AND KANGAMOTO AND
GARUDAS AND THUNDERBIRDS AND PIASAS AND
ANUNNAKI AND ILU AND THE LOFTY ONES
AND NEFELIM AND IGIGI AND ELOHIM AND AN-
NEDOTI AND MUSARUS AND THE REPULSIVE*

ONES AND HOMOSAURIANS AND REPHAIM AND
NAGAS AND DRAVIDIANS AND SERAPHIM AND
CHANES AND KUMBI AND JAGGA AND BATMEN
AND BIRDMEN AND CHIMERA AND SAURIANS
AND LANDLORDS AND LAWYERS AND SOCIAL-
ITES AND INDUSTRIALISTS AND POLITICIANS AND
THE WINGED MAN OF CONEY ISLAND? . . .
WHAT DO LIZARDS EAT? . . . THEY EAT MANY
THINGS . . . DRAGONS EAT KNIGHTS, COOK 'EM
AND EAT 'EM WHOLE; DEVILS EAT SOULS, EAT
'EM LIKE CANDY; VAMPIRES EAT FLESH AND
DRINK BLOOD, LIVE FOREVER, THAT SORT OF
THING; LANDLORDS EAT TENANTS AND CLEAN-
ING DEPOSITS; WEREWOLVES TAKE A BIT OF
FLESH NOW AND THEN; BLOODY THINGS EAT
OTHER BLOODY THINGS; MONSTERS EAT MAID-
ENS AND CHILDREN; SERPENTS EAT SAILORS,
SOMETIMES WHOLE SHIPS; DEMONS EAT LIVES,
HOPES, DREAMS, GOBBLE UP JUSTICE, BELCH EVIL,
SWALLOW GOOD, EAT HEARTS . . . WHAT DO
LIZARDS EAT? . . . NOW I GUESS THAT DEPENDS
ON WHAT TYPE OF LIZARD YOU'RE TALKING
ABOUT AND WHETHER IT IS A FLESH-EATER AND
WHEN IT LAST ATE AND HOW HUNGRY IT IS"—

 "Thank you Frank," interrupted Mrs. Dieseldorfer, cringing . . .

 —"NOW, IF YOU'RE TALKING ABOUT A REP-
TILIAN DRACO, LIKE THE ONES THAT LIVE UNDER
THE CITY, IN THE CAVERNS CONNECTED TO THE
SEWERS, UNDER THE SHOPPING MALL, THE MALL
WHERE THE KIDS KEEP DISAPPEARING FROM,
OH, I'D SAY THERE'S A COUPLE HUNDRED THOU-
SAND OF THEM, NINE-FOOTERS, RED EYES, POOR
TEMPERAMENTS, PARASENSORY, PSYCHOKINETIC,
TRANSDIMENSIONAL, PSYCHOTIC, NO SENSE OF
HUMOR . . . THEY'VE BEEN LIVING INSIDE THE
EARTH SINCE THE LAST PLANETARY GEOSEISMIC

FART THIRTY THOUSAND YEARS AGO, AND NOW
THAT THE OZONE HAS BEEN THINNED AND THE
TEMPERATURE ADJUSTED AND THE ATMOSPHERE
PROPERLY SEASONED WITH PETROCHEMICAL
EMISSIONS AND BIOSHIT AND SPRAY-CAN
FLUOROBIOCRAPS AND RADIOACTIVE MEGA-
HERTZIA THEY ARE READY TO COME OUT AND
COLLECT THE RENT . . . THEY ARE IRONING
THEIR FISHNET STOCKINGS AS WE SPEAK . . . IF
YOU'RE TALKING ABOUT THEM, WELL LET ME
SEE . . . THEY'RE BIG, AND THEY'RE MEAN, AND
THEY EAT . . . YOU!—Frank *suddenly looked around
the room, pointing frantically at the terrorized stu-
dents*—"AND YOU! . . . AND YOU! . . . AND YOU
AND YOU AND YOU! . . . AND YOU WERE
THERE . . . AND YOU WERE THERE . . . AND
HANK YOU WERE THERE . . . AND AUNTIE EM
YOU WERE THERE . . . AND I WAS SCARED . . . IT
WASN'T AT ALL LIKE KANSAS . . . WE WALKED
FOR MILES AND MILES TO THE EMERALD CITY . . .
WE THOUGHT IT WAS PARADISE BUT WHEN WE
GOT INSIDE AND PULLED BACK THE CURTAIN WE
SAW IT WAS JUST A LIZARD DISGUISED AS A WIZ-
ARD AND MY OH MY THERE WERE UNDER-
GROUND CAVERNS AND TUNNELS AND BLACK
HELICOPTERS AND MIND CONTROL AND BRAIN-
WASHING AND LASER KNIVES AND HUMAN-
ENTRAIL BURGERS AND LIVER SHAKES AND
HEART PATÉ AND DICED KIDNEYS AND BRAIN
NOODLE SOUP AND BABY POT PIE . . . AND YOU
WERE THERE AND YOU AND YOU AND YOU AND
YOU AND YOU! . . . YOU ALL WERE THERE! . . ."

The air was thick; a psychic smog enveloped the
room . . . Frank surveyed his kingdom: all was still; a
few of the other children stared back, their eyes calm
and empty as if their souls had vacated and were hiding on the far side of the moon, leaving the bodies of

*the helpless children to fend for themselves; Mrs. Die-*
*seldorfer was lumped at her desk, her face buried in*
*her shaking hands, frozen in time like a child para-*
*lyzed by an air raid siren; she lifted her face; greenish*
*sweat poured out of her pores; she looked like a zom-*
*bie . . . with great effort, she spoke:*

*". . . Frank . . . go to the principal's office . . ."*

*She was pleading with him, really, not command-*
*ing or asking or even suggesting; she was begging: she*
*was pleading with Frank as a swimmer might plead*
*with a charging twenty-foot great white shark . . .*

*". . . COOL . . . ," said Frank, who got up and*
*sauntered toward the door, whistling some tune, un-*
*doubtedly from a Walt Disney movie; of course, he*
*had no intention of going to the principal's office—an*
*understanding had developed with the school system*
*over the years: he did not want to see the principal,*
*and the principal did not want to see him; if in-*
*structed to see the principal, he was not required to*
*do so; the principal would rather lie down in traffic*
*than see Frank; the principal would rather eat lead*
*than see Frank; the principal would rather drink motor*
*oil than see Frank; the principal would rather stick his*
*tongue in a toaster than see Frank; the principal*
*would rather swallow steel shavings than see Frank;*
*the principal would rather soak in a bath of Drāno*
*than see Frank; the principal would rather cut off his*
*own head with a chain saw than see Frank; if in-*
*structed to see the principal, Frank was not required*
*to do so—and so he didn't—and instead he wan-*
*dered the halls, an unwanted psychosociopath, often*
*ending up at the school library, a happy-pretty place*
*with a sunny yellow paint job and cheerful self-esteem*
*posters, and he would wander the aisles and knock*
*Dickens and Proust and especially Darwin off the*
*shelves and put his muddy shoes up on the tables,*
*soiling the material plane as he did the psychic plane,*

*and he would sit there picking his nose while flipping through the tasteless pages of copies of* Fling, Hustler, Busty, Juggs, Skunk *and* Shaved 'N' Ready, *depraved magazines that he had brazenly lifted from the 7-11 downtown—he had just walked right into America's favorite convenience store (it was certainly convenient for HIM) smiling like a demonic, horny maniac as he strode purposefully to the porno rack, selected several mags off the shelf, and strode purposefully straight back out the door, waving the flopping magazines over his head and smiling like a psycho while a middle-aged woman in a red apron named Dot who took her job seriously and cared deeply about the concentric puddles of her actions and about her responsibilities on this earth fumed but dared not interfere—and no one dared to say a word in the library, either, as he whistled, gurgled, and hooted, loudly admiring the mammoth airbrushed "spreads" that unfolded before him, his booming psycho erotic rants echoing through the shattered academic stillness; the students gaped in horror, feeling the wetness, as Frank made no effort to conceal his actions or intents and let his small, stubby hand slide whimsically into his pants to massage his stained balls as he scanned the sticky magazine pages, groaning: Mary O'Leery, librarian, tried to mind her own business and ignore the hairs that were standing straight up on the back of her neck screaming WARNING! RUN FOR YOUR LIFE! and went about her business, making sure that Jane Austen was filed correctly, that the Hardy Boys mysteries were in proper sequential order, and that Dickens, Proust, and Darwin were picked up off the floor and brushed clean; she knew better than to confront Frank or to even make eye contact with him, with IT—she was twenty-nine, and she did not want to die—she did not want to go for a JOYRIDE—and so she averted her eyes and shuffled*

**53**

papers as Frank peered over the top of his *Fling* and looked her up, down, sideways, left, right, inside, and out; with the poised assonance of a particularly repulsive Eddie Murphy character, he spoke:

". . . AND WHAT DO YOU THINK ABOUT . . . GENITALIA? . . ."

Mary O'Leery felt a crimson wave move across her face and fear surge through her body; she tried to maintain her composure and poise and focus on her paperwork, which blurred before her; she tried to ignore this deranged lizard-fixated subhuman beast, but could think of nothing BUT Frank; his words climbed into her mind and his eyes bored holes in her blouse; she found herself unable to stifle the instinctive animal voice that squeezed her internal organs and squealed; she rested precariously on the edge of panic . . . Frank, meanwhile, was a lump of calm adolescent male ego, leaning back in a chair, fifteen feet away, a grade school Marquis de Sade: he cupped his hands into the shape of a megaphone and spoke:

". . . HEY TITS . . . TALK TO ME, BABE . . ."

". . . DIDN'T I SEE YOU IN ONE OF THESE MAGS? . . . WAS IT THE MAY *BUSTY*? . . . THE JUNE *FLING* MAYBE? . . . I SWEAR I'D RECOGNIZE THOSE FLOPPERS ANYWHERE . . ."

The librarian's hands were trembling; Frank began muttering in a gravelly, throaty whisper:

". . . OH YEAH, BABY . . . SHAKE IT . . ."

". . . THAT'S IT, TITS . . . MOVE IT FOR ME . . ."

. . . OH YEAH . . . THAT'S IT . . . OH YEAH . . ."

Frank edged closer to the librarian; she could feel the black energy spilling off around him in all directions; he spoke again:

". . . LEMME ASK YOU THIS . . . TELL ME,

**54**

*MISS LIBRARIAN . . . WOULD YOU LET DICKENS SUCK ON THOSE . . . HOW ABOUT HEMING- WAY? . . . VIRGINIA WOOLF? . . ."*

*The other students in the library ran for their lives; little Billy Smythe-Hardwick, being a particularly favored target of Frank's, dove to the floor and crawled behind the tables and out the door; Molly McSlide took the gum out of her mouth and, holding it between thumb and forefinger, deposited the lump onto the underside of a table and strode briskly out the door; Rusty Clips, who was nearest to Frank and whose path to the door was in fact blocked, moved discreetly toward the window, which he quietly pushed open: he leapt out, landing awkwardly on the cement below, breaking his ankle; Jack Bolt, class president, who was on his way straight to Yale and the Pent- house—he most certainly did not want to go for a joy- ride—bolted for the door at the first opportunity, knocking over Billy Smythe-Hardwick and several chairs as he ran . . . but Mary O'Leery, librarian, sym- bol of discipline and order, dispatched from the aca- demic pantheon to direct these wayward creatures, could not leave, could not run, could not hide; she could only quiver . . . Frank stared at her breasts . . .*

*". . . HEY TITS! . . . I'M TALKING TO YOU!"*

*". . . HEY! . . . I'M TALKING TO YOU! . . ."*

*". . . LISTEN, BABY . . . COME ON . . ."*

*". . . TAKE THAT BLOUSE DOWN A NOTCH . . ."*

*". . . COME ON . . . PULL 'EM OUT FOR ME . . ."*

*Frank's sadistic, impish expression became more menacing; his complexion took on a gray, textured ap- pearance and his eyes grew narrow and dark, as if a black storm cloud was gathering in his soul; his teen- aged soprano growl deepened, as if someone or* something else was about to use the vehicle named Frank to take a JOYRIDE, to commit a bit of random earthly mayhem; IT spoke:

". . . DON'T FUCK WITH THE REAPER, TITS . . . I SHOOT WHEN I SEE THE WHITES OF THE EYES . . ."

Frank the vehicle began moving away from this quivering young woman, this frightened lamb, this young librarian—who had once been content to just dust off Dickens and Jane Austen but would later do nothing but recite *Finnegan's Wake* at the top of her lungs while strapped to a padded chair unable to move because of the tight fit of a wraparound straightjacket, alone, so alone—so alone—in a lonely room with rubber walls and one small window through which only occasionally a young attendant with a heart of plastic and a pocket full of stolen drugs that he could sell for good money, real money—more than his lousy paycheck—would look through and with wide eyes gape at the freak-out queen and listen to the weird jive shit and shake his head and roll his eyes and feel a brief moment of pity—glandular re- gret, really—for such a pretty young thing gone to waste, just twenty-nine years old and over the edge so fast, so deep, and she landed so hard, her brains splattered all over the inside of her mind, and the doctors shook their heads and traced the genesis of this total collapse to just one particularly painful en- counter with a kid with muddy shoes and a breast fe- tish—hovering over her books, her poor, dear books, and wondering why—the eternal, unanswerable ques- tion: WHY?—and he moved away with slow, purpose- ful strides, the calm, measured strut of a sociopath, and approached the light switch by the door, stopping only to sneer at a young girl with ponytails who scam- pered awkwardly like a frightened colt in a lightning storm, and the poor librarian, her lower lip quivering, kept hoping IT would just GO AWAY, and she pretended not to hear him move or breathe and pretended not to move or breathe herself, and Frank paused as his bony fingers reached the light switch, and then he flipped it, off, and the room went dark, and as he began walking slowly back toward her a strange voice—a voice from somewhere else, unspeakably old and dark—emerged in toxic whispers from his small mouth; the words rippled forward in a slow-moving cloud:

". . . NOW IT'S DARK . . ."

# 4.

kicked in the head,
buffalo style

Frank's presence was required at school Monday
through Friday, and therefore Saturday quickly became his favorite day of the week; hell, Saturday was
everybody's favorite day of the week; Saturday was
AMERICA'S favorite day of the week . . . the synchro-
nized dancing cogs slaved away all week, so why
shouldn't SATURDAY be their day?; Monday through
Friday belonged to the Man and Sunday belonged to
the Lord—who didn't pay as well as the Man, which
isn't saying much, because the Man paid just enough
to keep bread on the table, or at least what PASSED
for bread in the modern processed world—which is
why people eat out so much, because the bread of
the modern world doesn't even taste like bread—it
has a do-it-yourself, name-it-yourself quality that invites
you to add your own comments, your own opinion,
about what the hell it IS, because it tastes like nothing, really, like bloated loaves of compressed air—and
so people eat at expensive restaurants with plastic
potted plants and put up with abuse from surly wait-
ers because the bread is actually BREAD and not
mulched preservatives, eight fifty for a small bowl of

*thin chicken stock with occasional floating carrot slices
and minuscule bits of meat product substitute loaf,
but it's WORTH IT because the package includes
REAL bread smothered in butter that may or may not
be alive—why can't LOCKHEED make BREAD?—
Saturday was all that was LEFT—and so the cogs
cogged during the week, and gave thanks on Sunday—for WHAT?—should they have been THANK-
ING God or should they have been tracking Him
down and kicking His Supreme Ass?—and Saturday
was theirs to do with as they pleased, to express their
spirit and individuality, if they had any . . . most didn't;
most simply PASTURED: they nibbled, they paced,
they puttered; they milled, they shuffled, they tended;
they did ordinary things, American things, suburban
things, small things: they attempted to rake up the
dead leaves that leapt from the undead trees that
looked with sticky unsleeping maple syrup eyes at the
pathetic humans and their odd Saturday lives and rustled; they staggered from the couch to the kitchen
and back to the sagging sofa with beer and chips;
they sucked vast amounts of radiation from the organized, sanctioned, National Security State-approved
bloodletting ritual sporting events that oozed out of
the almighty box in a seasonally rotating blur of
choreographed violence and implied blood: in the fall,
footballs flew through the air and war analogies filled
the airwaves: "bombs" were thrown, players were
"hit" and "stuck," "battles" were fought "in the
trenches," and the game was frequently interrupted
for commercials—commercials for WAR, really—
featuring the twin towers of advertising, BEER and
CARS . . . America was instructed to DRINK, to stay
"loaded," "tanked," geopolitically ignorant, socially
numb, cortexually incapable of pondering the morality
and implications of weekend wars launched on small
postage-stamp factories like Grenada; just DRINK*

*America, and DRIVE: get in your cheap metal cages
with the exploding gas tanks, where the BABES are,
and BURN, BABY, BURN the blood of mother earth,
suck the oil out of her flesh, just keep sticking those
needles into her veins and sucking the oil out so that
fat cats in big hats can sit on their old-growth porches
and look into the oily Texas nights and say hot-damn
as they stroke the expensive young butts of the not-
so-sweet young things from the local community college who are fucking their way through college but
have not yet realized that there is nothing after college but more fucking—they will fuck their way
through LIFE—yes, stick the needle into mother earth
and TWIST . . . the box showed them actual contrived
footage of an alcoholic actor from east Pasadena, so-
bered up for one day, one gig, his face pasted with
pancake makeup to hide the pits and prevent the
grease and oil from the late-night cheeseburgers and
endless cups of coffee from spilling out of his pores
and running down his face, a two-dimensional man
with perky amphetamine-bright eyes and a cocaine
smile sitting in his Dollar Rent-a-Car—thirty dollars,
actually, for a limping pile of tin-foil—and driving in
contrived contentment down the boulevard of airbrushed dreams, into the sunset of our imaginations,
smiling and laughing with his manicured and grotesquely pancaked family—an aging, pill-addicted former soap-opera slut queen and two young bratty
Hollywood snot-children whose parents are thinking
CAREER in large flashing neon letters when actually
the twitching little brain stems have merely postponed
destiny—the living death that is life in wageslave
smog hell—for a few short, fat years of teenage blus-
ter which will fly by like ants in a tornado and soon
enough they will find themselves behind the counter at
Greasy Cheese saying "May I have your order?" when
they really mean "Would you run over me and kill*

*me?"—driving contentedly into our minds, into our lives, telling America to shut the fuck up and DRINK . . . in the winter, legalized mayhem reigned in the form of ice hockey, where sticks met teeth and teeth lost and dental bills mounted until there were no more dental bills because there were no more TEETH: false choppers were simply removed before the game and replaced by Lockheed space-alloy stick-repellent miracle dentures . . . in the spring, uniformed gangs gathered in strange pants around grassy knolls, one man hurling a small ball at the heads of other players who attempted to knock the ball back through the teeth of the man who threw it until one man eventually hit the ball or WAS hit and scampered around first base and slid into second, super-lightweight Lockheed razor cleats flying high and wide and threatening the genitals of the nearest fielder, at which point the other players wandered off the bench and rustled about like angry, milling buffalo, snorting and clawing the ground as wraparound gold chains rattled about bull necks menacingly and yet elegantly, bull necks strengthened and buffed from passionate sessions of deodorized straining and snorting on reverse-gravity gyro-enhanced muscle-selective heart-monitoring post-Sears weight-training equipment, which left the players looking massively tight and stiff, like coiffed gorillas, milling about the field of the fan's dreams—the play-ers' dreams were elsewhere—lurking suggestive in the disco-neon lobby of the hotel adjacent to the sports bar out by the airport—dreams of fishnet stockings and PUSSY HEAVEN—with the field reserved for the smaller dreams of the fans, who lived for nothing but Saturdays, cheap beer, and millionaires in strange pants . . . in times of desperation, the TV barfed up bowling, the sport of dullards, hosted by the creaking Jackson—the fountain of Frank's father's sad and inadequate dreams—and Frank's father would stare* in open-mouthed rapture, his pineal gland strutting bravely forward, in an apparent attempt to CONNECT with Jackson—who, sadly, HAD no pineal gland—as he sat sucking up the excitement of the week's match oozing out of Cleveland or Des Moines or Reno—never anywhere civilized—there were no bowling matches from Manhattan or Cambridge—and the reflected images danced and leaped in his eyes: Ray Hall, plaid slacks, Kmart, bounded down the floor like an idiot and spun the ball with a limp hissing sound, like a balloon deflating, skidding in two-tone shoes, looking like a cripple and a fashion jerk; five pins toppled and he meekly tiptoed back to the bench to sit with head down and legs crossed and hands folded in his lap because he was now twenty-one—count 'em—pins behind, according to the tally announced by the venerable Jackson: Ray Perez, red shirt, was wiping the floor with this Hall cat, hurling the ball at high speed with a half-drunk Juan Corona leer—now that was BOWLING—the pins collapsed almost willingly, seeming sexually satisfied—SPENT—as they lay in the gutter, looking up at the stars, before being scraped up and set on their fat asses by a machine not engineered by Lockheed; Hall pranced down the floor and flicked the ball with a high-pitched chirp, but he jerked when someone chuckled and the ball veered and missed the front pin for an embarrassing leave—at this point it was becoming quite clear that nothing short of the greatest television-hosting performance of all time could make this genetic mismatch even remotely bearable, but things perked up suddenly when Jackson unexpectedly blurted out the line of the day—"What a set of pipes!"—as Perez was walking back to the bench after pulverizing ten more pins—he was one of those people who walked leading with their stomach—and dared you to say something about it—and Jackson became strangely quiet, because there were, sadly, no pipes of any kind in sight; apparently, the "pipes" remark had slipped out of Jackson's own private world and into the minds and hearts of America; apparently he had lost contact with reality and had been speaking to the nation from the seedy, one-way world of his own imagination, a world without street signs; there was no further mention of pipes and Jackson seemed to be behaving himself until a few minutes later when he suddenly exclaimed—"ONE OF THE TRULY GREAT MOMENTS IN PROFESSIONAL BOWLING!"—he had done it again—pilot to tower! MAYDAY! MAYDAY!—and Frank's father watched, transfixed, as Jackson unraveled and history apparently pivoted in the grooves before him: Pete McQuarrie, blue and red stripes, polyester, had roared from behind, knocking down hundreds of helpless pins to take the lead—but then Ray retook the lead—then Pete—then Ray—then Pete—then Ray—and the lead swayed back and forth like Ray's stomach—and then Jackson cleared his throat and announced "there it is . . ."—but CBS left his words hanging and cut to a commercial for the Popeel Expandable Food Storage Unit featuring the remarkable accordian construction system; Frank's father's eyes were wide and red with tears; Saturday was also HIS favorite day of the week . . .

Without school, without flesh and will to mold, Saturday afternoons usually found Frank working his way outward and downward toward the local 7-11, a regional landmark located on what in the sixteenth century had been an Indian burial ground, or at least the burial ground of ONE Indian, a particular fellow who had been killed—PULVERIZED, really—by a crazed buffalo avenging the death of two of his close relatives who were captured, greeted, befriended, apologized to, killed, skinned, eaten, belched up and

**63**

*shitted out by this particular Indian's extended family
of friends and relatives . . . this particular Indian, however, was not apologized to, befriended or eaten, and
his death was not avenged: he was merely cornered
and kicked in the head, buffalo style, falling to the
earth on nearly the exact spot where centuries later
would stand a five-cent-per-copy Xerox machine and
an Insta-Teller cash machine that could theoretically
be programmed to discreetly tap into the accounts of
any number of aging, senile millionaires and spit out
ten twenties a day every day from now until the end
of the instant replay that is time collapsing back upon
itself, and his Indian pal found him, apologized, and
then buried him . . . the clerk at the 7-11 located on
the sixteenth-century Indian apology and burial site
was a young Hindu woman from New Delhi named
Dot who had chosen a different and more difficult
path: to manifest goodness and hope and patience
and decency, to create an outward ripple of GOOD
that moved out into the world; to be a living example
of the divine origins of fleshy beingness and the vast
potential for growth and expansion of the soul in this
dimensional classroom; her life's work was to awaken
and to remain awake while those around her wandered through life like dazed cattle, using only about
two or three percent of their brains, living lives of accessorized boredom and episodic stagnation, sprinting
from their shadows and avoiding the opportunities
presented by their own higher selves in this cosmic
preschool to transform pain and transcend suffering,
avoiding the great work to WORK—which is the
American way, really, to live only for the fulfillment of
small, immediate, transitory pleasures while at the
same time silently crucifying those annoyingly blissful
freaky Zen types, those mystic nutcases with their
eyes wide open, all THREE of them, who see all and
everything from their perch on the magic mountain*

*and radiate the light of majesty and brilliance that fills
their outwardly expanding inner worlds, the arresting
beauty spilling from their hearts like sunlight—if a million suns filled the sky—those walking, leaking, oozing
manifestations of the ultimate, all-encompassing and
annoyingly unknowable bottom layer of reality—
BEDROCK reality—the last stop on the evolutionary
interstate, the final rest stop and eternal home of
Christ, Buddha, Merlin, Quetzalcoatl, Dot, Beethoven,
Lester Bangs, Bach, Coltrane, Pythagoras, Newton, St.
Augustine, Swedenborg, Twiggy, Barney, a thousand
Sufi poets, a hundred gaggle of monks, five thousand
lamas, ten thousand yogis, fifteen hundred Amazonian
shamans, four hundred seven Eskimos, nine hundred
fifty-four American Indians, fifteen vampires, twelve
thousand hyperboreans, seventeen hundred dolphins,
four whales and two Draco . . .*

*Dot smiled a lot as she was swearing under her
breath in cracked, dusty Hindi; she didn't speak much
English except to ask "soft? . . . box?" or "lemon-
lime? . . . cherry?"—two questions of prime importance to 7-11 target consumers; she knew numbers
and prices, though, was gifted in that way, and no one
EVER bought a ten-cent Laffy Taffy from her for a
nickel, as was known to happen at other 7-11s where
the clerks were less attentive—word got around about
places like that—but all the kids knew that the chick
they called DOT was tough: nobody conned her on
prices; nobody scammed her; nobody lifted ketchups
from her or plied extra sips from the self-serve Big
Gulp machine; nobody switched price tags and got
away with it; nobody beat her . . . she was tough, poverty tattooed on her soul, and she kept her third eye
peeled for creeps like Frank, psychic boulders blocking
the path to her earthly awakening, fleshy obstacles to
overcome on the high road to evolution and salvation,
the raw ingredients in the transmutation of the her-*

metic gold; she locked eyes with Frank as he walked loudly into the store (beep beep) and moved directly toward her; from her position behind the counter, she felt the power invoked by laser blasts of Free Will fired from the diaphragm outward in Tesla waves, emanating from the dark place inside him where where evil lurked and goodness choked . . . Frank looked at her and she wilted like a dead man's penis; her eyes, bright and attentive, suddenly lost all glow, like those old fifties TV sets that faded from the bizarrely hunched shoulders that WERE Ed Sullivan to a dot that got smaller and smaller until Ed was trapped again in that invisible television hell where he remained every week until the next Sunday at eight when he reanimated and wedged his shoulders back into your living room; her eyes lost all life; she smiled yellow-white-green teeth and swore under her breath; Frank rolled his fat tongue over his greasy lower lip . . .

" . . . THE SPECTACLE OF A CHILD BEHEADED BY A TRACTOR TRAILER MIGHT CAUSE A PERSON TO SLIP BETWEEN THE CRACKS OF THEIR FLESHY VEHICLE, BUT ONLY FOR A MOMENT . . . FEAR WILL DRIVE THEM BACK . . . ONLY AN ACT OF GOD CAN BRING OUT GODLINESS . . . IF GOD STRAPPED DYNAMITE AROUND HIS ROBE AND TOOK A SENATOR'S NIECE HOSTAGE IN A SALAD BAR AND SMEARED HER WITH MACARONI SALAD AND COTTAGE CHEESE AND DEMANDED A HELICOPTER, A MILLION IN CASH, AND ASYLUM IN ISTANBUL, PERHAPS THEN AND ONLY THEN MIGHT HE GET PEOPLE'S ATTENTION AND PERHAPS A TWO-MOVIE DEAL AND A *VANITY FAIR* COVER . . ."

Dot looked upon Frank, this THING from the postmodern gene-pool mud puddle, this abomination of Trumanism and television, this small, powerful mon-

*strosity, and, inside her head, all was silent; no*
*thoughts formed; the language of psychic violence, the*
*rhetoric of Frank's malicious INTENT, transcended*
*translation and her mind froze, the way the mind of a*
*man turning a corner in a video store might FREEZE*
*if confronted by a nine-foot, twelve-hundred-pound*
*Alaskan brown bear with an H&K machine pistol and*
*an erection to scale; she felt her stomach ripple as if*
*her liver was pounding on the walls of her abdomen*
*attempting to escape: she felt her bowels empty and*
*flood her slacks with a greenish surge of brown rice,*
*chick peas, and steamed okra that left a warm,*
*greenish brown streak on her red 7-11 apron, like a*
*moss-draped log floating lazily down a sea of blood in*
*the steamy mist of a quiet nuclear winter; she quiv-*
*ered . . .*

"Box . . . soft?"

". . . THIS IS A WORLD OF LIES . . . THE LIES
CANNOT BE STOPPED . . . THEY HAVE MOMEN-
TUM AND THERE IS NOT ENOUGH INERTIA TO
STOP THE MOMENTUM . . . THERE ARE SIMPLY
NOT ENOUGH UNSOILED SOULS AND TOO
MUCH SOIL . . . THERE ARE MOSTLY EMPTY
SHELLS LEFT NOW, VAGUE WAREHOUSES OF
FLESH WITHOUT ORIGINAL THOUGHT BUT WITH
NICE SOCKS . . . A LIE IS A LIE IS A LIE, BUT AFTER
THE THIRD LIE THE FIRST LIE DOESN'T KNOW IF
THE SECOND LIE IS LYING ABOUT THE THIRD LIE
AND THE FOURTH LIE IS BORN INTO EXISTENCE
FROM JUST THAT ONE THOUGHT AND THE LIES
MULTIPLY LIKE A PYRAMID SCHEME UNTIL THERE
ARE MILLIONS OF LIES AND A SMALL COLONY OF
ABOUT SEVENTY-THREE TRUTHS HUDDLED TO-
GETHER IN AN ABANDONED WAREHOUSE NEAR
THE APPENDIX AND SOON THEY ARE INFIL-
TRATED BY A SMALL SQUAD OF SMILING LIES
WITH FURROWED BROWS PRETENDING TO BE

*TRUTHS AND THE LIES POISON THE WATER SUP-*
*PLY AND FOUL THE OXYGEN AND THE TRUTHS*
*SLOWLY SUFFOCATE UNTIL THEY NO LONGER*
*KNOW THE LIES FROM THE TRUTH AND THEY*
*BEGIN SMILING AND COMBING THEIR HAIR*
*STRAIGHT BACK . . ."*

*Dot was gripping the air in her stomach and slowly
compressing it into small suitcase-shaped compartments, which were being portered frantically by her organs in a futile attempt to escape to somewhere,
anywhere; she was stiffly propped against the cash register, her right index finger wedged tightly against the
CLEAR button, causing a continuous, quietly painful
beep—that droning consumer call-to-arms, that march
of a thousand ninety-nine-cent deaths—that damnable
BEEEEEP—and the sound reverberated through the
cracked furrows of her brain; Frank spoke:*
*"CAMELS . . . BOX . . . MATCHES . . ."*

*He picked up a Laffy Taffy, a ten-center, and me-
thodically unwrapped and wedged the caramel-colored
square of processed food matter into his mouth, into the
crack where a tooth was sprouting from his gums, waiting to fill out the space like a tree filling out the black of
the night sky; still sucking the waste off the bottom of
her soul with his eyes, he reached into the back pocket
of his black jeans and scratched out a nickel with the
edge of his thumb and casually flipped it across the
counter: it landed on its edge and began slowly to wobble in a concentric, descending circle, like a planetoid on
a doomsday ride into a whirlpool spiral down a black
bottomless vortex to the place beyond nowhere . . .*
*"CAMELS . . . BOX . . . MATCHES . . . NOW!"*

*DOT's right hand was still frozen, rigid, the tired
whine of the cash register echoing somewhere in the
padded cells of her withdrawn personality; with her
left hand, she reached below the counter and in a
stiff, plastic motion pulled up a fresh, shiny hard pack*

of Camels, complete with the Masonic imagery, the pyramids, the eye, all that shit, and she put it down on the counter, gently and yet quickly, as one might put down a dead baby; she smiled, and air hissed through the cracks around her parched lips . . .

"Have Nice Day . . ." she said with attempted civility; the words fell out of her mouth like broken toys; Frank smiled:

". . . WE ARE THE PUDDLE THAT LEAKS . . . AND WHEN SOUTH BECOMES NORTH LAYERS OF MUD WILL COME TO LIFE AND WE WILL DIE . . . WHEN THE EARTH TURNS OVER, ALL EVILS DOUBLED, SOUND WAVES WILL TRAVEL THREE TIMES AROUND THE WORLD AND POISON ASH WILL FILL THE SEAS FOR ONE HUNDRED MILES . . . THE LIZARDS WILL SQUEAL IN DELIGHT . . . AT LAST THE CYCLE WILL BE COMPLETE . . . DECAY WILL BE REALIZED . . ."

He picked up the cigarettes and slipped them into his pocket without offering to pay for them and grabbed a book of matches—the cheap ones that always go out just after ignition but have those you-too-can-draw-sucker scams on the inside flap, where one might look and study closely between puffs in a dreamy sort of way and see a different, smaller world—and as he put them in his pocket he broke his psychic choke-hold on the decaying bottom parts of her soul, which receded into a position of fetal indifference from which it might take hours for the notion of time and space to finally snap her back into somewhere, anywhere, near where what had just been the perimeters of her well-defined and orderly reality, but was now, well, MUSH . . . Frank then began his slow march toward the door; under his breath he was humming one of Uncle Walt's American Dream pinko Nazi mind-control theme songs . . .

"SOME DAY MY PRINCE WILL COME . . ."

**69**

# 5.

## a fleshy lump named Frank

Frank was a cosmic thug, evil, foul, an asshole, a prick, a jerk, a soiler of lives, a stealer of souls, one-hundred-fifty-proof evil . . . all of this was clear from the beginning; and as he grew older, as he grew wiser, as his life unfolded like a decaying lotus, his personality gave way to a sense of completeness, a summation, a willful mass . . . a rampaging IDENTITY: in that regard he was lucky; most people spend lifetimes looking for SOMETHING, ANYTHING, to give purpose to their small lives and meaning to their meaningless existences; their quest is for form, for definition, for PURPOSE, for a goal or a career or a nametag or a uniform or a badge or a title or an office or a business card or an appointment calendar or a desk or a mug or a gold watch or a hat or a gun or a bicycling outfit or inflatable tennis shoes or a hooded sweatshirt or a mortgage or a business card holder or a credit rating or a profession; their quest is to be more than just THEMSELVES, more than just NOTHING—although, ironically, if they actually WERE nothing, they might actually BE something: to exist OUTSIDE of the choice of boxes supplied is to be FREE, to exist

70

*independently, to choose NOT to choose; to be noth-
ing HERE is to be that which has come from THERE
and leaked through—that is why we exist alone, independently, in BODIES, free to sprout upwards or sideways or down into the ground or in circles, free to
define our individual worlds from WITHIN, free to
choose courses of experience or growth or ignorance
or sloth or art school or radiant goodness, as we so
choose, hopefully ascending upward and outward and
away from this backed-up toilet and toward someplace REAL, someplace where civilization is less civilized and more civil, where plants talk and people
listen, where music sits in chairs and speaks whimsically of lost notes and favored chords, where angels
smoke and cough and tell dirty jokes, where God
takes a long sauna and leaves the message machine
on, where evil is a fading memory, where love and
hope are not mugged by Sinatra wannabes in cheap
suits, where there is no Max Factor Beauty Museum,
no Oscar Meyer Wiener Mobile, no World's Tallest
Office Chair, no Tupperware Awareness Center, no
Spam Museum, no Cranberry World—no pathetic ca-
thedrals to capitalism of any kind—a place where life
is more than a leased cadillac and a ranch house and
a young wife and a swimming pool and lawn furniture
and a stock portfolio and a dishwasher and a sixty-
inch TV and two smiling plotting children counting the
days until mommy and daddy are stone cold dead so
that all of THIS can be theirs, a higher world than
this one . . . but in the meantime, THIS is it, HERE
WE ARE, and most find it EASIER just to slip comfortably into the warm prefitted parameters of a paint-by-
numbers connect-the-dots universal-barcode-box-life, as
instructed; they pass on the high hard road to enlightenment; it is far easier to be fat and stupid in the
middle than to be lean and hungry on the EDGE,
where life cuts and bleeds, and so the vast majority of*

the herd postpones the evolution of their immortal souls, offering up any number of lame excuses— paperwork, tennis match, aerobics class, shopping, dentist appointment—although failure to evolve carries a REPEAT sentence: offenders return again and again and again, and again, until they get it RIGHT, and if they keep SCREWING UP they never graduate, never elevate, never float on up to cloudville, heaven, motel nirvana, the galactic hostel that actually exists, somewhere, but somewhere else, certainly not here; if these poor sucker-punched souls understood the gravity of the matter they'd forget about restaurants and carpeting and four-wheel-drive vehicles and mortgage points and concern themselves with nothing less than the evolution of their own soiled souls, the soil that does NOT wash out; they would drop the defensive clichés and elevate, graduate, from this twirling garbage dump, leave this cosmic preschool behind, cut their losses, get the hell out of the game, knock the board over and start the game over . . .

Frank was lucky: his personality had been steamrolled, waylaid, ambushed, cluster-bombed, by the THING that came from somewhere else, the crystallization of the being, the fleshy lumping of the essence that came striding forward not long after birth, all that he HAD BEEN and WOULD BE, and it manifested itself in a lump of solid matter, a fleshy lump named Frank Booth, who appeared to him one night—as if out of a poorly lit dream—and said "BABY WANTS TO FUCK" . . . it was a cold and stormy Thanksgiving night and Frank was drunk; he was thankful for that much: he hated holidays, he hated hypocrisy, he was not giving thanks and god he hated turkeys; he was loitering about his apartment, throwing down Pabst Blue Ribbon sixteen-ouncers and mug shots of Jagermeister after having spent the better part of the afternoon careening his cab around the city and finally crashing into a downtown corner news-stand, sweeping right through it, detaching the small structure from its foundation and carrying both the structure and its wide-eyed occupant on his front bumper for several harrowing, terror-filled blocks, dis-tributing newspapers, cigars, condoms, lumber, Harle-quin Romances and copies of *Fling, Busty,* and *Penthouse* and sending dazed tourists and panicking commuters sprawling for cover before finally broadsid-ing a police cruiser and hurling what was left of the fractured cubicle and its bruised occupant over the top of the cop car and onto the center divider of a major thoroughfare; it had been his first day on the job, and his last day, his first job, as a taxi driver, the first of many jobs he would hold before finding himself incorporated in the dead Christmas tree business, the business of jingle-hell memories; he had been fired with enthusiasm by his boss, a small man with a red whisky face, and then promptly arrested by a rat-faced policeman with an automatic weapon; he was released on bail after vomiting profusely and returned home and was now loitering about his apartment, one minute staring at Ed Meese on CNN and belching whenever Meese lied like a grinning, cornered dog, and the next saying FUCK IT and moving out into a dark and cloudy world which by the time the night was over would still be dark and cloudy but would have a certain shimmer to it, a glow like the sad slip-pery light of Jackie Kennedy's eyes, a world which would never ever be the same, especially for Frank but also for the rest of the world, a blue velvet night; he wandered downtown, occasionally stopping to rant at groups of tourists, who scattered like pigeons, until he found himself near where earlier that day a news-stand proprietor had been harmlessly barking out "Get yer afternoon paper!" when he should have been

73

screaming "Run for yer fuckin' lives!"; Frank craned his neck to look up at the tall buildings, at the ghosts of the imprisoned nine-to-five souls; he felt the wind whip against his cheeks and slipped into a familiar alley that led to a door with peeling paint, the back door of the theater where he had first been exposed to *Babes in Toyland*; he quietly wedged himself in . . . *Blue Velvet* was playing; he liked the title, but he had no idea what the film was about; he was hoping for nothing more than to be mildly amused, hoping for one of those traditionally American films, something generic, something grotesque, something with lots of blood and mindless killing, something with that auto accident excitement, that blood-ritual energy, that blood-sacrifice-at-the-pyramids feel, that psychic Jolt Cola feel, that adrenaline SPLAT that gets people EX-CITED and makes producers think that THIS is what we want to see—films that arouse us only because it is in our GENES to be aroused, a bad habit dating back to when we were dodging giant lizards, not because it is GOOD for us to be aroused—we need to get our hands OUT of our genes—and yet these sleazy Hollywood bozos keep pushing the arousal buttons without stopping to think about what we might DO with this extra blood-sacrifice-at-the-pyramids feel and then executives are shocked and stunned and horrified and saddened when the bones of thirty-four teenagers are organized by bone type and laid neatly in rows in a shallow grave next to the apartment complex where the cross-eyed crossing guard with the weird smile and the baseball card collection lives—OH MY DEAR GOD HE HAD EATEN THOSE CHIL-DREN—and the producers feel TERRIBLE about the whole thing—really they do—they hold a celebrity benefit golf tournament—but they don't feel bad enough to STOP MAKING those ultra-violent Masonic-blood-ritual films because, well, THAT'S WHAT THE

**74**

*PUBLIC WANTS, and, anyway, they need the
MONEY, and, HELL, this is a free-market economy,
this is DEMOCRACY, this is AMERICA, the BEST
DAMNED COUNTRY THERE IS, and GENERIC
CLICHÉ, and TIRED FRONTAL-LOBE WORLDVIEW,
and OVERBLOWN NORTHISM, and, anyway, times
haven't been that good and you know how it is and
after the deductions for dinners and drinks and hotel
suites and air fare and limousine service and location
shooting and unscheduled reshooting and unforseeable
post-production cost overruns and reasonable, healthy,
respectable, outlandish profits, well, there just isn't
THAT much left over and there are studio costs to
pay and mortgages to pay and ex-wives' mortgages to
pay and mistresses' mortgages to pay and vacation
home mortgages to pay and lawyers to pay and
shrinks to pay and thugs to pay and film critics to pay
and theater owners to pay—these people need to be
PAID—although what WE perhaps need is to be EN-
LIGHTENED and UPLIFTED rather than glandularly
mauled, but it's too late for that NOW because there
is NO WAY that we are going to sit through the ten
fucking commandments or the sound of fucking music
when sex and blood and rock and roll are playing on
the other seven screens at the octoplex; our decay is
playing at a theater near you; it's too late because our
DNA has bounced off the end of time and we are on
a roll, backwards, into the black hole from which we
emerged; we are moving away from Shakespeare and
back toward Attila the Hun . . . sure, they were "just
films," but films are an eerie precursor of reality;
somehow the future leaks through the cracks and
floats out there in the thinning ozone where screen-
writers and novelists and reporters for the world
weekly news grab slices of the future and cut and
paste them into the nightly news and tabloid TV
shows and cheap novels and producers buy up these*

toxic time leaks cheap and hire hacks without hearts
to crank out scripts which are paired with the dream
star of the moment, Cary Grant or Meryl Streep or
Darryl Hannah or Henry Fonda or John Travolta or
Lee Majors or Doris Day or Demi Moore or Molly
Ringwold—it doesn't really matter WHICH star—they
are more or less interchangeable—and these trashy
nightmare futures are made into FILMS, the stuff that
defines and consumes our life, the junk food of our
souls, cheeseburgers of consciousness, and these fu-
tures leak into our world, the mass psychosis that is
the future flooding the present, where they fill our
minds and become even more real, the path even
more clearly defined; there is no escape from tomorrow when tomorrow leaks in and colors today . . .
*Blue Velvet* was the future puddling darkly into the
present: Frank saw his own fouled gene pool dripping
from the spiraling decay that was THE NEIGHBOR-
HOOD; the creature wrapped around his soul like a
snake had finally wobbled out of a Pabst Blue Ribbon
nightmare and revealed itself: he WAS Frank Booth,
the flesh-and-blood döppelganger of the two-
dimensional antihero of the ultimate anti-movie, a fictional image inhabiting a three-dimensional vehicle; he
was Poe's maelstrom extended into the real world,
"the wide waste of liquid ebony," the wide waste of
liquid HUMANITY, the manifestation of an archetype,
a THING, a FORCE, a creature that resonated the
pure, fluid BEING of the modern disease with such
resolute clarity and perfect dissonant pitch that his
mere existence had shaken the balance of the world
itself, and the world had SHIVERED and RECOILED,
the very fabric of global thought, the lace of our combined souls, caught off guard, flipped and pinned like
a harmless old lady suddenly attacked on the sidewalk
by a malicious, grinning street sign . . . that was the
POWER Frank had—there was no need to differen-

*tiate between the film Frank and the flesh Frank: they
were equally REAL, mirror images inhabiting parallel
universes, parallel NEIGHBORHOODS . . . Frank
Booth, film creep, had been INSIDE him all along, hiding, just as some people insist that CHRIST is inside
THEM, until he just pops out one day, into their field
of awareness, into their consciousness, and from that
moment forward they do whatever they want in HIS
name: it is okay for them to preach the scriptures fer-
vently in the soiled pagan aisles of the local Wal-Mart
in an attempt to convert people who are attempting
to purchase shampoo and are not the least bit interested in religious salvation; it is okay because they are
doing it in HIS name, because HE is in them, because
they have seen the LIGHT . . . well, Frank had seen
the DARK: his identity had emerged fully formed from
behind blue velvet curtains; suddenly, he WAS Frank
Booth, and it was okay for him to take people's
hearts and turn them inside out, to take people's
worlds and substitute his own; it was okay because he
had seen the DARK, which was inside of him, puddling outward . . .*

    *Blue Velvet WAS Frank's world, the world that
defined him, and it unfolded before him like a battle
plan; the NEIGHBORHOOD leaked out and enveloped the theater like a fog; he inhaled deeply,
knowing he would carry this world out of the theater,
where he could spit it out onto those around him,
where it would STICK; just as Frank Booth was more
than merely the embodiment of a tacky film creep
with a taste for lipstick and warm beer, Blue Velvet
was more than just "entertainment": it was an
AGENT OF CHANGE, a vehicle of consciousness that
interacted with and influenced the world around it, a
psychic burger with fries that left the assembled
human flock simultaneously stunned, excited, aroused,
enraged, barely able to breathe let alone think, unable*

*to stop themselves from hauling this new reality out of
the theater, out into the world, where the film exists
independently in the ether and grows like a fungus . . .
years later, looking back in summation, Frank
would reflect upon life in general and upon Blue Velvet and this day in particular, the day "it" all fell
apart, the transdimensional moment when Europe
reached critical mass and the Middle East boiled over
and Africa vomited and the United States staggered
and lurched, the MOMENT when life on earth fell
and could not get up, and it occurred to him that all
these massive simultaneous stab wounds had in fact
not been inflicted by Henry Kissinger or General Electric or Mitsubishi or Gorby or Ronnie or Saddam or
Millie or Slick Willie or Dirty Bob or Socks or Gumby
or Biff Henderson or the people or the left or the
right or the liberals or the conservatives or the bol-
shevics or the chia-pets or runaway capitalism or runaway socialism or runaway inflation or cloned
stewardesses or washer-dryers or booze or drugs, but
rather by a sudden, massive psychic shock—a
GLOBAL MINDFUCK—that had been triggered, as
death is TRIGGERED by the outwardly concentric impact of a shotgun shell against a smiling, sweating
face, by too many too people seeing BLUE VEL-
VET—either the movie or the world behind the
movie, it made no difference—on the same fucked
and doomed night; the world can only stand so many
bad trips at once: if enough people have a bad trip at
the same moment then THE WORLD has a bad trip;
and that night, that peculiar night in this strange
world, Gurdjieff's SHOCK, the global synapse jolt that
was needed to propel the human race to a higher octave of consciousness, occurred in REVERSE: the shock
of Blue Velvet, the intrusion of Frank's World into
our own, propelled the human race BACKWARDS,
into a lower spiral of existence; that night, Frank put*

his disease in all of us as sure as he put it in Dorothy Vallens; that night, he took us ALL for a GENETIC JOYRIDE . . .

Frank staggered out of the theater that evening and the world was a different, stranger place: the sky looked like Dorothy Vallens's darkly ordered apartment, glowing with that reddish tint that looked like faded blood; the clouds were alive; the trees were moving; the streets were pink and wet, like Ben's Place; the houses were black and still, like the eyes of Jeffrey Beaumont who looked out through black shutters into Frank's World, through the cracks in his own mind and into the black souls of Frank and his joyriding neighbors, from his world of sense and logic and crisply ironed shirts and into a world of underworld suits, string ties, hunched shoulders, amphetamine grimaces, ether masks, Pabst Blue Ribbon, and candy colored clowns, and what LOOKED BACK was the dark, soiled reality that is the fundamental identity of the HUMAN neighborhood; he looked into the rotting DNA of humanity: Frank Booth looked back and said "WHO IS THIS FUCK"; he looked into the void and saw mommy and baby and blood and pain and violence and decay and sickness and despair and dogs on the floor, lurking and scratching: baby wanted to fuck, and mommy did it for daddy, for the ear, for Van Gogh, for blue velvet, and through his mind's shutters he saw everything he didn't want to see but that had been there all along, daddy mommy baby hit me hit me hit me hit me HIT ME HIT ME HIT ME THUMP . . . and then it was dark—FINALLY— and Frank gave thanks, because the world was different . . .

Frank Booth was BORN that night when turkeys were ritually broiled and offered as sacrifices to the great god capitalism, the night when Frank sucked up the leaking ooze of the neighborhood and carried it

*with him out into the streets . . . suddenly, the world
that HAD BEEN no longer WAS; Frank's World had
seeped up from somewhere in the all-American lawn
of Jeffrey Beaumont's Lumberton and puddled, and everything that had looked so SWELL suddenly upon
closer examination didn't look swell at all; upon closer
examination, the red roses had sharp thorns and the
white picket fences had sharpened tips and the American Dream was as cold as a dead Vietnamese peas-
ant; IT was loose and running around, the America of
stolen hubcaps and shattered dreams, having crawled
from beneath the manicured lawns, the pink flamingos, the lawn furniture from Sears, from beneath the
Giant Balls of Twine and the World's Largest Catsup
Bottle, from beneath the manicured excuse-me dog-
fight that was life within the surreal illusion that was
America, from a parallel world of shadows, from a
place of dark and slimy spaces wedged between tiny
bits of light, from a place where ants devour butter-
flies and dog shit alike and carry the remains down
their holes, deeper into the dirt, where the lizards
await; Frank knew that it was a short distance—in
TIME rather than SPACE—from roses and picket
fences to blood-sucking thorns and Vlad the Impaler,
from Bedford Falls to Potterville, from Disneyland to
Mei Li, from Lumberton to Frank's World . . . that
night, staggering out of the theater, eyes glazed but
pulsing, surging with identity, Frank felt like Richard
Nixon, invincible—inhuman—and as he emerged
from the theater he immediately deposited his film
commentary on the sidewalk; the people milling about
looked at Frank with frozen expressions of squalid disgust; the corners of Frank's mouth were like tiny hollow logs with bits of tomato and pizza crust hanging,
clinging, dripping from his lips in a slow red sauce of
tomato spit vomit; Frank was smirking, beaming, and
yet his eyes were glazed, unfocusing beyond this world*

into the spinning realms of vomit hell; slowly, with
great effort, his mammoth lips parted once again—
the people scurried—and a visible, hazy blue-green
belch emerged, traveling slowly, drunkenly, expanding
in a random, fractal pattern across time and space:
the world itself was disgusted; he had not yet met Viv
LaFrance, grocery-store mind fucker, barroom queen,
waitress with a heart like downtown Baghdad, but had
she been there to see Frank spill his opinionated film
commentary all over the sidewalk, she would have
been impressed . . . a few blocks away, a man—tall
and dignified and polished and refined and reflective
and educated and grandfatherly and humble and wise
and powerful and educated—was standing on a gran-
ite bridge, admiring the vista, gazing out serenely and
pondering the evening moon as it slowly rose in full
round splendor through a vivid blue-black sky and
loomed majestically above the gently rolling water,
casting a brilliant, shimmering reflection that stretched
across the water like a silver snake; he carried a compact, well-used pipe, and took occasional long, comfortable puffs, releasing the smoke in small satisfied
clouds that dissipated and floated into the night; he
was a content man who wore his wisdom in his eyes
and his riches in his confident, patient stride and meticulous suit and wide-brimmed fedora; he walked with
a dignified limp, the result of a childhood injury suf-
fered during the revolution as he fled to China where
he was raised with the thoughtful and deeply reverent
attitudes of a young scholar while still carrying within
him the massive heritage of his homeland, the big
bear of a presence that extends back as long as time
and as wide as half the world . . . he moved slowly
from one edge of the bridge to the other, thinking,
musing; he leaned his finely crafted, polished walking
stick against the stone retaining wall and stood very
still, his hands in the pockets of his great wool over-

*coat, the folds of the collar flipped up to cover his
ears: from behind, he was merely a long, bearlike
coat, a colorful hat and gentle, floating puffs of smoke
that appeared and drifted, small, precise concertos of
smoke, dancing worlds of thought that dissipated and
floated about, scattering to the gentle winds that
moved calmly above the waters of the river that contained nameless fish and unborn dreams . . . he had
been here before: his thoughts were everywhere,
thoughts from months and years before that loitered
around the comfortable nooks of the bridge like playful white ghosts; they would collide with his new
thoughts, carried in waves of smoke, and ideas would
emerge, emotion colliding with dreams, ideas that
would hang briefly in the night sky; sometimes he
would reach up with his mind and grab them, and the
ideas would be lodged into his fine, ordered world,
where they would be in good time worked into his polished worldview; sometimes the ideas would linger, un-
heeded, floating about lazily, and he would leave
them behind, and someone else would wander by, lost
in thought, and they would pull in the ideas, and
would go home not knowing where these wonderful
new ideas—these creatures, these thoughts—had
come from . . . that is the way ideas traveled: they
floated, suspended in time and space, until someone
came along and grabbed them out of the sky . . .*

   *Several blocks away, several short blocks, a man
with mottled hair, a fractured grin and a strange,
otherworldly odor had just staggered out of a crumbling downtown film theater . . . Frank Booth, drunk
on the creepy residue of a malignant film thug, dizzy
with identity, reeling in the majestic glory of a heritige
uncovered, a PURPOSE revealed, an identity CON-
GEALED, wobbled into the dimly lit street glowing in
blue velvet shades: he wandered into the neighborhood, carrying the NEIGHBORHOOD, inside of him,*

*leaking out around him, and he could feel the cold
and dark sensation as it flowed out of him, through
him, and flooded the night air, hiding in cracks and
behind trees and in corners and shadows, where a
man, lost in thought, would be sure to walk past and
catch these dark thoughts, these joyride thoughts, with
his mind, just a quick passing glance at the black
shapes in the shadows and the thoughts would
become his, and he would go home unrelaxed, tense,
nervous, edgy, carrying these new thoughts with him
and he would snap at his wife and kick at his dog
and yell at his children and experience sudden crav-
ings for uncooked meat swimming in blood, his mind
filled with dark and devious thoughts, and he would
grab his frightened wife that night and push her face
into the pillow, one hand holding her hair and pulling,
the other wrapped around her thin neck, soaked with
her tears, and he would fuck her quickly with a violent
lunge and then roll off and fall asleep within seconds,
his mind clouded with images of horror and death, his
dreams foul; he would wake up feeling better, but
only a little; his wife and children would look at him
with fear and loathing, as they would look at a
demon, which, for one evening at least, was what he
had been . . . Frank walked on, leaking, his thoughts
swimming with visions and sounds: switchblades, Roy
Orbison, dancing fat women in short skirts, severed
ears, toppling detectives in yellow suits, ether masks,
knives, smeared red lipstick, pussy heaven; he was
whistling "In Dreams" and wishing to god he had a
cold sixteen-ounce Pabst Blue Ribbon; he wobbled
down the street another block and came to an old
bridge; he leaned over the side of the bridge, looked
down at the water, thought about jumping, wished
there was someone there he could push, or better yet,
THROW—a small baby, perhaps, maybe a month
old, two months, not old enough to know what the*

*hell was going on but old enough to cry his little guts out for mercy, mercy which would NOT come, that he could hold high, in a ritual sacrificial pose, as the child's entire family—mother, aunts, grandparents, brothers, sisters, cousins, in-laws, family pets, lost uncles, old college roommates, neighbors, teachers, babysitters, the family doctor, the dentist, the auto mechanic—looked on in horror, and he could feel their pain and sorrow, he could taste it, he could feed off it, and it was like a Thanksgiving feast, like a glorious mouthful of bloody, meaty stuffing, and he could suck their fear for minutes that seemed like days, and then hurl the child, screaming, over the edge of the bridge, to its small, barely audible death as it landed with a tiny splash in the calm, rippling waters one hundred feet below—and he fumbled at the zipper of his greasy jeans and pulled his knobby penis out with a reverberating groan and hung it over the side of the bridge, stroking it gently, and he sent a long, proud, arcing flow of brown-yellow liquid, like oil leaking from a grounded tanker, spilling into the water below, and he thrust his small head back, his hockey-puck lips spread to expose brown teeth, and began singing in a truly wretched, demonic voice, a howl, almost . . .*

*". . . IN DREAMS . . . I WALK . . . WITH YOU . . ."*

*On the other side of the bridge, facing away from this wretched spectacle, a bear of a man in a large overcoat felt his thoughts scatter like frightened sheep; startled, he turned to see a wobbly creature leaning precariously over the edge of the bridge, draining his foul juices into the community's drinking supply; he approached the groaning man and spoke in a concerned voice . . .*

*"Excuse me there, young man . . . if I may be so kind, might I suggest that, until you cease to wobble unsteadily about as you are now doing, it may be in*

*your best interests, and mine as well, and for the community at large, if you gather yourself up and find a safer place to answer the call of nature . . . I would hate to have to address the issue of diving into the river after you . . . the water is quite cold this time of year and I would deeply regret having to get my coat wet, my good man . . ."*

Frank continued peeing, continued singing in his twisted Dino-on-speed howl; the yellow river stretched farther, surging with pride, and he shuffled another step closer to the edge, wobbling precariously, looking down at the steaming oil spill forming below . . .

". . . IN DREAMS . . . I TALK . . . TO YOU . . ."

The large gentleman sized up this unusual creature; he took a long, slow puff on his pipe and thoughtfully blew the smoke in small rings into the air; he smiled gently and took two confident steps toward Frank . . .

"Well, young man . . . if you insist on persisting in this display of exuberant acrobatics, perhaps I may assist you by steadying your arm while you finish what you have started . . . after all, it is a dark and beautiful night . . . it has a strange glow to it, don't you think? . . . and perhaps you are not aware of the fall that awaits you should you stumble and fall over the edge you are leaning over . . . in all seriousness, may I be of assistance? . . ."

Frank was smiling; a small river of drool formed at the left corner of his swollen mouth and ran down his chin . . . yes, it WAS dark . . .

". . . IN DREAMS . . . YOU'RE MINE . . . ALL OF THE TIME . . ."

Frank wheeled and squirted the last quart or so of his foul fluids all over the fine wool coat of the large, well-mannered gentleman; he surged, quivering, as the last of his piss trailed away, dripping off the edge of his cock; he rubbed himself, smiling . . .

The gentleman stood perfectly still, a startled but composed half-smile on his face; his soft eyes looked down at his coat, which was steaming; his eyes burned . . .

"My goodness . . . what have we here? . . . I must say, forgive my mild annoyance at this sudden turn of events, but you have indeed startled me, my exuberant young friend . . . perhaps it is my fault . . . have I frightened you with such talk of falling? . . ."

Frank looked at his brown-yellow DNA dripping from the man's coat; his piss smelled of death and decay; he belched . . .

". . . I AM AN ANT THAT'S GOING TO CRAWL INTO YOUR EAR AND SLOWLY NIBBLE AT YOUR BRAIN AND CARRY IT OUT IN PIECES AND I WILL COOK IT UP AND EAT IT AND THEN I'LL COME BACK FOR MORE AND CLIMB INSIDE YOUR HEAD AND YOU'LL DREAM OF A BUZZING SOUND, THIS RELENTLESS CHAINSAW BUZZ, AND THAT WILL BE ME, AND THEN YOU'LL BE DEAD . . ."

The man looked at Frank silently, sternly; his chest puffed out reflexively; being a rather large bear of a man, he could have squished Frank like a rotten banana, which is what Frank was, but he just stood there, frozen, wobbling slightly in anger, staring at Frank like a bewildered tuna sizing up a fisherman from the deck of a boat . . .

". . . I don't know what to say, young man . . . you have caught me off guard . . . what is it you want from me? . . ."

Frank lifted his left leg and swung it over the side of the railing; he broke into a broad madman's smile and turned his head to look back at the man; the moon scampered behind clouds . . .

The man took a step toward Frank and reached out . . .

"Good lord, my son . . . may I suggest that you

*gather yourself together and return home before I cease to be amused by your rather frightening and, may I say, FOUL antics . . . young man, come to your senses! . . ."*

Frank leaned back, feigning a fall, and at the last instant caught the edge of the stone railing with his hand; for a moment, he remained stiffly propped over the edge of the bridge; his eyes were glued to the eyes of the old gentleman, as if through a rifle scope and into the eyes of a frightened deer that knows something is wrong but is not quite sure WHAT; with a psychic lunge, he extended himself, extended his force, through the man's eyes and into his soul . . . the gentleman steeled himself: he had been around the world many times and had seen many things; he had lived through two world wars and a revolution; he had watched his father die; he had seen cruelty in hundreds of its shapes and forms; he had felt knives creep into his back and bullets whistle past his ear; he had felt the sting of a bullet lodging in his chest; he had faced death with courage and faith in God and Christ; but never—NEVER—in his seventy years on this earth had he seen anything quite like this monsterous little demon: he braced himself and spoke . . .

"I do believe, young man, that you had better move along or I shall be forced to seek out the authorities and have you arrested! . . . I shall have you locked up and shall personally throw the key over the side of this bridge! . . . you, sir, are a public nuisance and a threat to humanity! . . . I warn you . . . BE GONE!"

Their eyes locked; Frank steadied himself; he looked into the soul of this strong man and sucked . . .

" . . . GOD? . . . WHAT IF GOD IS JUST ONE OF US . . . WHAT IF GOD IS JUST A LARGE, OM-

NIPOTENT VERSION OF THAT GUY OVER THERE BY THE PHONE BOOTH SCRATCHING HIS ASS . . . OR THE GIRL OVER THERE SENDING THAT HAA-GAN-DAZS TO THE SIDEWALK WITH THE HELP OF HER INDEX FINGER . . . OR THE GUY AT THE POST OFFICE HURLING YOUR CHRISTMAS GIFTS AGAINST THE BACK WALL OF THE DELIVERY TRUCK . . . OR THE SMILING POLITICIAN PICKING HIS TEETH WITH YOUR DREAMS . . . OR THE DAZED REFUGEE SLAVING AWAY SEVENTY-TWO HOURS A WEEK—THAT'S FOUR THOUSAND THREE HUNDRED AND TWENTY MINUTES— SHREDDING PROCESSED IMITATION CHEESE LOAF SUBSTITUTE AT THE PIZZA-RAMA . . . OR THE SOLDIER WITH THE SMELLY FEET AND THE UZI PICKING OFF CHILDREN AS THEY SCAMPER ABOUT THE STREETS OF ONE OF SEVERAL CIA-SPONSORED THIRD WORLD COUNTRIES . . . OR THE PENNZOIL-FACED LUMP WITH THE DONUT-HOLE EYES AND CHEESEBURGER SMILE WHO IS WATCHING *JEOPARDY* WITHOUT REALIZING THAT WHAT IS INDEED IN *JEOPARDY* IS NOTHING LESS THAN HIS IMMORTAL SOUL? . . . WHAT IF GOD IS A TEENAGER AND THIS IS HIS VIDEO GAME? . . . WHAT IF DEAN MARTIN'S OVERSOUL IS GOD? . . . IN THE NAME OF GOD, WHAT THEN? . . ."

The old man's eyes were wide and sad: he had been visibly sucked; he appeared to flatten out, like a deflated balloon; air hissed from his mouth, filling the sky with emptiness and scattering the clouds of thought . . . without taking his eyes off Frank, he took three weary strides toward the edge of the bridge; he paused momentarily to take his hat off and placed it carefully on the stone railing; he then threw his broad wool coat, soaked with the urine of a living demon, transdimensional maelstrom, over the side of the

88

*bridge; it flapped upward, like Superman's cape in freefall, and hit the water like a bird hitting cement, making a thunderous racket as it splashed one hundred feet below . . . older, tired, broken, corrupted, beaten, clocked, stiffed, marked, johned, joked, gerbiled, planted, fruited, vegetabled, the man turned and wobbled away into the empty street, an emasculated Hemingway, a broken Oscar Wilde, a sucker-punched Rimbaud, moving slowly, erratically, in the general direction of his large and prominent life which had—in the flash of an eye—had lost all meaning and proportion and had become inconsequential, expended; the neighborhood lived inside of him now, growing, leaking . . .*

    *Frank drooled uncontrollably . . .*

# 6.

jingle-hell memories

There comes a time in every young man's life when he leaves his family or is pushed and moves out into the larger world, and the THING that he has become enters the public bloodstream like a virus; for some, life then becomes a firm handshake and a nice smile and nice teeth and that special twinkle and a ho-ho-ho and a how-are-you and did you hear the one about the nigger and the jew or how about the one about jerry brown and the dyke and what a marvelous day and we are so lucky and you gotta be thankful and it could be worse and there are people starving in China and love it or leave it and we all have to make sacrifices and who the hell are we to complain and it's a grand old flag and whistle a happy tune and I wouldn't know what to do without work and you gotta look out for number one and you gotta believe and it's none of my business and I didn't pull the trigger and it saved lives in the long run and you've gotta be cruel to be kind and a reflective mind is the devil's playground and I've got work to do but I can't tell you how great it's been to see you and you're looking so well and johnny must be fifteen by now and as big as

*a house ha ha ha and how's the little woman perfect*
*marvelous outstanding dandy howdy shooty well swell*
*wunderbar golly fantastic shucks wowee happy happy*
*happy . . . others, like Frank, hurl themselves upon*
*the arena of life with a vengeance; they impale the*
*world; Frank plunged himself into the ever-expanding*
*experimental malfunctioning American social machine*
*like a nuclear weapon, a kamikaze soul; the circles of*
*his psychic stab wounds extended outward in every di-*
*rection, puddling wider and wider, forever, outward in*
*every direction from EVERY VICTIM; the excurrent*
*wounds inflicted by Frank stretched outward from the*
*great beast and impaled those in the way and THEY*
*CARRIED THE DISEASE WITH THEM in progres-*
*sively larger circles into and through the people that*
*they too encountered and unwittingly contaminated;*
*and as the range of his psychic weaponry increased,*
*as his sphere of reference expanded, his effect on the*
*world at large, the gradual swallowing of our world by*
*Frank's World, increased exponentially; Frank*
*SPLASHED in the gene pool . . .*

*He was armed with an IDENTITY— careening*
*transdimensional soul agenda—but you can't EAT*
*identity . . . Frank still needed a JOB; it would seem*
*everybody needs a job; it would seem there are plenty*
*of good jobs, but not enough good people to fill the*
*good jobs, due to the poor state of our DNA (RIP); so*
*we fill the good jobs with bad people and, instead of*
*moving forward, as we assume ourselves to be, we*
*move BACKWARDS, as if wandering through a film*
*being projected in reverse, as if time is shrinking back*
*into its hole after the end of the world and carrying us*
*with it as we breed merrily downward into the Ken-*
*tucky backwoods of our souls, floating aimlessly about*
*the seas of life, dialing for dollars, wrapped in plastic,*
*waiting to be gobbled by the thugs of the world that*
*roam the waters, feeding and shitting; where once*

reigned a proud and noble species now breeds a milling herd, nourished by television, reactive cogs swimming in rollicking seas of mere DATA, free-floating clouds of information sucked up by cheeseburger-enhanced senses and filtered through the old war-horse reason, nicely compiled and attractively packaged but incorrectly correlated, grotesque piles of mashed statistics, imaginary representations of what someone somewhere perceives may be real but never is . . . there are more people sucking up good and spitting out evil than there are cosmic janitors to clean up the residue left behind; evil is like glue; if allowed to dry, it STICKS . . .

In the meantime, stumbling over the cardboard residue of ten billion served, striving toward an advanced or at least advancing range of qualities and beliefs, are the GOOD (applause) who through force of WILL have overridden the lower urges and have chosen to project kindness, sensitivity, compassion, and love; the world NEEDS these people: teachers and nurses and faith healers and plumbers and farmers and poets and mentors and scholars and monks and gurus and guides and curmudgeons and stargazers and starwatchers and stardancers and shamans and magicians and musicians and dancers and ranters and pranksters and clowns and hopefuls and have-nots and give-aways and used-to-be's and slackers and bikers and lickers and lovers and sexologists and hookers and gigolos and free lovers and cross lovers and interbreeders and bird lovers . . . but none of these jobs pay well, and so the good labor on, toiling toward enlightenment, dragging behind them the baggage of humanity, smothered by the lumbering minds of millions of lesser members of the larger herd, FELLED by the FALLEN, killed by the hate, foiled by the FRANK in us all, shunned, spat upon, vilified, crucified, damned, dammed, persecuted, hexed, boxed, bottled, canned, corked, capped, canceled, edited, rewound, pan-fried, beheaded, microwaved, blended, toasted, buried, humbled, trashed, trampled, burned at the stake, grilled with electromagnetic grids, roasted with rumor, basted with television, refrigerated, disposed of properly . . . QUANTITY kills QUALITY . . . the lesser hound the great until the great willingly submit to the social grid or in exceptional cases are celebritized into submission or are simply IGNORED to death and left frowning in their graves, wondering what the hell that little shudder was about, that LIFE, what it MEANT, such a STUPID experience, lying there in the dirt right next to—even in death, no escape—the rotting, smiling face of some idiot in a polyester suit—in life, T-shirts with stained armpits and soiled jeans hanging low and wide below fat and pimpled guts exposing the cracks of raw, well-scratched butts, and in death, polyester suits—somehow it all makes sense, in a twisted Big Mac with fries kind of way that only the lesser can understand, lying there rotting . . .

Psychic thugs are neither interested in nor qualified for the aforementioned positions; a psychic thug is not qualified to GIVE but rather only to TAKE; a psychic thug cannot be a farmer, for example: a psychic thug cannot GROW something, cannot give energy to something; a psychic thug can only suck the energy from something, KILL it, EAT it; if the psychic thug has the good fortune to come from a well-to-do family, from a well-heeled lineage of bleached thuggery, from a manicured legacy of deodorized mayhem, from a discreet history of cruelty, greed, wealth, and spin control, from a gnarled family tree of inbred transgenerationally dysfunctional polished prep-school elitism, from a house—not a home—with skeletons buried behind gilded walls of money, power, silk and tennis and lies shoved in the powdered cracks between layers of denial and negation, if the child comes from such a

**93**

place, success is INHERITED; the human "race" was designed BY such people for their OWN benefit, to extend their oligarchy and expand their fortunes; "civilization" is nothing more than a strategic virus, a MASTER PLAN, thought up by soulless gangs of well-dressed, scrubbed, pedigried semi-humans conditioned over generations to NOT feel, incapable of seeing beyond the next THING, shallow ponds of cultured thought without consciences but with Cadillacs, creatures without friends but with furs, perfumed thug-families that consider the physical plane their personal playpen . . . if the psychic thug is one of THEM, if the psychic thug comes from a place with a manicured lawn, a security fence and a butler's pantry, where the rugs are insured and the gardener looks the other way when the Lord grabs the maid's butt, which is quite often in the lust-palace of his imagination made real, and the Lord says FUCK and she fucks the sad creature with the repulsive, bulging eyes and the shriveled, fatty skin, the creature that over generations is mutating into a not-quite-satisfied devil-in-embryo— what choice does she have?—if the psychic thug comes from such a place, then a JOB is not NEEDED . . . the young thug will be placed squarely on the gold brick road to Wall Street and given a swift kick in the direction of the proper prep school, to be properly propped up and PREPPED, to learn the rules of THEIR game—that MONEY indeed DOES buy everything one needs to get along in the world of sharks, chilled Cliquot and lightly grilled salmon steaks, the world that feeds politely off the downward decay of the human race—to learn to lie, to cheat, to steal, to drink, and to fuck—in that order—to throw down the credit card of choice and buy teachers and grades and functionally secure an "education" . . . and then it's off to COLLEGE, the tree-lined, alcohol-fueled pussy heaven that is the "Ivy League," the by-

*invitation-only club full of polished and handsome young thugs, attractive in an EMBALMED sort of way—like a LAWN that looks great from the window of a passing car but in actuality contains a world of rotting decay teeming with worms and bugs and ants and slime and mold and pesticides and carcasses and lizard shit and dog shit and fleas—who will spend four drunken years with their dicks hanging out of their pants forging future senatorial contacts and business arrangements over fifths of Black Label and cases of cheap beer at bacchanalian frat parties, vomiting enthusiastically with other future power brokers—erecting BONDS etched in vomit— cementing contracts with nudges and winks and building industriopathic sociocorporate bridges that will last generations and shape history and perpetuate industries and prop up Third World governments and keep armaments flowing and bullets flying from Indiana to Istanbul and cement places in history and secure fortunes glued together by vomit over the outstretched backs of the working class, COLLEGE, where Thuggy will meet and fuck the woman of his mother's dreams, the well-connected empty shell who will become the coiffed, credit-drunk wife, the pathetic and long-suffering mother of the dysfunctional brat-children, COLLEGE, where the seeds of the future will be planted in beds of vomit and nurtured with discreet transactions involving alumni groups and pension funds until the pearly gates of law school swing open and the lesson is once again reinforced—remove credit card from wallet; hand card to clerk—and the party that never ends will begin once again: golf swings and tennis tans will be perfected and pipelines laid for future extraction from the wallets of the taxed and burdened public; Thuggy will learn to turn the tap of the great one-way funnel of government spending, to suck up the public's MONEY through the industrial* matrix before returning it with interest to the padded fortunes of the governing few; then, drawn by the laws of social gravity, the career opportunities will material- ize—law firm partner, junk-bond trader, power bro- ker, landlord, slumlord, political consultant, campaign manager, corporate director, politician, sleazoid, lobby- ist, international influence peddler, "import-export con- sultant" CEO, VIP, CIA—and before Thuggy can say "caviar dreams," the CAREER will be launched—man the torpedoes—and he will be transformed into Lord Thug, a walking corporation with cemented contacts and millions if not billions in cold, hard, sweet, stolen, paper, cash, the oil of the American Dream, cherished by all, hoarded by few, protected and counted and re- counted and stored in other smaller countries where economic procedures are loose to say the least and the money travels about through shady lanes and re- produces by feeding off the blood and dreams of real people with broken hearts . . .

NOW, if the psychic thug comes from an ORDI- NARY neighborhood, an almost anywhere place out- side of San Antonio or Bakersfield or Topeka, a sad place with broken dreams, a place where kids slide through cracked fences and chase each other through the richness of their Kodak moments and find love and trust and friendship and community and compas- sion or perhaps are bitten by a dog with spots or sprayed by a skunk or psychically mauled by a young embryonic suburban thug-in-waiting and drained of all life force by the putrid resiliency of words, the stench of barbed language, SLIMED, more dead than alive, doomed to live without dignity, rotting liver, rotten life, a swollen bag of organs in a wheezing body, roughly ten percent alive, virtually dead, a place with shit on the shoes and piss on the tires, a place where noise— the splendid rhythmic chaos of LIFE—fills the air and the sky is thick with the addictive scent of tomorrow's crushed electric dreams, if the young psychic thug comes from such a place and does not find a way to ESCAPE—by befriending a politician's son or impregnating a debutante or running guns for a spook—or is not one of the few token lesser fodder-beings that are actually allowed, as a precautionary measure, for the sake of appearances, to maintain the charade of democracy, to participate in the ILLUSION of success—which is itself an illusion, a collective hallucination—by squeezing through the gates into the right prep schools, colleges, law schools, and law firms, allowed to squeeze into the CLUB, allowed to slip UP through the one-way glass ceiling where the rich look down disdainfully at that sad gray place of cracked walls and poor slobs and blue-collar dads and stained diapers and starving siblings and frozen foods and frayed collars and scuffed shoes and heroic *Life* magazine cover stories and heart-warming Oprah episodic parables and bloated Phil testimonials and over-blown Geraldoisms and punctured dignity and bruised pride and tested character and low pay and deductions and dentists and taxes and insurance payments and rent and bills and second jobs flipping burgers and pushing brooms and endless yes sir Mister Havilland-Smythes and no sir Mister Periwinkles and yes sir Mister Alibasters and no sir Mister Olivenoses and the WORK the WORK the WORK—THE WORK—and the toil and the sweat and no tennis tan and no golf blisters and no lawn chairs and no croquet, allowed to slip UP through that small one-way crack, away from the only tired cliché in this world that works, away from LOVE, and into the embellished splendor of the PENTHOUSE, to taste the caviar of soiled dreams, to sip the champagne of spiritual decay, to hail the limousine of soul death, to become THINGS without a world, despised both from above and from below, allowed to scratch and claw up, through the cracks, as a public relations spin-control rim shot, and into law school where they can cheat and steal themselves into positions of power and authority within the system . . . if the young thug does NOT escape, then the gravity of life will pull firmly in one direction—DOWN—and he will be sucked into the maelstrom between the cracks in the holes, down among the rats, propelled into a life of crime: life will INSIST on a life of crime; the job opportunities within the crime industry are limited—drug dealer, con artist, drug dealer, grifter, pimp, thief, killer, collection representative, drug dealer, hustler, burglar, drug dealer, drug dealer, drug dealer drug dealer drug dealer DRUG DEALER DRUG DEALER—and one choice reaches out with long tentacles and grabs young men of low character and pulls them in: it is the choice of default; if one does nothing, one will be sucked in, like a fly down a storm drain, awakening one morning from uneasy dreams to find themselves suddenly transformed, DEFINED, by this monstrous, multi-tentacled career choice that has them tightly in its grasp and will not let go . . .

The privileged, inbred, educated psychic thugs—with their cold, vacant eyes, Yale rings, nice suits, cracked creased faces, frozen smiles and slick skin oozing oily, fatty overpriced restaurant food—steer the huge herd of free-range thugs toward their favorite shadow industry: the cattle drive proceeds into the box canyon of DRUGS, where opportunities for profit await within the fluid global geopolitical twilight zone called the drug industry, a free-floating shadow organism exempt from congressional oversight and taxes and regulation, a smooth-running, well-oiled, LIVING profit-being crossbred and streamlined over hundreds of years, a planetary virus, the perpetual bio-engine of Capitalism, the single greatest achievement of Ivy League social engineering, the ultimate system, the *last MACHINE, self-sustaining, unrestricted, trampling beyond national or ethical boundaries, without a soul or a conscience, sucking PROFIT, operated recklessly by a mad cabal of banker-thugs and leader-thugs and propped-up Central American and Southeast Asian hand-picked CIA-funded drunken-operative dictator-thugs, a three-headed machine oiled with public funds and greased by the enforcement/logistics wing of the multinational profit-junkie money machine; transactions are completed without fanfare and profits arrive discreetly into the accounts of the caviar whips and chains crowd to fund the continued exploits of the great perfumed thug-families with revenue pledged in earnest self-interest by the deluded working sheep; the wholesale barter currencies are drugs and weapons, an exchange that has kept both parties partying and the world largely at war for centuries; it has also kept the sheep cooperative and docile while forging massive opportunities for private profit from public investment; the drugs move smoothly through well-established channels into large cities to be distributed among street thugs who get hooked and sell to other street thugs who get hooked and sell to other street thugs who get hooked and sell to businessmen and athletes who get hooked and sell to grandmothers and teenagers and soon the drug "problem" has expanded concentrically, exponentially, until EVERYONE is hooked, one way or another—some hooked on NOT being hooked—some hooked on the mush-mouthed just-say-no rhetoric—some hooked on Major Dad—some Hooked on Phonics—some hooked on sweating that second mortgage and flipping deathburgers at that second job after shaking strange hands all day with something different than sweat oozing from their palms, something stickier, PRIDE maybe, stifling that cough and tugging at that damnable TIE, that LEASH that is too tight—some hooked on SLEEP, who refuse* to WAKE UP, who say leave me alone I'm enjoying this DREAM, who collapse on the couch and say God Bless America and think how LUCKY they are—they aren't even smart enough to know they're IN hell AL-READY—they are living in the BASEMENT of possibility and they don't even KNOW IT—even DRUG DEALERS have disdain for these plant people . . . and so the flotsam and jetsam of humanity drifts toward the world's largest, quietest industry, the manufacture of illicit drugs, the distribution of HOPE and FANTASY, a multinational superindustry supported by the film-loop sales pitch that never ends—Capitalism—and delivered door-to-door by the ultimate salesman, the friendly little grinning box-god in the living room that fills the air with empty hopes and flat dreams in which the color is never quite right, a two-dimensional reality full of stiffs, props, and plotted lives . . . DRUGS and TELEVISION are but two symptoms of the same disease, and the thugs of the world make sure the flow of HOPE is relatively constant and the quality of FANTASY relatively high . . . in a strange way, the drug trade also provides a certain twisted sense of gung-ho frontier integrity for these creatures that have fallen through the cracks, dishonest work for dishonest people, which is HONEST, in a back-wards sort of way, although drug dealers do not nec-essarily THINK of themselves as dishonest: they think of themselves as THUGS; they look like thugs, they behave like thugs, they SMELL like thugs; they dress like thugs, retro-gangsters, modern neopantheonic anti-gods; they surround themselves with armed guards and fully automatic weapons and cruise con-spicuously about town in white stretch limos, black Mercedes sedans, Silver Cloud Rolls-Royces and purple Jags, attracting as much attention as they possibly can; even their MOTHERS know they are thugs . . . Frank, on the other hand, had no desire to take

*PRIDE in his work or to move about town escorted by an armed entourage seeking the twisted admiration of confused and spiritually malnourished children; Frank wanted only to suck up souls . . . hell, he didn't NEED the advantages provided to the Ivy Leaguers; there were no doors anyone could open for him that he couldn't just as easily kick down himself; he was a creature without conscience, steamrolling through life, following the hewed pattern of his desires and destroying anything in his path; if he wanted to, he could have taken the easy way out and with a minimal expenditure of energy become one of the greatest drug lords in history: a few discreet phone calls, a few quiet murders, and he could have quickly risen to a position of power somewhere near the jugular vein of a tightly disciplined and streamlined corporate body of pure evil that would have provided him with a comfortable tax-free annual income of, oh, fifty million or so, cash, and also the perhaps more rewarding satisfaction of having hurled a few more rocks into the gene pool, fried a few million more brains, ruined countless lives, amplified the ripple of dysfunction so that it would expand outward through the wreckage of the next TEN generations—THAT would have been an accomplishment—but somehow Frank sensed it would have been too damned EASY, too predictable, too SAFE, like walking through a wide-open door without even getting a chance to pick the lock; Frank wanted to feel the bones crack; he wanted to slip inside people's hearts and earn their trust, coil his tentacles around their hearts like countless pythons, wedge himself into their good will, nurture their admiration and open-hearted support, and then sucker-punch their souls, psychically maul them, create rips that would take lifetimes to repair, slip into their quiet worlds while their guard was down, kill their guard while their guard was smiling and shaking hands, slash their guard's throat, offer toxic candy to the inner child, smile, spit on the corpse; Frank preferred MINDFUCKING . . . the POPE, he thought: he could become the fucking god-damn POPE . . . nah: the Pope was already too much like a drug dealer, parading around in that pompous Popemobile . . . CHRIST: HE could be the Second Coming . . . nah: he pitied the poor soul who actually WAS the new vehicle of Christ: he knew THAT poor sucker would be rounded up and CRUCIFIED for his trouble; the herd will trample its own savior WHEN-EVER he arrives throughout the endless pasts and fu-tures as far as time stretches in either direction; THE WORLD does not WANT to be saved . . . SANTA CLAUS: he drooled at the thought; he could be SANTA . . . his eyes twinkled as he envisioned parents with bright eyes full of hope and wide-open hearts full of love sticking their precious dream-bags on his bony lap with swelling pride—their brittle little babies, their lives, their hopes, their dreams, their unfulfilled fanta-sies—those little fleshy bundles that represent their dismal lives full of failure and disappointment and the second chances that they themselves would not get except through the vicarious sucking on the failures and crushed hopes of these smiling, unsuspecting little varmints, their children—the happy little bastards looking up into Frank's soul-sucking eyes, their little ra-diant features glowing as he encouraged and nurtured their greed, inspiring them to feed their own inevitable spiraling decay, to gorge themselves, to demand more more more more more MORE MORE MORE bigger bigger bigger better better better BIGGER BETTER BIGGER BETTER, THINGS, more THINGS, better THINGS, bigger THINGS, things, things, things, THINGS, THINGS, brand names, designer labels, tags, prestige badges, emblems, hood ornaments, to keep asking and begging and crying and demanding and screaming and pouting and manipulating and with-*

*holding and smiling and snuggling and smugly lying*
*and promising and faking and kissing ass and proposi-*
*tioning and hard-balling and politicking and short-*
*selling and power-broking until it's mom and dad that*
*are broke and bitter and beaten and bartered and*
*foreclosed and nothing is good enough anymore and*
*everyone hates everyone else, and then Frank's bony*
*little yellow quivering hand, extending in stiffly righ-*
*teous anger just below the crisply pressed white furry*
*cuff of the red happy Santa outfit, could discreetly slip*
*onto the little bundle's leg and massage his little thigh*
*and arouse a primal, unborn urge in the little sucker,*
*dredging up inappropriate feelings of embryonic de-*
*sire, staining his little mind and forging perhaps even*
*a small, lunging all-American boner, or, if the child-*
*thing was a girl, he could massage her upper leg until*
*her thoughts became moist and the future cheer-*
*leader housewife sex-addict confused neofeminist was*
*nervous and excited and aroused and vulnerable and*
*uncomfortable all at the same time and Frank could*
*slide a verbal penis into the psychic hallway outside*
*the doorway to the bedroom of her mind and whisper*
*something dripping blood like it hurts to feel this good*
*or it feels good to hurt or good is evil or evil is good*
*or pain is pleasure or you will be confused for the rest*
*of your life and unable to enjoy your body or anyone*
*else's for that matter and you will blame every man*
*who comes into your life and you will die a bitter old*
*vodka sniffing thrice-divorced witch after dancing on*
*the tables of your dreams looking for something you*
*didn't know you had lost . . . he could be SANTA*
*CLAUS; and yet, somehow, it STILL seemed too*
*damned EASY . . .*

*Frank's career choice came to him, as did all*
*things worth waiting for, as he was absorbing the ra-*
*dioactive teachings of the Great Master, the godlike*
*Oz-box that leads beyond two dimensions and through*

the doorway to a greater collective mind that is at once National Security and Disneyland; it was a wonderful life, and he sat there watching *It's a Wonderful Life,* his mouth funneling drool as director Frank Capra—director of thought, really—manipulated images through the vehicle of film, the vehicle so much larger than his puny earth body, and created an ALTERNATIVE Bedford Falls, an alternative to the ONE inevitable happy-ending Bedford Falls that radiated out of sets across the land and into the hearts and minds of millions of tragically bored housewives who cried every Thanksgiving like clockwork, the cheeseburger-and-fries world where George Bailey was hardworking and kind and honest and trusting and giving and caring and the people really did care about each other and everything worked out at the end even for Clarence the angel who saved George from tragedy and bankruptcy and alimony and child support payments and pain and suffering and heartache and heartburn and indigestion and cramps and death and decay and social stigmatism and liver spots and clogged toilets and knives and collection agencies and compound interest rates and kneecapping and fast food and lines and crowds and traffic and idiots and fools and scum and bums and heat waves and foot fungus and earthly damnation—he EARNED his wings—and he flapped away (cheery music) and life was swell from that day forward in every direction, happiness everywhere, fade the fuck out; it wasn't a FILM, really, it was a damn COMMERCIAL for all the factories and the stinking industrial hellholes and the plastic cubicles that awaited workers and their crying wives when, after stuffing themselves with excessive portions of ritually roasted bird carcass and ceremonial blood-wine—a virtual Visigothic orgy—they collapsed in toxic holiday shock and spent the next forty-eight hours fending off the assault of bad food—forty-eight hours

*of belching and wheezing sloth, punctuated by vague
attempts at the raking up of the dead leaves that
have jumped from the evil trees and dominated by an
eight-hour injection of flying bodies and snapping
necks, a mass immersion in the gruesome spectacle of
college football, an overdose of that blood-sacrifice-at-
the-pyramids feel—and then, in an approaching, staggering haze, as if out of a dream, comes Monday,
when the "habits" are resumed and the workers take
their proper places as cogs in the giant wheel of the
machine that supplies unlimited champagne and pussy
to the endless generations of boys from Yale, the boys
with the gaudy lifestyles who do not WATCH football
games—they LIVE them—Spartan encounters where
they guzzle champagne, throw caviar, pounce on ex-
otic naked women, lick, sing, snort, fuck anything that
moves, immersing themselves in Roman holidays last-
ing for weeks that leave them with the burnished,
chipped glow of men that have spread their seed, the
proud peacock glow of men that have FUCKED . . .
FRANK wasn't looking at THAT Bedford Falls, the
"happy" Bedford Falls: he was watching time bounce
off the end of the world and land in the ALTERNA-
TIVE Bedford Falls, the parallel reality—"Potterville"—
where Bedford Falls and cannot get up, the
wrong-turn other-side Bedford Falls that exists, somewhere, always, everywhere, nowhere, only a moment
away in the eternal parallel future present past, an
evil cold hard oily sticky dirty wet moldy foul putrid
stale frankenplanet place that makes slave-wage hell
Bedford Falls seem positively heavenly by comparison;
Frank knew that there are, indeed, BILLIONS of Bedford Falls, infinite Pottervilles, whole galaxies of spinoff
Pottervilles, millions of funhouse mirror worlds coexist-
ing together and yet alone, like two sides of the same
coin; Frank knew that most people live in Potterville
and dream of Bedford Falls, live in hell and dream of*

the place of happy-myth-perpetuated happy endings acted out by worker-ant TV families—Ozzie and Harriet, Ward and June, Mike and Carol, the Huxtables, even the Bundys and Roseanne—the artificial global village—the mythic sperm bank—maybe not Roseanne—but Frank knew that THIS, the mythic here and now, was the ILLUSION, while THAT—the dripping urban America of Potterville—the sick and twisted world of Frank Booth, Bobby Peru, Ted Bundy, Hannibal Lechter, Charles Manson, Travis Bickle, Jeffery Dahmer, Roman Polanski and Rupert Pupkin, a world where the sidewalks are stained with the blood of broken dreams, the blood that DOES NOT wash out, a world that leaks into places like Bedford Falls and stays as long as it likes—Frank knew that THAT was the far more REAL place . . . Bedford Falls was the dream; Potterville was the reality . . .

Frank knew that in addition to parallel worlds there were parallel HOLIDAYS; for each mindless idiot giddily waving a flag in a grim parade of weekend patriots lumbering down Main Street, hot dogs and flags, waving frantically in a hollow beer-fueled gesture of frenzied nationalism on the happy fucking stupid Fourth of July, there was another man, a veteran with half a leg missing, lying on a bed somewhere in Cleveland, blasted after that second "holiday" pint of Relska vodka and a few of those little yellow pills that help make the world go away—it gets fuzzy but never COMPLETELY goes away—and neither does the image of the kid with her head blown off or the spongy, one-way feel of the land mine that blew off his foot, the foot that had, in his recurring dream—or was that his childhood?—skipped in blissful symbiosis with his other foot in a transcendent dance chasing the small footballs that bounced off the caverns of his memory, his mind colored by the stains of the soft green grass, the putrid rot of Vietnam, and the si-

**106**

*lence, the death, behind every root and shrub and bush and then that damn dream started again—or was THAT reality?—and he slid back and forth between now and then, here and there, somewhere and nowhere, from Vietnam to the end of the world and back again, trapped in the cage of a memory he can't remember, a prisoner in a war that will never end: he can't hear the parade or see the flags and he doesn't give a rat's ass whether the Cowboys beat the Vikings—THAT foot was like Potterville, rotten and dead somewhere in the jungles of Vietnam, but VERY REAL . . . YES, there are, indeed, parallel holidays . . .*

*Like many great thugs before him, Frank decided to exploit the opportunities for profit and soul-sucking that exist in the world of parallel holidays: he acknowledged the existence of the inevitable "happy stream" of reality—brimming with Christmas mirth and grinning people in ill-fitting suits exchanging presents and faking boundless joy and seasonal mirth and heavenly thanks—he couldn't stop THAT—but he COULD certainly COUNTER it by creating an ALTERNATIVE Christmas reality stream full of rusted memories, "holidays" so long and sad, so massively lonely, that they would not be forgotten, lingering like Vietnam, lingering like the guy in the leather vest who hangs out on the corner by the bridge across from the high school smoking cigarettes and showing little girls with black eyeliner the tattoo of a goat on his lower back; Frank could create Christmas memories that would be like small wars, raging and bleeding in the memory, regional conflicts fought inside the heads of his victims, living hells, JINGLE HELLS . . . Christmas: the holy day that Christ was allegedly born, although scholars insist he was born in July and that the Christ-mass is actually a Catholic spin-control holiday tacked onto a preexisting pagan celebration of the winter solstice, a mass ritual offering to mother earth which is coun-*

tered by the "modern" holiday when we cut down trees, "decorate" them with glass ornaments and strings of small, electric lights and gather in surly family units and insist that we are NOT overweight, underloved, resentful, angry, broke, depressed, wanting nothing more at the core of our beings than to put on a pair of diapers and sit in a large pen with our thumbs in our mouths . . . Christmas: the day marking the opening of the door to the sacrificial shopping dimension; the day children learn to wallow in reinforced greed and addictive consumerism; the day millions pretend to care when actually they still pretty much hate each other just as they did the day before and would the day after and they drink and smoke and argue and yell and exchange the cheapest gifts imaginable wrapped in cheap paper and they loathe the cheap gifts they get in return, and they measure people by the cost of their gifts, by the degree that they have raped society to stockpile paper money, paper trust—by the degree that they CAN'T be trusted, really—the day when the family unit collectively sucks up enough food to feed ten Vietnamese villages, emerging bloated and in toxic shock, in the holiday tradition, with forty-eight hours of dazed sloth required for the body to attempt to digest this massive holiday blood-feast, and here comes Monday, and with added bulk they once again dive into the rushing waters of the insane river of working life in the modern world . . . Frank decided then and there, to become the proprietor of a Christmas tree lot: he had been partial to trees ever since that day when Walt Disney indoctrinated millions of children in that classic scene from *Babes in Toyland* where the kids are assaulted by thuggish trees in The Forest Of No Return but get outta there thank god and away from nature, saved by the toymaker and trained to resume a healthy life of addictive material greed; in Uncle

*Walt's crafty hands, the mighty tree, supplier of oxy-
gen to the world, was cut down and hurled on the
metaphorical fire, burned at the virtual stake, trans-
muted into something evil and dangerous, a force to
be tamed, an enemy to be conquered, an animal to
be herded and carved into logs and burned ritually on
Christmas Eve . . . he would FUCK UP CHRISTMAS:
he would become an executive in the mine-field
industry of alternative parallel holidays, Christmas
Division . . .*

    *He began work the next morning, the morning
after Frank Capra had invited the workers of the
Western world to pick their hells: Potterville, which
can be quickly and efficiently implemented in a matter
of days by the Federal Emergency Management
Agency—so don't try anything funny—or the happy,
giddy Bedford Falls, where angels earn their wings and
good triumphs over evil and people work long and
hard; the workers, of course, always pick the lesser of
the two hells, apparently unaware that there are an
infinite number of hells and corresponding heavens
. . . the morning after the blood-feast, Frank scurried
down to the shopping mall for his next meal: "The
Day After Thanksgiving Sale"—the blood is still warm
from one holiday and already the nation prepares for
another—and he worked his tongue across his lips
and eyed the shoppers who fought and pushed and
shoved and sweated with bulging eyes and open
purses and closed minds and all in anticipation of saving ten to twenty percent on endless things: tele-
phones shaped like loaves of French bread and pulse
striders and easy gliders and toss pillows and throw
pillows and satin sheets and leather furniture and
electric massage machines and digital blood-pressure
monitors and closet organizers and singalodeon portable stereo karaoke units and curling irons and para-
keet food and cashmire dog sweaters and compact*

disk players with digital to analog filter transposterators and megahertzian rhapsodic antifloradefibrillators and projection televisions and coke machines and cuisinarts—who needs a CUISINART? ever try to stab someone with a CUISINART?—and leashes and choke chains and dog food bowls and blindfolds and rubber thigh boots and studded collars and fishnet stockings and rubber dresses and latex miniskirts and spiked latex bustiers and hoods and corsets and latex cat suits and studded dresses and irons and cords and whips and ropes and belts and spiked knee pads and dildos and studded dildos and spiked dildos and gags and tawses and stretch racks and branding irons and chains and slit dresses and spiked rubber couches and rubber body suits and rubber riding trousers and spurs and rubber harnesses and gas masks and ankle restraints and arm binders and ball gags and bar gags and body corsets and chastity belts and dildo harnesses and cock and ball straps and harness suits and wrist restraints and hog ties and leather dildos and leg spreaders and masks and spankers and paddles and saddles and suspension devices and wrist restraints and handcuffs and stockades and torture tables and headlocks and designer furniture and designer sheets and designer children—mom and dad's little cloned bundles of greed and wasted youth, their ties to their OWN designer past—and the high and wide rows upon rows of TOYS, toys that are everywhere, like some social virus conditioning tool, toys that are getting smarter each year, more human, more HUMAN than the HUMANS, cartoon tie-in toys, movie tie-in toys, breakfast cereal tie-in toys, welcome to TOYLAND, Mr. Two-Car Garage, where your National Security State Cog-In-Training son and your Future Consumer Shopper Housewife Basket-Case daughter are shaped and molded by the toys that surround them and call out to them, BUY ME: the don't wake

**110**

daddy color-matching action game and the fisher-price magic money machine and the fisher-price supermarket (packed with shopping fun!) and the fisher-price magic vac (sounds real!) and the fisher-price bubble mower and the little tykes laundry center and the little mermaid roller skates and the snow white electronic talk 'n view magic mirror and the talk 'n teach doll potty and the mattel mcdonald's magic hamburger snack maker and the potty-time drink and wet quints with magic diapers and newborn baby shivers and baby feels so real and the fashion magic deluxe jewelry-making set and the barbie we girls can do anything game and the barbie queen of the prom game and barbie roller skates and the barbie golden dream motorhome and the barbie fold 'n fun playhouse and the barbie lamborghini (with phone!) and wild style barbie (with leather skirt and thick gold chains!) and bath magic barbie and pretty in plaid barbie and dazzlin' date barbie and the barbie backyard cookout and the ken scooter and the barbie mermaid 'n swan playset and the barbie spray 'n play pool and the barbie splash 'n fun raft (a floating world of bathtime fun!) and the barbie starlight bed (with spinning disco ball!) and the barbie dress 'n go mountain bike set and the barbie vanity and the barbie refrigerator/freezer and the barbie armoire and the barbie slut 'n fuck rambler and the barbie fun phone center and teen talk barbie ("love to shop, don't you?") and barbie pretty surprise cosmetics and marine corps barbie and totally hair barbie and rollerblade barbie and switchblade barbie and jamaican barbie and mermaid barbie and alpha draconis barbie and pretty surprise barbie and hollywood hair barbie and hyperborean barbie and the barbie chocolate shop and the barbie dream house and the barbie spin pretty dryer and the barbie press pretty iron and the barbie wash 'n watch dishwasher and beach barbie and bath magic barbie and sun sensation barbie and snap 'n play barbie and cool times barbie and barbie trading cards and barbie memory lane postcards and flight time barbie and ski fun ken and dance magic ken (with reversible disco/ballet suit!) and sparkle surprise ken (with handsome new face!) and superstar ken (with campy outfit and mustache!) and ice capades ken (with spandex stretch pants!) and the barbie party bake oven (big enough for barbie's head!) and rappin' rockin' barbie (with leather skirt and boom box!) (condoms not included!) and the barbie corvette (with power steering!) and the barbie fun rider jeep and the barbie hamburger stand and the barbie porsche (with real working headlights!) (watch out for ken!) and the barbie '57 chevy (with trunk that opens!) (perfect for stuffing ken's body!) and the barbie ferrari and madison avenue barbie and fifth avenue barbie and west fifty-seventh street barbie and south central barbie and bowery barbie and magic needle barbie and the barbie magical mansion (with flickering fireplace!) and the hanky panky magic hat and the super nintendo wheel of fortune game and the my first sony electronic sketch pad and the sparkling tools jigsaw (with realistic working sound!) and the big dude radio-control monster truck and the x-men versus evil mutants pinball game and the incredible crash dummies (explode on impact!) and the crash dummies bash 'n crash chair and the ninja turtles 3 manhattan project game and the wet shots sponge blaster target game and the nerf bow 'n arrow and the nerf blast-a-matic and the electronic mighty sword III (with slashing sounds!) and the tomorrow's hero video command talking battle leader ("drop your weapon! open fire!") and the trolls on the go police patrol and the terminator 2 judgment day game and the crossbow and arrows game and the doctor mindbender master of mind control-action figure and the penguin commandos and the g.i. joe fully armed multi-

deployable headquarters set and the g.i. joe patriot
missile launcher and the earthquake ground-ripping
combat vehicle and the air commandos one-man ae-
rial attack craft (armed with pivoting submachine
guns!) and the terminator 2 action figure (with missile
launcher and secret chest weapon!) and the terminator 2 bioflesh regenerator and the tyco pong bazooka
and the eliminator TS-7 electronic laser and the
beretta 86 (with fixed blade front sights!) and the
thompson 9mm semi-automatic and the mossberg
590 (tube fed!) and the colt king cobra and the glock
20 and the walther p-38 and the walther p-88 and
the weatherby mark five and the sig/sauer 226 and
the CA 75 and the h&k P2M13 and the colt python
and the h&k P7M13 and the h&k 91 assault rifle
and the h&k 94 carbine—CAN'T YOU SEE YOU ARE
BEING TOYED WITH?—and it was like taking candy
from children—EASIER than that, really: it was like
GIVING candy to children—and within twenty minutes
Frank had taken possession of eleven credit cards
hanging out of purses virtually demanding to be lifted
and was "in business," grinning, whistling, infested
with that damnable "Christmas spirit," and down to
the A-1 Rent-A-Lot he went, to rent a truck . . . he
picked out a particularly threatening-looking specimen,
fifteen feet of rumbling four-speed double-steel smog
machine, and slapped down the American Express
platinum card, Bank of Tokyo, which he had lifted
from a drunken, broken-down socialite with creepy
furs that he had bumped into rather aggressively at
the perfume counter at Nordstrom's before apologiz-
ing extensively for rubbing against her with his soiled
clothes and the tentacles of his black vortex soul and
offending her with his foul, smelly, grinning presence,
with his very EXISTENCE, to such a degree that she
did not notice that he had relieved her of her purse
and all it contained—it had been enough of a trauma

*that he had INVADED her world: her existence from birth on had been defined by AVOIDANCE of pond scum like Frank and the erection and maintenance of social barriers and fences to keep the small and smelly peasants of the world out of her life; in her perfumed mind there was no room for people like Frank, no room for a situation such as this, no room for objective analysis or compassion or cool-headed self-defense, no chance of her dropping and rolling and whipping out a Glock 20 with hollow points and dropping fifteen rounds into this disposable street creature, this rubbish of society, depositing his brains against the sidewalk with a vengeful, hip coolness, no room for anything except the swollen vision of Frank that stuck in her throat and took up all available space in her small mind . . . Frank, meanwhile, was off with a wink and a smile to collect more goodies, off to do more shopping—he was growing fond of these shopping malls—MAULS, really—and he skipped like a child, making his way through the wide-eyed drooling hordes of junkie consumers, collecting credit cards and souls as he went . . .*

*Frank loved the idea of TRUCKS: he WAS a truck, really, the human equivalent of one of those grotesquely oversized monster trucks with ten-foot tires and death-head paint jobs that roll around the great holding pens of the midwest like giant cattle, characters in a capitalistic opera, searching out and crushing other, smaller cars—defenseless Toyotas and helpless Yugos—before facing off against each other and colliding grandly and toppling over to the sick de-light and guttural hooting of the assembled beer-bellied, cholesterol-laden crowd, the leading edge of our downward-spiraling DNA; Frank WAS a truck, ramming his oversized frame, his swollen soul, into un-suspecting, helpless bit players in the great American opera that never ends . . .*

**114**

*Frank sat in his rented monster vehicle and fought off thoughts of ramming fences and driving into schoolyards and through walls and into classrooms— where he really could fuck up some lives, disrupting fingerpainting sessions by literally ramming through walls and crushing desks and presumably teachers as well, fingerpainting on a larger scale on the canvas of life in the colors of blood and fear—and instead he steered his thoughts toward the transmutation of Frank's Dead Christmas Trees, Inc., into a malignant reality: he needed two things: trees and workers . . . getting workers, of course, would NOT be a problem, here in the "land of opportunity"—the land of OP-PORTUNISTS—where people from around the world line up for participation in the grand deceit that is their receipt for the American Dream that they can pick up the day after tomorrow, the tomorrow that never arrives; in America the entire world is available for employment; Frank could just drive his monster dream truck—the bigger the truck, the bigger the dream—downtown, any downtown, and casually nod to any of the millions gathered on thousands of street corners deep in the kidney of the heart of the belly of the beast, where the blood pumps, where the blood spills, where the coffee is thin and the whisky warm, milling about, grazing, waiting for that windfall job that will cement their futures and lead to the fat pay-checks and the Italian suits and the big houses in Bel-Air and the harems of blond fetish queens and the caviar memories and the Lincoln Town Car dreams and the hot-tub nights and the champagne mornings and the million-dollar views of the night sky over Big Town with its oil-sucking lights that never turn off— they just sit there and glow and people stare at them and say god, that's nice, and soon everyone wants a view and real estate prices start climbing and soon there are more lights—why not get a place overlook-*

ing BAGHDAD?—and homes staffed by small armies of imported maids and gardeners and au pairs from Mexico City and Guatemala and Nicaragua and Vietnam who are paid less than minimum wage and smile while swearing under their breath because they know they've been cheated—they're not THAT dumb—and just so Mr. Two-Car Garage could save a few pennies by BUYING INTO the ILLUSION with a currency more valuable than gold, his humanity, but the joke's on him, because the day after tomorrow, or the day after that, or the day after THAT, THEY will reach out and squish his little fantasy, devalue his currency, knock over his stock market, declare martial law in his neighborhood, close his bank, repossess his house, seize his assets, knock over the board that is the game that is his life, and the more things that he HAS in this little world the tighter their grip around his neck becomes, and the more he HAS to lose the more he WILL lose, and they'll leave him behind, SEE YA, BYE-BYE, scratching his ass and wondering what hit him, stealing bread crumbs from the little kid on his left, the skinny kid with the big eyes . . . all Frank had to do was pull up to the curb—any curb—they are more or less interchangeable—and whistle, and the very STUFF of the American Dream would scamper out from the cracks and line up for the slaughter . . .

The morning after the great turkey shoot that is Thanksgiving, when America awakes from uneasy dreams to find itself dazed and dulled from food and implied mirth, Frank pulled up in front of the Greyhound Bus terminal, the terminal of soiled dreams, the place where dreams go to die, and whistled, and the sad humanity scampered out like cockroaches; Frank picked out a half dozen or so of the strongest, stupidest young men he could find, and he smiled broadly like a shopping-channel costume jewelry salesman, pledging loudly to pay these losers twelve tax-free gringo bucks an hour to CUT TREES, nothing more, just trees, little trees, cut 'em down, easy worko, no problemo; he supplemented his presentation by waving a reasonably crisp one hundred dollar bill in the air, conspicuously fanning himself, and even THAT wasn't real: he had cut the corners off of four hundreds and glued them to a one dollar bill—but how would THEY know?—and as he waved the bill teasingly, he had no problem getting help that day: they came like metal shavings to a magnet, like pigeons to a bread crumb, twelve hundred pounds of raging dreams and illusory aspirations from throughout the cardboard democracies of Central America, and soon they were packed in and bouncing about the enclosed sheet metal prison of the monster rental truck, deep inside the whale, getting quite scuffed and bruised, like a cargo of fleshy peaches, rolling down the great highway, the ribbon of dreams, and Frank couldn't help but smile and think of Mr. Potter of Potterville, to whom the herded workers of Bedford Falls were but CATTLE, on this day, the day after the harvest blood-feast, his first day in the satisfying business of alternative, parallel holidays . . .

It was less than an hour before Frank and his bruised cargo left the civilized brown-gray world of asphalt, smog, and blood stains behind and found themselves approaching the undeveloped industrial blue-green wonderland, the wide open spaces, or, in this case, the wide CLOSED spaces: Frank had chosen to select his inventory from a National Security State Park, where members of the general public were required to purchase permits for the privilege of looking at trees which they themselves owned; it was a place where they were not allowed to live, but merely to "vacation," where children were discouraged from touching the board-footage or chasing the squirrels or

*throwing rocks in the lakes or kissing in the meadows
or swimming naked and watching the big fat trout
with silver streaks leap out of the pure blue acid-rain
water, catching a glimpse of the cursed upper world,
just a peek, before diving headlong back into their
own dying world, away from those crazy humans and
their dwindling DNA; no, the land was off limits to the
public and reserved for spotted owls and bureaucrats
and corporate logging executives who were occasionally spotted admiring the crystal lakes from limousine
windows, watching the chipmunks wiggle their noses,
looking upon the beautiful trees, calculating the mag-
nificent board-footage to be harvested, hauled off and
mauled, turned into boards for coffee tables and desk
chairs and bed frames and bookshelves and baseball
bats and electric guitars and picture frames and designer decks and luxury yachts and all kinds of other
useless American shit . . . Frank considered himself a
logger—of souls—and so he approached the locked
gate leading into the park with the intention of grant-
ing himself a "permit"; he gunned his rental monster
truck and smashed into the gate as the cargo of
loosely packed Latin Americans rolled around the back
of the truck like empty beer cans, two of them
smashing their heads against the side walls and losing
consciousness, mumbling something about the blessed
Mary just before fading out—mere hours before they
had been agitated nationalists trading peppered in-
sults but now their eyes were wide with solidarity,
fear, surprise, and dazed confusion—the same feelings a steer experiences on the way up the ramp
when hearing the muffled warnings from ahead and
FINALLY realizing WHAT the HELL is GOING ON—
suddenly, it ALL MAKES SENSE—the pens, the shots,
the food—it finally occurs to the poor steer that its
DESTINY in life is to sit steaming in butter sauce
aside a baked potato and vegetable du jour—and the*

*dust flew and the steel gate gave way under the insistent thrust of the truck's bumper and a small trickle of drool formed on Frank's creased chin and dribbled down his pitted neck; he was going to like this job . . .*

*The truck took out the gate and bounced down the dirt road leading into the bowels of the park as the white-knuckled minorities with the scrambled Robin Leach highlight-film dreams clutched their worn crucifixes tightly and prayed to the almighty virgin mother who allegedly watched over them—or at least WATCHED them—perhaps stifling laughter and throwing down tequila shots—as they prayed for her to please not let this maniac KILL them, prayed to the same virgin that mere hours before had given them this JOB that would define them and transform their small and sad lives into grand and glorious ever-expanding pleasure domes, whirlpools of sensation not unlike* Dynasty *and* Dallas *or even* The Cosby Show *and they would wallow in eternal happiness like happy pigs in the endless comfort zone that is every-where in this land or at least around the next corner or the corner after that, the comfort that is America, land of the world's nightmares and let US pray that the world one day wakes up from these infant dreams and wipes the crusty sleep from its eyes and goes about the business of lifting itself from the mud and EVOLVING—and what does a virgin know, anyway?—and they prayed for their wives and for their children that they might never see again as Frank's vehicle lurched through the undeveloped rows of trees, end-less trees; Frank slammed on the brakes, and the cargo tumbled forward like an advancing herd of slam dancers: a crucifix impaled the back of one of the watched-over hulking drunken Catholics who—from the perspective of the ones doing the WATCHING, at least—from the perspective of Clarence the angel, for* example, who, incidently, was chosen for the job of fucking with George Bailey's head only because GOD, a chatty collective of twinkling wiseass stars, had declared that "he's got the IQ of a rabbit and the faith of a child"—looked like CATTLE—and that also pretty well described the motley crew of wide-eyed tumbling dwarves—including Sleepy and Groggy, still out cold—that flew about the back of Frank's truck like Christmas gifts in the hands of the postal service—and the dust swelled and swirled and Frank reached for a cigarette and the mayhem slowly subsided, and the labor force slowly regained consciousness and they gathered their wits about them as they realized the truck had stopped moving: one by one they hopped, fell, staggered, or—in the case of Sleepy and Groggy—were hurled out of the truck, their hearts more or less POUNDING with excitement—the way a torture victim is more or less excited when the whip stops ripping into their flesh, even if only for a moment—and the dream once again flared dimly in their hearts as they prepared to begin the work that would cement their hopes and dreams; their prayers had seemingly been answered thank you virgin and they could already feel the money piling up, five cents, ten cents, and some of them were actually SMILING—shock can have that effect—but Frank WAS NOT smiling: he emerged from the cab of the truck wearing the glazed, psychotic leer of a serial killer, waving a forty-five around like a conductor's baton, and he fired two slugs into the air and the shots boomed and echoed into the space between the immigrants' ears, and the world was suddenly deathly, absolutely quiet: Frank was giving orders in the international master-slave language, gunfire, and they lined up without Frank saying a word, looking at him like they were looking at God, and they weren't thinking about their crucifixes or praying to the bitch-virgin—

*they knew, deep down, that the real GODS were*
*TELEVISION and GUNFIRE, that the messengers of*
*the gods were psychic bullets from the box and hol-*
*low-tipped angels that flew on steel wings from the*
*barrels of polished and spit-shined mechanical*
*penises—guns, millions upon millions of guns—and*
*rained the wrath of the gods upon this low and foul*
*world and reigned, really—they knew THAT much—*
*and as the echo of the fallen angels reverberated*
*from Frank's gun, echoed off the walls of possibility,*
*all was quiet and still; Frank felt like Snow White with*
*her army of dulled, conditioned dwarves, and he*
*grinned slightly as the words slipped through the*
*cracks in his teeth:*

*". . . HEIGH HO, HEIGH HO, IT'S OFF TO*
*WORK WE GO . . ."*

*Frank stood around picking his teeth with the*
*edge of his gun for the next six hours, drinking Pabst*
*Blue Ribbon from a cooler he kept in the cab of the*
*truck—he had stolen two twelve-packs from 7-11—*
*and he kept whistling "Heigh Ho"—the Uncle Walt*
*worker death-march theme, the eerie melody that the*
*doomed and traumatized immigrant workers would*
*carry with them to their graves, the song that they*
*would not be able to forget—the song that would*
*WHISTLE ITSELF—while the Frank's Dead Christmas*
*Trees, Inc. labor dwarves hacked down trees with*
*chain saws purchased at Sears with the credit card of*
*an unwitting Mr. Hank Johnson, a small man wearing*
*a Chicago Bull's cap who kept his wallet in a tattered*
*backpack attached to the rear of his mechanized*
*wheelchair—easy pickings for Frank—and the*
*dwarves harvested several hundred youthful firs that*
*day that would have been perfectly content to remain*
*in the forest, NOT attacking children, and, on the con-*
*trary, making prolonged human life on earth POSSI-*
*BLE by doing their chemical dance and pumping*

*oxygen into the atmosphere, if they had been given a
choice, which they never are, trees that really meant
no harm to children or anyone, but that will now be
killed and carted off to parceled suburbia where their
carcasses will be propped up inside people's homes
and covered with electric lights and razor-sharp tinsel
and glass ornaments that shatter and rip the flesh of
young children, all in the glorious and grand celebration of the birth of CHRIST, who was born in July: a
strange ritual, this Christ-mass . . . but to Frank,
Christmas was a gap in people's souls, a little smiling
opening into which he could wedge his psychic time
bombs, which will tick for years, quiet, deathly loud
tick that comes from nowhere but WILL NOT go
away, the tick of the big clock on Main Street in
downtown Potterville that will finally explode in a
killing spree in a McDonald's in San Diego—
cheeseburgers and blood, everywhere—or in the
squeeze of a trigger that kills a tourist in the back of
a stolen Volvo or in the slice of a knife across a child's
throat in the woods outside Lakeport or in the tug of
a phone cord around the neck of a woman in Fresno
or in the words that kill children and children's children and cause death to ripple out timelessly, the tick
that forever screams KILL or BE KILLED . . . Frank
watched the workers cut the life out of the trees, and
he waved his gun recklessly, as Zeus might have, in-
structing the seven dwarves that remained conscious
to load the trees into the back of the truck, and when
the trees were crammed and packed in like cattle at
the slaughterhouse, like slabs in a freezer, trees upon
trees upon trees, Frank raised his gun and fired two
more shots into the air: two more angels of death
whistled into the late afternoon sky; Frank waved his
gun about as he guzzled his last Pabst Blue Ribbon;
he threw the can over his shoulder where it tumbled
limply and lay still; he climbed into the cab of his*

*truck and started the engine, which groaned loudly, a monster awakened: he turned the truck around and in a cloud of dust and smog jammed the accelerator to the floor and left behind him two unconscious lumps on the ground and seven dazed immigrants who looked at each other and suddenly all their regional differences evaporated—they knew that they had been robbed of their dreams as the real America un-folded before them in bloody red, blinding white, and bruised blue; never again would they be able to look at a tree without feeling massively sad, or stand on a street corner without feeling sick, or watch a Walt Disney film without cringing, and they watched Frank drive away, united in the black solidarity of hate . . .*

*Frank declared the next week or so a company holiday, laid low, and ditched the trees in a large stor-age locker rented with the credit card of Mrs. Gladys Schrapnel of Fort Wayne, Indiana, who had been strolling past Macy's admiring the windows when Frank lurched into her field of vision and vomited on her purse; startled, splattered, she willingly surren-dered her purse to Frank after he apologized pro-fusely with rank breath reeking of pizza and immediately offered to clean the purse for her and she knew she was making a big mistake but every-thing was happening so fast and soon Frank was mer-rily waltzing down the main boulevard of the mall, whistling, a vomit-covered purse hanging from his shoulder; he also used Mrs. Schrapnel's cards for a short vacation trip to Las Vegas where he collected several more credit cards and about five grand in cash from small-time cons of drunken people with too much money—it was a fair exchange: THEY had plenty of money and yet were miserable; their small minds could not understand why; they needed some-one to blame; along came Frank; Frank scammed them in some small, unimportant way and both par-*

123

ties emerged fulfilled: Frank had his money, and they had someone to blame besides themselves for the sorry states of their small, floundering lives . . . transactions like this are more common than one might think: the world RUNS on such exchanges—and soon Frank found himself stretching out on a comfortable bed in a luxury suite, slurping champagne and feeling the dried vomit crack and peel on his chin . . .

After a week of discreet fund-raising, Frank returned to make the final arrangements for opening his business; he rented a large vacant lot next to the video store and advertised for high-school-aged workers seeking "internships"—"interns," of course, are never paid—and within three days he had convinced four eager students that they were going straight from his Christmas tree lot to Yale and Harvard and from there onto luxury yachts and Caribbean islands where the rich ride comfortably upon the broken backs of the working class . . . as it turned out, the eager interns WEREN'T going anywhere near Yale or Harvard, although they WERE going to learn important lessons about the business world from Frank: they would learn to never match drinks with an alcoholic; they would learn to hit the ground running at the sound of gunfire; they would learn to never take small pills from strange men; they would learn to never play "William Tell" with .45s and beer cans; they would learn to never apply for "internships"; and they would learn the most important of business lessons: that most people are shark bait, and to survive one must become a shark, one must develop a taste for human flesh, one must EAT or be EATEN . . . the interns arrived on their first day promptly at 10:00 A.M., dressed in pleated slacks and button-down shirts with crisp haircuts, polished shoes and Ivy League smiles; they found their boss lying in a massive pile of refuse behind a tree, a drunken heap stretched out awk-

124

wardly on a bed of empty sixteen-ounce Pabst Blue
Ribbon cans; the ground was littered with cigarette
butts, some of them still smoldering—a nearby tree
lay burned and charred—along with two pairs of
soiled panties, several .45 casings, and a long bull-
whip; Frank groaned and wedged his eyes open—he
looked like a Draco with a hangover, his narrow eyes
glowing bright red—and he sneered at his new workers, grunting, and they looked at the ground and
shifted their polished shoes in the dirt . . . Frank
moved his mouth and a sentence fragment fell out:

". . . CHECK'S IN THE MAIL . . ."

The boys looked at each other, sickly, and the
tallest of the four spoke, a spunky young prep with
manicured nails and a tennis sweater:

"Good god . . . excuse me, but we're looking for
Mister Booth . . . we've been hired as interns for his
corporation . . . do you know him? . . ."

Frank sneered again and the boys instinctively
stepped back, tripping over beer cans . . .

"RAYMOND . . . SHUT THE FUCK UP . . ."

The young yuppie held his ground, grinning, and
said:

"Excuse me, but my name is WALLACE, Wallace
Fontleroy, not—"

"SHUT THE FUCK UP . . . YOUR NAME IS
RAYMOND YOU STUPID SHIT . . . I JUST TOLD
YOU THAT AND I DON'T LIKE TO TELL PEOPLE
THINGS TWICE . . . DO YOU UNDERSTAND
ME? . . . NOW, RAYMOND . . ."—the yuppie boy
snapped to attention—". . . VERY GOOD,
RAYMOND . . . NOW I WANT YOU TO GET PAUL
OVER THERE AND BEN—. . . BEN, HOW THE
SHIT ARE YA? . . .—AND GET TO WORK . . . I
WANT THESE FUCKIN' SHRUBS PRICED WITHIN
THE HOUR . . . SMALL ONES IN FRONT, LARGE
ONES IN BACK . . . SET THEM UP ACCORDING TO

THIS MAP I'VE DRAWN"—*Frank pulled a dirty nap-kin from his pants, upon which had been scrawled a primitive layout for the lot*—"AND SO HELP ME GOD IF ONE OF YOU LITTLE BUMS SO MUCH AS LOOKS AT ME THE WRONG WAY I WILL SEE TO IT THAT YOUR LEGS ARE BROKEN IN SUCH A WAY THAT ONE WILL BE EIGHT INCHES SHORTER THAN THE OTHER AND NOT ONLY WILL YOU NEED TO HAVE YOUR SUITS CUSTOM MADE BUT YOU'LL ALSO NEED A HIP TRANS-PLANT EVERY FIVE YEARS AND YOU'LL NEVER WALK AGAIN REALLY BUT RATHER HOBBLE LIKE A CAR WITH THREE FLAT TIRES SO HELP ME GOD AND SHOULD YOU DECIDE TO STEAL FROM ME, WELL THEN, I PROMISE YOU, I HOPE THERE IS A GOD, FOR YOUR SAKE, BECAUSE YOU BETTER GET DOWN ON YOUR KNEES AND PRAY THAT YOUR GOD SUCKS YOU UP AND OFF THIS EARTH BEFORE I CUT YOUR BALLS OFF WITH THIS CHAIN SAW AND HANG THEM FROM ONE OF THESE TREES AFTER WHICH I WILL DRAIN THE BLOOD FROM YOUR BODIES AND DRINK IT AFTER WHICH I WILL TAKE WHAT'S LEFT OF YOUR CAR-CASSES AND THROW THEM INTO THE STORM DRAIN UNDER THE MALL, AND DO YOU KNOW WHAT HAPPENS THEN? . . ."

The boys did not want to know what happened then . . . and Raymond interrupted—"yes sir, Mister Booth, sir . . ."—and they scampered off, heigh-ho . . .

Frank's map was clear, but unusual: it was a Christmas tree lot as designed by Gaudí, full of other-worldly twists and bizarre strangeness; one entered the lot surrounded by the smallest, cheapest trees, and then followed paths that wound toward the cen-ter of the lot; the place was laid out like a maze, with paths twisting and doubling back; aisles led nowhere;

*paths twisted in circles; others led deeper into the maze; the perimeter of the lot was well lit, but the light grew faint toward the center, provided only intermittently by flashing strobes that lit the area like a frozen scene from a bizarre David Cronenberg film: patrons were alternately blinded and blind, staggering in shock, falling into trees, cutting their hands on beer cans, jabbed by tree limbs; the area near the center of the maze was like one of the gates to Hell itself: strobes blazed, beer cans and cigarette butts were everywhere, trees stood smoldering and charred, and one song, unbearably loud, played in an endless loop that radiated from giant speakers—. . . "YOU HAVE STUMBLED IN, YOU HAVE BUMBLED IN . . . NOW YOU CAN'T GET OUT" . . .—it was the "Forest Of No Return" song from Babes in Toyland—and occasionally someone would recognize the song from their childhood—from happier times—and smile reflexively; the children, however, would hear the shrill cry of the trees—"NOW YOU CAN'T GET OUT"—and would panic and break free from their parents and stagger through the nightmare strobe world tripping on empty beer cans and falling facefirst into cigarette butts, trapped in what appeared to be some sort of Revenge of the Trees made-for-TV movie; the tallest and most expensive trees were of course in the center of the lot, in the heart of the Forest Of No Return, and Frank took great pride in escorting patrons, smiling—at first—through the maze, walking briskly, jogging almost, with the happy family—husband, wife, children, seeking nothing more than to dutifully consummate the Christ-mass by purchasing a ritually sacrificed tree to adorn with small electronic icons of technology—scampering to keep up, with no idea they could become lost within a Christmas tree lot and led into some surreal nightmare world of trees, dead-end paths, queer music, beer cans, strobe lights and ciga-*

*rette butts . . . by the time they realized what was happening it would be too late: they would be hit by the white wall of strobes, the parents freezing like deer caught in headlights, not really sure what to do, and for the young children it might be fun, at first, a sort of adventure, but as they became more and more frightened and disoriented and kept tripping on cans, the smell of charred trees and beer filling their nostrils to the point of making them dizzy, and that song, that damned song, surrounding them and THEY COULDN'T GET OUT and they would run along the narrow path, stumbling over cans, bumping into trees and suddenly the trees themselves would begin mov-ing and shaking and the kids' eyes would bulge and their little hearts would race and the trees would move and shiver—it would be Frank, of course, stand-ing behind the trees and shaking them—and some-times he would poke his head out and shout in a low gurgle "HEEEERE'S DADDY!" or "NOW IT'S DARK!" or "I'LL SEND YOU STRAIGHT TO HELL FUCKER!" and sometimes he would whisper frantically to one of his assistants, it didn't matter which one:— "RAYMOND! . . . 'CANDY COLORED CLOWN' . . . HURRY!"—and "Raymond" would scamper back to the office and return with a Roy Orbison cassette tape, and Frank would interrupt the endless loop of "Forest Of No Return" and would insert "In Dreams," and he would mumble to himself, nodding—"THE CANDY COLORED CLOWN THEY CALL THE SAND-MAN"—and then he would start chasing kids through the maze until one was cornered in one of the dead ends, pinned against trees, and he would lean over the shaking child, his hot steamy breath in the kid's face, his mouth covered with smeared red lipstick, and he would hold an auto mechanic's lantern against his face and sing along with Roy Orbison in a low moan: "IN DREAMS . . . YOU'RE MINE . . ."*

*Most customers elected not to purchase trees from Frank's Dead Christmas Trees, Inc., but nevertheless found themselves trapped in the lot for twenty to forty minutes, at first wandering and later running for their lives through the maze; and when they finally escaped, they sprinted to their cars and locked themselves in and hugged each other, glad to be alive; the women and children cried, and Frank knew joy: he knew that THIS would be a Christmas season not easily forgotten: this would be an Anti-Christmas, paved with Jingle-Hell memories . . .*

## 7.

Frank was holding up the bar, so to speak, while in REALITY—as opposed to the dream that never stops sucking on YOUR life, IT won't go away, YOU have to go away, YOU have to leave this cesspool—hell, even the MYTHS are living on the boulevard of broken dreams—Sinatra, Brando, the Ramones, sitting at the same bar, telling the same joke over and over, killing the pain—KILL THE LIGHTS: the dream never WAS, the DREAM never ends—it's like that Uncle Walt propaganda training flick, *Bambi,* the one about the young steak with wobbly legs that became increasingly steady as he quickly realized that life was not a party, more like a shooting gallery, and that for no apparent reason this creature MAN would like nothing better than to blast his fuzzy little hide full of buckshot; and so one day, he's out with his mom, grabbing a bite to eat, having a few laughs in the meadow, and mom blurts out "RUN BAMBI RUN! DON'T LOOK BACK! RUN AS FAST AS YOU CAN! RUN BAMBI RUN! DON'T LOOK BACK! RUN AS FAST AS YOU CAN! DON'T LOOK BACK!" and she gets blown to bits by a playful shell from a twelve-gauge and then roasted *and served with a nice apple-spice sauce and a dry zinfandel; then Bambi gets tangled up with a big-eyed doe and a new era of grief begins: first he has to deal with her asshole boyfriend, then he has to protect her from a pack of marauding dogs—he gets mauled for his trouble—then he gets shot in the butt, THEN the forest catches fire, and THEN the doe drops TWINS!; a butt full of buckshot and two more mouths to feed! . . . Frank LEARNED: don't wait for the fire, RUN to the nearest deserted crossroads and pray for a mothership to materialize out of the forty-ninth octave and catch yourself a lift straight off this pink pile of preservatives, this earth, but be sure that it's the RIGHT ship—don't get snagged by THEM—they'll either throw you in a vat or put you to work on the CIA's post-ozone summer home, MARS—and watch out for those little GRAYS, too—they may be small but they're not DUMB—hell, GRAYS don't eat TV dinners—GRAYS don't watch The Golden Girls—GRAYS don't sing "Achey Breaky Heart"—in REALITY, the bar was holding up Frank; the sturdy aged oak was supporting his limp body as he ordered his twenty-seventh and final double Jagermeister of the evening . . . "IT'S HERBAL," he croaked, as a sliver of brown drool forged a path through a forest of rough whiskers and down his grotesquely crusted chin, where it puddled concentrically on the bar . . .*

*The bartender—attractive, bouncing, busty, bright-eyed, blonde—a bimbo—the type of young outsider sex object that bar owners hire in the hopes of reeling in the masses of idiot suburban four-wheel-drive twenty-something commuter working dead, so desperate for companionship that they will drop twenty bucks on three shots of cheap tequila and two beers just for the privilege of saying "hey . . . nice place!" to an actual human female before wobbling out in a haze to their polished trucks and driving er-*

*ratically home where they will put on a Suzanne Vega cassette tape and masturbate—but what the bar owners or the bartenders don't seem to understand is that the PROS—the hard-core one-hundred-proof straight-no-chaser get-out-of-my-way psychotic lunatic soul-eaters—the FRANKS—did not go to bars to DRINK, per se—drinking was a means to an end, a key to a lock—but rather to SUCK MINDS, and there's no brains they love to suck more than those of twenty-two-year-old wide-eyed black-leather-hip bartender chicks who foolishly take on drunken psychotic lunatics like Frank in one-way they-lose mind-suck death-chess in sleazy, dead-end bars in black-hole corners of the clogged toilet that is earth—the toilet that WILL be flushed—and TWIST . . .*

*"IT'S AFTER THE END OF THE WORLD . . . DON'T YOU KNOW THAT YET? . . ."*

*Frank's baritone heavy with alcohol, boomed into the dark corners of the bar, bouncing off walls, slithering into corners, rattling about in cracked harmony; echoes leaked outside, discoloring moments, staining the fuzzy neon night; Frank was quoting Sun Ra, a former exchange student from the planet Saturn and the great benevolent mindfucker of jazz; Frank backed up his comment with a look that would have frozen a side of beef; the sides of beef stared back, not sure if he was KIDDING; he wasn't—from his perspective, the world HAD ended; it WAS after the end of the world—it was after the end of THEIR world; now they were living in HIS . . .*

*"DON'T YOU KNOW THAT YOU'RE DEAD? . . . HASN'T IT OCCURRED TO YOU THAT YOU'RE LOOKING BACKWARDS INTO THE REARVIEW MIRROR OF YOUR MEMORY? . . . HASN'T IT OCCURRED TO YOU THAT WE HAVE REACHED THE END OF TIME, THAT TIME IS GOING BACKWARDS NOW? . . . HASN'T IT OCCURRED TO YOU*

*THAT YOU HAVE TO RELIVE THE WHOLE DAMN
NIGHTMARE OF HISTORY BACKWARDS? . . ."*

*In his exuberance to explain his theory of time
bouncing off the end of the world, Frank teetered
and began falling off his barstool; the stool fell with
him . . . he saw the floor approaching and soon found
himself eye-to-eye with a cockroach; he disengaged
himself from the grotesquely mangled stool and rolled
over into a semi-fetal crouch, looking up at the spinning wheel—consensus reality—with his eyes bulging
out of his head like eggs emerging from a hen; he
thought for a moment that his eyes were going to fall
out of his head; perhaps they were: he prepared to
catch them if they popped out and fell into his
hands . . .*

*"ALIENS INVADE! . . . SINISTER VATS
APPEAR! . . . GOVERNMENT PANICS! . . . FILM AT
ELEVEN! . . ."*

*Frank lifted himself unsteadily, preparing to rise
to yet another moment of Hitleresque triumph; from
his position on all fours—as a crowd of numbed,
blurred faces, bleached and warped with success,
rage, confusion, and cheap booze, looked on—Frank
swelled like a titanic whale, forcing his weight onto his
back legs and hoisting his mighty swollen frame up
into a swaggering, semi-upright stance; wavering, he
used the wobbling, broken barstool for support and
grabbed the bar with both yellowed hands, straining
like Zeus on bad acid to lift himself up, first balancing
both feet on the quivering stool and then stepping
with eighty-proof pride and blurred dignity directly
onto the bar itself, which seemed to almost CRINGE,
and he slowly walked the length of the bar, kicking
over glasses, sauntering, styling, moving with the swaggering assurance and venerable poise of a R&B sax
man marching the blues in a sleazy after-hours club,
the orgasmic honking gurgles spurting from his horn*

**133**

and creating deviant thoughts where before there was only the empty smell of booze; Frank cleared his throat loudly and prepared to deliver the sermon of his life, the sermon after the end of the world, the backwards sermon that bounced off the end of time . . .

"THEY HAVE NO SWEAT GLANDS! . . ."

He stopped and surveyed the crowd: the shapeless faces were without individual identities, passively reactive cells in a larger organism, immersed in some sort of ritual ant-hive mentality, possessed by some lesser, community mind . . . and yet, for the moment, this greater being was strangely silent, curious, sensing perhaps that this walking cocktail was MORE than just another ranting drunk on top of the bar talking about giant lizards . . . was it the booze talking? . . . or was he relaying to them some higher, cosmic, primal secret, some mythic truth? . . . was this strange twisted tale some type of WARNING? . . .

"BEWARE MOTHMAN! BEWARE DRACO! BEWARE REPTILE! BEWARE SNAKE! THEY LIVE! CONSUME! REPRODUCE! MARRY! SMILE! OBEY! BE—"

"AAARRRRGGGGHHHHTTTTHHHHLLLLL-AAAAAUUUUHHHNNNNBBBBBLLLEECCCHHHHH-HHH . . . BEWRAR! PHLEMGAAAAAB" . . .

Frank had THROWN UP; with an exploding slow-motion spin-toss—like the compressed swivel of an Olympic discus thrower—he had developed sufficient torque to unleash an outwardly swirling spiral composed of Jagermeister and bits of pizza fragments—shrimp, anchovies, zucchini, garlic—that spun through the air in slow-motion Picasso fat lady stretched oozing glory and quickly enveloped anyone and everything within a substantial radius, which was a considerable gathering of souls and furniture; it all happened so fast that the moment was frozen, a slow-motion fast-forward freeze-frame time pause, one

134

*of those moments when time becomes fluid, flexible, when days can last seconds and seconds can last life- times, and the vomit hung suspended, an eternal ooze, a timeless drip, a wave—a fluid standing sine wave—of majestic, Olympian vomit . . . twenty-seven double shots and an extra large pizza: recipe for di- saster . . . the incredible volume of material was liquid and yet semisolid, the molten Jagermeister providing a bond like mortar to brick; the pieces of partially di- gested pizza soaked in sticky herbal liqueur attached themselves with a vengeance to everything they hit, which was most everyone and anything in the room . . . panic ensued; panic engulfed; it was as if the Blob itself had escaped from Japanese film hell and oozed into the sweaty world of real people with real problems—or so they thought—and then THIS: the world ending in a foul tidal surge of VOMIT—and SLIMED it, the translucent gel seeping from the invisi- ble hand concentrically and people ran, scratched, bit, bellowed, screamed, lost any sense of order, dignity, calmness: Frank watched the humanity pour out of this pack of wild animals like juice exploding from an orange squeezed by a Goodyear truck tire: they DE- FLATED before his very eyes . . . the panic, of course, amplified the time freeze, and things continued to move slower, as if God had pulled over to watch the aftermatch of a horrific traffic accident: people tugged at each other, clawed their friends, punched their spouses, developed traumatic sociopathic bonds that would last lifetimes, tore at the flesh of their fellow man, screamed till their ears bled, ran into walls, smashed their fists into tables, sliced their arms on shattered shot glasses, slipped on vomit, stuck to each other, had slices of sticky zucchini mashed against their faces by hordes of trampling wide-eyed slow- motion people going nowhere, fighting to go anywhere but really going nowhere in a frantic, semi-real strobe-*

**135**

*light snuff film that was going backwards . . .*

*The only reasonable response to this turn of events was to remain CALM, to wait this melee out, to light up a cigarette and wait for this animal surge to recede, for the dicks to go limp, for the eyes to cease to bulge, for the throats to relax and the mouths to close, for the fists to stop flailing and for the panic to stop, and this is exactly what one stag-geringly gorgeous blonde did, standing alone against a far wall—she was just TOO beautiful; some women COMMAND a circle of space around them; they un-derstand their power; they know how the game is played; they know how to get whatever it is they de-sire in this reflexive world, this sadly predictable globe that spins around the revolving whims of beautiful women and their batting eyelashes; and so they are often seen alone, between whims, scouring the hori-zon for victims, while the men cower at a range of ten to fifteen feet, looking at their shoes, circling, eye-ing their prey, fearing the powers that they don't un-derstand, the spell they are under, fearing the GODDESS before them; Viv LaFrance—alone but not lonely—leaned nonchalantly against a wall in the far corner of the bar, striking a sculpted pose straight out of the summer Paris Vogue, legs teasingly long and silky calm like a tiger's, eyes soft and half-closed like a cat's, body loose, coiled like a panther's, an urban goddess of debauchery taking huge manly puffs off a Camel with long, smooth drags and with absent-minded precision blowing rhythmic, perfectly formed smoke rings in the air, looking through coolly detached eyes at the bedlam after the end of the world, slightly amused . . . Viv was a waitress by profession, a cock-tail waitress; she was Venus in a short skirt; she had seen everything there was to see, twice; she knew ev-erything, intimately; she knew nothing about politics or business or sports or gun-running or law or industry or*

**136**

*computers or medicine or education or the arts and
yet she knew everything that MATTERED about anything that moved; she knew that ALL things were but
sublimations of the all-encompassing SEX DRIVE of
the gods: history reeked of sex; culture dripped sex;
civilization WAS sex; all human interaction was either
derived FROM or was a substitute FOR or was a commentary ON or led directly TO sex; all communication
either led TOWARD sex or AWAY from sex; each
word from every mouth was a declaration of sexual
intent; yin and yang and light and shadow and night
and day were but earthly manifestations of the great
YES-NO of the gods; the American Dream itself was
but a massive sexual sublimation, a cultural dildo, a
national jack-off; the American War Machine was but
a gigantic, lumbering erection wedged into the tight
pants of Democracy, stifled until the outburst of war
prompts congressional rubbing and legislative foreplay
and the uncontrollable spurting ejaculation of bombs
and missles ensues as the nation COMES on the
heads of a nation of Third World villagers . . . as a
cocktail waitress, Viv walked the finest of lines, the
slim crack between yes and no: she fed the primal
urges with flashes of cleavage and thigh, fueled the
looming desire with liquor, fired fantasies with implied
suggestion, stoked imaginations with playful hey-baby
eyes, inflamed the hordes of attacking glands encouraged by Budweiser and stilled by fear with the occasional discreet and semi-intentional hip-thrust
body-nudge, the defining gesture of waitressing, the
GREAT SECRET of waitressing, the hermetic path to
greater tips, the alchemical transmutation of lust into
cash, the laundering of lust, the greasing of the seduc-
tive palm that stokes the eternal imagined fire; she
felt the loneliness loom like a wall preventing the hims
of the world from proceeding to follow the customary
route to establishing the groundwork for increasing the*

*possibility of perhaps building a fragile relationship which might lead to a contemporary romance but probably not; she sensed the bad teeth behind tense jaws as the visits increased in frequency and leaden intensity, precisely imagined interactions wedged into grotesque five-minute chunks that grew longer and heavier as the years piled up and the waists grew limp and uncaring under the burden of the rising tide of beer and pretzels; she tamed the all-seeing EYE that lashed out; she met the furtive glances launched through clouds of smoke at THE woman, ALL women, she who touched once and never always said never yes but never not no; she sensed the pulsing of the cracked hearts left open and vulnerable as they thrashed about the sticky barroom floor; she watched the sorrow swim in the ice cubes and the double scotches and cower in the sweet folds of the margaritas; she sensed the cloudy hopes and soothed the dreams gone awry and listened patiently to the misguided staggering rants; she smiled as the greasy-spoon decay rubbed off . . . as a cocktail waitress, she knew that life itself was nothing more than the eternal dance of cock and pussy . . .*

*SEX: the world is made of sex; flecks of sex on distant decks cause train wrecks; sex sells farewells; the smell of sex is everywhere . . . in the sewers, in the amber waves of grain, in the clouds, in five billion pairs of underwear; sex makes the world go round, spinning in a sexy, provocative, slightly skewed way, as if trying to pick up Venus with a nudge and a wink and a sexy cloud formation—once the earth had a lover, the moon, and she drew the moon into her orbit, seduced the poor fellow, then changed her mind and rejected him, he was too small and gray, with a bad complexion, like 200 million miles of bad road, and she just left the moon hanging out there to rot, embarrassed and humiliated, a broken hulk of ele-*

*mental dust, and the moon just rolled over one day
and died of a broken heart, and just sits there late at
night staring through dead gray eyes at the earth,
longing for the shapely blue-green bitch goddess, circling the woman of his dreams that he can never
have—the lizard people inside the moon, they
couldn't care less about this interplanetary sex dance:
they're too busy tending to their large vats filled with
floating organs and genetic material, kind of like a gigantic Safeway meat department—except that
YOU'RE the meat—making noisy lizard-vat love,
drinking homemade lizard-vat beer, waiting for orders
from the transdimensional eminently smelly lizard
kings of the hollow under-earth, waiting for the return
of the cruel and unusual landlords of the playpen that
is earth, the caretakers of the overgrown garden of
delights that needs weeding—and why IS it that tenants simply WILL NOT tend to the garden? do they
resent the fact that PLANTS don't have to pay rent
and uproot themselves every day and go to WORK?
do they resent the ageless beyond-the-dawn-of-the-
gods tenant-landlord hierarchical social matrix game?
do they express their unrequited resentment at this
systemic injustice by killing innocent soft and fluffy
lawns and grinning dandelion patches and poppies
with families at large teenage social gatherings where
the male urine flows ritually like waterfalls of waste
into the unkempt rental gardens of America and the
yeasty high-school vomit puddles discreetly in the dark-
ened corners of yellow suburbia? do they gain a small
sense of VENGEANCE by killing plants that just happen to LIVE THERE, occupying that particular point in
space and time, plants that would just as soon run for
their lives but are not able to move about or drive, really, so THEY don't have much choice?—THEY don't
WANT to be rooted in "someone else's yard—but
soon, very soon, the space weeders will come from the*

place where there are no tenants' rights groups,
where property disputes are settled with large tails
and extra-dimensional psychic switchblades, justice dis-
pensed quickly and without paperwork or defense at-
torneys or gumshoes or court battles, without any
hard feelings at all, without any feelings, really, and
they WILL NOT be pulling plants out by the roots;
they will be weeding the garden of human souls, har-
vesting the crop that is humanity: they will be collecting the RENT . . . perhaps the earth knows this; she's
been shaking badly for the last few decades; she's got
holes in her ozone and she's losing her hair; people
keep sucking her blood and using it to run their cars;
planes buzz her face like flies; she has become tem-
pestuous, her mood swings pronounced; does she
have AIDS? have the humans INFECTED the earth?
will the other planets get sick and die if they get too
close to the old gal? do the other planets talk about
her behind her back, like gossiping, fleshy paralegals
with grotesque hats hunched over four-dollar drinks
with miniature umbrellas and atmospheric slices of
decaying pineapple in run-down cheap plastic fern
bars with cardboard walls where the lights are hot
and the talk is oily and the air smells like lies and
even the ferns themselves are fake, as they debate
the doubtful fertility of a particularly broken-down,
slouching, once-wanted-to-be-somebody, suicidal, inept
claims adjuster two stools down as he bends over his
lifeless Long Island iced tea making terse slurping
noises through a plastic straw, imagining that he's
seven years old again, sucking the milk right out of his
cereal bowl as he sits in front of the TV screen, his
best and only friend, the giant Zenith, literally bigger
than he is, bigger than life, an angel, a devil, a god,
sucking in amber waves of radiation that will cause
his hair to repeal at twenty-three, watching Johnny
fucking Quest fight the lizards and live the two-

*dimensional four-color good life like a young, cartoon
Hemingway, wishing his mom and dad were there to
hold him and tell him that everything was alright and
to promise him that life would not become boring and
predictable and that he would not wish for death
while slurping booze in a death-disco fernless bar
while being watched—and he KNEW it—through
small eyes by two dead-fish women whose bitterness
was oozing through their skin, literally, oozing, only to
be held in check by a wall, a fortification, really, of
caked-on, buckling makeup, psychically pin-pricked by
these lumps of plodding DNA? do the other planets
suggest, in cosmic tones just loud enough to be heard
over the tinkling of stars at the galactic cocktail party
that never ends, that the earth should consider wearing . . . well, you know . . . a CONDOM . . . out of
consideration for the other planets and as a badge of
shame and a symbol of its disconnectedness from its
own vital fluids, a symbol of its own severed electromagnetic heritage, a scarlett bag? should the entire
sphere be enveloped in a giant, black-budget-financed
Lockheed-engineered National Security State approved
massive latex über-condom, a super-project of such
immensity as to call for the unlikely marriage of the
conceptual vision of Christo and the sleazy contracting
gusto of Bechtel, Inc.?—if the National Security State
had an office, it would say BECHTEL on the door—
and it doesn't have an office—a public-works project
dwarfing all others, an engineering opus for the ages,
and who would unroll this giant condom, who would
unfurl this flapping flag of cosmic concern? would
GOD himself be hired as an oversized subcontractor
to slip the eternal rubber-gloved hands lovingly, or with
DISGUST perhaps, stifling the almighty urge to
vomit?—what happens if God vomits? is that IT? is
that the end of the third act? is THAT the BIG BARF,
the ever-expanding concentric vomit launch?—but let*

*us assume LOVINGLY, under the earth's parts and guide the old gal safely into the snug harbor of the largest condom ever made? would this condom have advertising on it? would it be sponsored by Nippon or Fuji? would there be a McDonald's promotional tie-in? would it be the no-frills buck-fifty one-shot might-work might-not lubricated mini-pouch, the type purchased by teenage boys with sweaty hands and fiery glands and carried with swelling, lunging pride for sometimes years on end, hidden in the folds of their wallets, just in case, the kind carried, like a concealed weapon, by pragmatic, bitterly single women utterly repulsed by the thought of spreading their hallowed loins for one-shot gorilla-in-a-tie slam-bangs, just in case, the kind that floats loosely in the harbor of love, requiring occa-sional anchoring by a rubber o-ring obtained from the hardware store which costs about five cents but if the manufacturers knew it was being used for sex the price would go up to a buck fifty and they'd paint 'em pink and advertise on TV, inserting the idea into the mass consciousness that without a rubber o-ring to se-cure their free-floating, wandering condoms, their life-jackets, the public will swim the sea of flesh and DIE—expired, finito, stiff, snuffed, fried, mulched, bagged, boxed, DEAD—or, would it be the leather-bar yuppie-party-joke high-tech pleasure-pain smart weapon that looks like an underground genetic experi-ment gone awry with rippling folds of hardened plastic and small missilelike Lockheedesque extentions and mutant multidirectional Claes Oldenburg nubs, a friendly-fire power tool, a VIRTUAL DICK? will the other planets be moved by this gesture of heartfelt sincerity or will Jupiter and Saturn be disgusted and move their orbits even farther away from the twirling slut and her dead lover? will Mars be moved by the earth's gesture and invite her over for coffee? will Venus be aroused by the condomic projectiles and slip*

excitedly into the earth's orbit with a bottle of wine
and a Meryl Streep video? . . .

Viv could summarize the history of the world in
a word—THUMP!mmmmmmmmmmmmmmmmmmmw
wwwwwwhhhhhaahahhhhhhblblblblblblblolololoololol
oloodbloodbloodeelsslkalsslsldllorrqqqmsdsadaddaadada
adaddaaddadadaddaadddaaawwaawawawwdsdsasfuuuyu
yuuyuyuuyuyuytewvvvdvdfttddstddaeweqczxĉm,bnbvcxx
cvxxcvxxxzxzxzxzzxzzxzxzxzxzxzxẑxẑxẑaxzzxxxzxxzzx
xzzxxzxxzx̂zx̂azx̂ax̂x̂xdasdd̃aseeaggdfcvxccvbccvjunj
mhmjmmjjjjhhjcmbgjgmvcnhjrwws5u89488w0eþ09!!te
uuq903qutoouuu9t38167349349ut3761561 = tj6%t
761 = = eurjsjsjhrh84911 = = $$lu4jjcjjxclkxchhvfirrihrr
rrþa!90[jjrjndd883qhakfiiasueuerefjncnm̂ĥdu/hu899þ
48hnfnnvnzvn;̂lnv;̂zn#5828865868774592923235453456/,./ > < ?!@    #&< > < ? > ))(*&*\%%$$$$$
$@@!!@%%%BOOM!—shortened to
THUMP!BOOM!—which summed up HER life as
well—and yet her own heart resembled downtown
Baghdad, smoldering and choking in dust; she was a
bewildered ghost in a postwar zone, compromised and
propositioned and assaulted by so many psychic thugs
attacking from so many directions and positions and
dimensions, all simultaneously thrusting verbal dildos
and astral penises at her without warning or sense or
meaning, that there was simply nothing left to bomb:
the missiles continued to plow into the rubble of her
heart and stir up dust and move the debris around,
but nothing was left better or worse than before;
there was no damage LEFT to be done; her emotions
had run for cover; her heart lay wounded and near
death in a dark corner of the underground bomb shel-
ter of her mind . . . when one's heart shatters like a
plate of thin glass, one does not DIE: one plods along,
partially alive; one ceases to live and merely exists: if
the heart has only been hit ONCE, if the bombing has
not been continuous and relentless, if a grinning smart

bomb has not trailed the limping heart down a vent
and into the bomb shelter of the mind, THUMP!
BOOM!, if the heart in question does not resemble
postwar Baghdad or postindustrial Detroit, if the heart
in question is not TOTALED, if there remains HOPE
and a fragile FAITH that the world does not consist
SOLELY of thuggish bands of psychos that roam the
subterranean tunnels of the mind destroying the fragile architecture of hopes and dreams, then repairs—
although costly and labor intensive—are at least
possible; but the heart of Viv LaFrance was beyond repair: her heart resembled the MOON, choked with
dust; her world was bladerunner-dead; she cried acid-
rain tears . . .

Frank was still standing on top of the bar, a
wobbling, vomit-drenched übermensch, a fluid sculpture of pizza and pride; he belched and thrust his
sticky fist in the air in a grand salute to the gods that
made such a vomit-filled world possible and allowed
him to be here at this glorious place and time; he
drooled uncontrollably . . . at nearly the same infinite
moment in selectively fluid time, a small, seductively
meandering rivulet of gin-tainted saliva posed and
sauntered down the sleek, perfect runway of Viv La-
France's chin; Frank saw this holy glimmer of spit and
was moved; he relaxed his grip on mankind and
turned to face this she-beast of his dreams: he looked
inside the trenches that were her eyes and a CON-
NECTION was made, a switch was thrown; it was—
LOVE is not the word, ADMIRATION perhaps,
respect, recognition, understanding, KNOWLEDGE—it
was a look two grandmasters might have thrown at
each other during a championship chess match—the
look an electron might have flashed a proton—and he
sensed that from across worlds, from across space
and time, from between the small infinitely large
cracks in the dimensions had suddenly come someone

EQUALLY UNEQUAL who KNEW, without a word or
a thought being exchanged, WHAT Frank WAS, what
it was that leaked out and puddled, and what they
both KNEW at that moment was that SHE would, at
a time and place of her choosing, suck up Frank's
soul like a Hoover sucking up a match; we are drawn
to our mirror images; we melt in the face of our own
reflection; we bend to the whims of our unseen, omni-
present döppelgangers . . . even Frank . . .

    There are three types of people in the human
food chain: there are SHARKS, there is SHARK
BAIT—the sharks feed on the shark bait—and there
is a small population of dolphins that keep a low pro-
file and meet discreetly to discuss matters of progres-
sive cosmic importance and metaphysical permanence
and occasionally whap a shark or two with their noses
and kill them; but the dolphins are not interested in
overthrowing the sharks or saving the bait; they know
that the bait cannot be saved; they know that the bait
would not know what to do with itself without the
sharks; they know that the bait exists only to be eaten
by the sharks and the sharks exist only to eat the
bait—and so they mind their own business while the
vast majority of humanity—shark bait, floating about
the seas of life—do the same, providing fodder for
the wars and labor for the factories . . . "what" the
factories make is irrelevant: General Motors makes
pickup trucks that explode; General Dynamics makes
flying saucers; the process, not the product, is what
matters . . . the factories, manned by shark bait,
make THINGS which are then sold BACK to the bait
at a high markup—resulting in profit, money, cash,
scratch, grease, glue, which is collected and counted
and hoarded at the top of the corporate ladder, which
certainly is not a ladder at all but rather more like an
elevator that says GOING UP but stops well short of
the Penthouse, an elevator that goes DOWN really,

*an elevator that says PENTHOUSE but actually takes
the occupant straight down to HELL, and the smiling
shark bait, whistling after a hard day's work making
things that he himself will buy back at a later date,
after they have been marked up, gets on this elevator
and thinks he is going UP, straight to the top, when
actually he is going DOWN, further down into slave-
wage hell, down to the basement of possibility, where
the bait gets off, still whistling, thinking he has arrived
at the Penthouse, smiling cheerfully as he tips the
creepy elevator attendant, his mind saturated with
generations of radiant slave-wage TV families, conditioned to assume that, due to the assorted potted
plants scattered about, the Warhol prints, and the dis-
penser of tasty soft drinks against the wall, that he
has actually reached the Penthouse and achieved the
Cleaver or Brady or Huxtable preprogrammed paint-
by-numbers Dream, when, in actuality, he is still in
HELL, a hell he has arrived at out of his own efforts,
a hell he has never left, a tastefully decorated hell he
has created with his own well-meaning but misguided
hands, a happy hell of his own creation but a HELL
nevertheless; the ACTUAL Penthouse, of course, is
beyond the range of his small thoughts, with solid gold
fixtures, marble floors, crystal chandeliers, silver chal-
ices, private screening rooms, silk wallpaper, room service, champagne baths, whips and chains, silk sheets,
studded thigh boots, revolving beds, air conditioning,
oxygen masks, amphetamines, all this and more that
the ordinary situation-comedy-molded mind cannot
even conceive of, THINGS that money and power can
buy, THINGS that make the world go round, THINGS
that make pretty French girls scamper off to Hollywood after spending too many grimy Paris nights
watching too many overproduced blockbuster Hollywood love stories, brainwashed to think that America
is, really, just one big happy c'est la vie with three*

*acts and a happy ending in every three-bedroom
home on every clean and well-lit street and the cam-
era pulls back and pans the achingly beautiful horizon
to reveal the family, arm in arm, standing on the lush
lawn feeling the cool grass slip between their powdered and manicured toes as they watch the sleepy
sun sag behind the horizon of another perfect day in
the Penthouse of the American Dream—and then
they wake up from this silly dream as the rattling DC-
10 deathtrap—a pickup truck with wings—skids to a
quivering, spurting stop on a pitted runway and they
get herded off the plane, pushed and shoved like cattle, and the smog hits their eyes like a wall of fire and
their lungs burn and they climb into a groaning cab
with dried cum on the back seat and take a greasy
fifty-buck ride to Melrose in the coagulated heart of
Hollywood only to be barfed on energetically by some
homeless, stinking street wino ranting about his
crashed stock market portfolio and bladerunner lizards that live under the shopping mall; the Penthouse—where the French girls are invited only if they
spread their legs with vigor and feigned enthusiasm
for the men of power—is roomy, comfortable, and
tastefully decorated; the sharks live in the Penthouse
and the bait is kept in pens out on the south forty;
the many are PASTURED by the few; the sharks have
no intention of letting the bait get anywhere near the
Penthouse, and as a precaution they create an illusory,
cardboard-cutout Penthouse to keep the bait on the
hook—in the event they get a wild spur in their gene
banks and decide to take back what is rightfully theirs
and recapture their diverted reality stream—even
though the bait would not know what to DO with the
Penthouse, just as the CATTLE would not know what
to do with the ranch house if they lynched the Bark-
leys and took over the Big Valley; without shark paranoia, the bait would just lie there on the hook and*

rot . . . Frank surveyed the crowd with shark eyes and clenched teeth, a psychic eating machine sizing up a meal; the crowd was frozen in time and space, suspended in the backward highlight film that Frank was creating: the panic had subsided and the sides of beef just stood there gaping—the world had NOT ended—or if it HAD it didn't end the way THEY EXPECTED it to—with the white-hot afterglow of a mushroom cloud—or the dusty thud of a meteor—or the flesh-ripping winds of a grinding pole shift—it had not ended like a MADE-FOR-TV MOVIE—and the crowd seemed at least partially relieved to discover that they were not following some grinning bitch in a white dress up a tunnel of light toward a radiant white dot around the corner from infinity, which is really what most people are standing around waiting for—their OWN demise—and Frank looked about with smoking, empty-chamber eyes at the wreckage of booze and bodies, the legacy of his tainted bar walk; people were sitting, gaping, examining their wounds, trying to figure out what had happened, afraid to touch anything, afraid to move, afraid of life, afraid of death, just afraid; Frank's attacking film-hell vomit had induced others to vomit—behavior is like a contagious virus for which there is no cure—and the room seemed to float in a thin film of living gel; people looked about and stifled the living lumps in their throats . . .

". . . THEY'RE . . . HERE . . ."

Frank was working the room like a Las Vegas master, like Wayne Newton or Vic Dana at the Sands; Sinatra himself would have been impressed as Frank grabbed space and time by the throat and force-fed his WILL into the minds of his audience: Sinatra himself would have been glued—more or less literally—to that floor, his eyes riveted on the Werner Erhard of bodily fluids, his eyes fixed on Frank . . .

". . . THEY'RE HERE . . . THEY'RE NOT GOING

AWAY . . . THEY'RE OVER SEVEN FEET TALL . . .
THEY LIVE IN HUGE CAVES AND TUNNELS THAT
CRISSCROSS THE EARTH . . . THEY HAVE PSYCHIC
POWERS BEYOND YOUR COMPREHENSION . . .
THEY HOP ABOUT INTERDIMENSIONALLY AND
HIDE IN THE CRACKS OF TIME . . . THEY CON-
TROL MINDS AND THOUGHTS AT THEIR CONVE-
NIENCE THROUGH PSYCHIC MANIPULATION,
MASS HYPNOSIS, SELECTIVE IMPLANTATION, REVI-
SIONIST SEDUCTION, DOGMATIC HYSTERIA, RELI-
GIOUS PROGRAMMING, BIOMAGNETIC BEHAVIOR
MODIFICATION, REMOTE MIND CONTROL, PER-
SONALITY RECONSTRUCTION, SUBLIMINALS, TELE-
VISION, FOOD CHAIN MODIFICATION, FORCED
INTERBREEDING, GENETIC INTERVENTION, WON-
DER DRUGS, WONDER BREAD, WHIMSY, WILL,
WACKENHUT, AND THERE'S NOT A CHANCE IN
HELL THAT YOU WON'T END UP IN A VAT SOME-
WHERE BOBBING UP AND DOWN WAITING FOR
YOUR ORGANS TO BECOME A SIDE ORDER AT A
LIZARD BUFFET . . . THIS IS THEIR PLANET AND
THEIR PARTY . . . THEY'RE BACK, THEY'RE HERE,
THEY'RE ANGRY AND THEY'RE HUNGRY . . . THE
LEASE HAS EXPIRED AND WE'VE FORFEITED THE
CLEANING DEPOSIT . . . THE DRAGONS HAVE
CLIMBED OUT OF OUR MYTHS AND DUSTED
THEMSELVES OFF . . . THEY'RE IN OUR HISTORY,
OUR ANCESTRY, OUR BLOOD, OUR GENES, OUR
MEMORY, OUR MOVIES, OUR VIDEO GAMES, AND
NOW THEY'RE IN OUR BACKYARDS: THERE IS NO
HOPE . . . THERE IS ONLY BOB HOPE . . . IT'S
AFTER THE END OF THE WORLD . . . DON'T YOU
KNOW THAT YET? . . ."

As the women of the world move about the
game board of life they encounter a broad palette of
men, and yet the encounters themselves fall neatly
into ordered patterns of action and reaction; the

*pieces are complex and yet the game itself follows a
short list of rigid rules, unwritten and implied; the
rules are the matrix on which the game floats, like
waves on the ocean; to fight the unwritten rules is to
drown in the game; those who KNOW the rules win
the game; women like Viv always win: THAT is one of
the rules; men like Frank eat lesser women like candy
but are in turn gobbled up whole by women like Viv;
the moment of conquest is, of course, SEXUAL; the
moment of victory is the instant of SURRENDER, the
instant the man gives of himself willingly, completely;
he gives his fears, his dreams, his flaws, his pain . . .
he gives his GENES; he leaves THIS world on wings of
imagination, tasting eternity for an instant; eternity
COMES, arriving in many layers, fluid waves of blurred
sensation that radiate in sequence from every direction; the armies of sperm, 360,000 strong—down a
few divisions from the half million that spilled from a
man in the Renaissance—the glory days of DNA—are
but the forward wave, trailed by the invisible legions of
SPIRIT and ESSENCE, at first hesitantly and then in a
joyous scramble as all that IS and all that WILL BE
tumbles in through the doorway wedged open by re-
lease and acceptance, flooding the moment with
supra-knowledge and trans-peace, wedging eternity
into a fragment of time that at first wobbles hesitantly
into infinity like a child on unsteady legs but later radi-
ates concentrically like a proud beam of sunlight,
never ending, never beginning, existing beyond the
concept of time, SURROUNDING time, ARRESTING
time, BOOKING time, charging time with the illegal
maintenance of an ILLUSORY REALITY, hauling time
off to the clink, hauling time off to DO time; in a flash
comes the snapshot of infinity, the split second of VI-
SION, the glimpse of the canvas beneath the painting,
the silence beneath the song, the seed beneath the
flower, the next page in a one-page book, the sequel*

*to the film that wasn't made, the MIND that maneu-
vers the invisible hand: EVERYTHING arrives in the
flood of waves that flow through the door that is
wedged open; to move with the waves is to find bliss
and power; to kick the door open and leave it open is
to find paradise . . . the opening of the inner door required the shutdown of the external senses, and
Frank's eyes were bolted shut as he attempted to
transcend the smells and sounds and textures and
thoughts—the SMELLS, the THOUGHTS—and especially the IMAGES that arose in his mind: the fisted
black latex-glove that forced its way IN like the Queen
of England wedging her way in a five-star French restaurant through the back entrance by the kitchen
where the cooks swim in decaying food scraps and
smoke cheap cigarettes and the flies on the wall are
fat and sassy and the greasy bums outside are sus-
tained by the smell of the rot alone and the rats wait
patiently in the cracks behind the stoves for the banquet that never ends to begin; the twelve-year-old girl
sucking on an imported cigar and giving him a hand
job; the eighty-year-old twins; the men, bent before
him: Ernest Hemingway, drunk, bent before him; Mister Ed, in beatnik shades, bent before him, reeling off
fractal stream-of-consciousness raps about international spy rings and flying carpets and Morse code
and Mae West and jazz and 900 numbers; Richard
Nixon, bent before him, mumbling strange confessions
into a tape recorder; Ed Sullivan, bent before him, ad-
libbing an introductory monologue for the Rolling
Stones; Keith Jackson, bent before him, a blue velvet
rag stuffed in his mouth; Robert Hilton, televangelist,
bent before him, clutching a small prayer cloth, ranting—"HALLELUJAH Brothers and Sisters . . . GOD
has sent you in front of this TV to give me your
MONEY . . . to SEND me a THOUSAND-DOLLAR
vow of faith, AMEN . . . I have been to the CROSS*

and DIED so that I can reach into your PURSE and
take your PLEDGE . . . get out of that CHAIR . . .
pick up that PHONE . . . open your HEARTS . . .
open your WALLETS . . . take DOMINION over the
demon of poverty . . . take GOD as your SENIOR
PARTNER . . . invest in the LORD . . . steal from your
children . . . cash in your insurance . . . send us your
jewelry . . . sell your children and send us the
money . . . BA SABBA HA! BABBA CANNA BA
SANNA! HABBA NANA!"—and phones are flashing
everywhere, ringing like crazy, handled by "prayer
ministers" in white suits with rings with walnut-sized
diamonds and it sounds like PBS pledge night, except
that, in televangelism, EVERY night is pledge night—
no, his asshole fantasies would have to be put aside
for now—and Frank stopped trying to see and merely
existed within himself; he stopped moving forward and
just floated; he drained his nostrils of smell and his
fingers of touch; his mind went blank, spilled into infinity, and he felt the pleasure stampede begin, leaking from somewhere else, flowing from a dimension of
immense size that surrounded him and was beginning
to leak through, an ocean of imagination, and he felt
the waves surge forward, from nowhere, everywhere,
hell, heaven, and the waves grew in size and intensity
and he felt himself lifted out of his body, his expanding awareness rising with the waves until it stretched
from the floor of the great ocean to the crest of the
highest wave, an ocean of thought, great waves of
feeling, and he felt his soul envelop and swallow the
ocean, knowing every creature and every pebble and
every thought within, tasting every scent and feeling
every textured ripple of life, and the ocean became so
big that he could exist within a single molecule, within
the endless infinities between the spaces, and at the
same time his soul became so immense that it enveloped the sky, the stars, the space, the black holes,

*the red giants, the godly vomit, time itself; Frank be-*
*came so big that he enveloped the entire dance of*
*cock and pussy . . . he surged several times, rolling*
*with the waves, and quivered slightly, feeling a calm-*
*ness fall over him; when he opened his eyes the world*
*was fuzzy: he looked at Viv's face: it was full of plea-*
*sure and power; he moved his eyes slowly down her*
*warmly glowing body to her fleshy breasts: they were*
*moist with pleasure and power; he looked down be-*
*tween her legs at the exhausted flanks of an army of*
*sperm: they loitered, satisfied and spent, on the her*
*edges of her vagina, which radiated pleasure and*
*power . . .*

# 8.

after the fall
comes the winter

And God said, "GET LOST, I'VE GOT MY OWN
PROBLEMS . . . I QUIT!" and then there was nothing—POOF—and man was alone with his thoughts,
his portals, just he and the wind and the rain and his
leaking vents through which evil fluttered in on oily
wings and stuck sometimes; just like that, alone; and
so it came to pass and stick that God liked the ar-
rangement, he liked being left alone, and so we,
like him, were, are, alone, each of us, completely
alone . . . and so it was and is a lonely old world and
the sharks among us roam the seas of our imaginations, feeding on the leaks in our souls, the space between our bodies, wandering through life, feeding,
alone, even THEY, even FRANK, who, like God, en-
joyed being alone, and never more so than when he
stared at the box, his mentor, his lover, his demon, his
friend, his portal, his whipping boy, his master, his
mirror, his SONY, because he wasn't really alone because the box stared back and SUCKED, the sleepless
low-resolution face radiating in his eyes, wiggling and
squirming into his world, creeping into his dreams,
bleeding through into his reality . . . the TV dominated

*his life as it dominated a world full of small lives,*
*flooding the small thoughts of a dying planet and*
*surfing into the mass consciousness of the human*
*race on turbulent waves of twenty-four-hour-a-day liv-*
*ing color—and the box SPOKE:*

*"I've fallen and I can't get up! . . ."*

*The old bag HAD fallen: she looked like a rat in*
*a winter storm, alone; like the last car in a train*
*wreck, crumpled, alone; like like a two-dollar steak in*
*a frying pan, alone; like a flash-frozen woolly mam-*
*moth staring up without eyes through two hundred*
*feet of ice glacier, alone . . . she twisted slightly, her*
*leathery, decomposing frame dominating the screen*
*like the lumpy and tensely mangled croissantlike*
*shoulders of Ed Sullivan; she rolled slowly back and*
*forth, cringing—this looked so REAL that for a mo-*
*ment Frank was confused: was she actually HAVING*
*a heart attack or was she merely PLAYING someone*
*having a heart attack? . . . sometimes it was hard to*
*tell the difference—and Frank leaned forward, smiling*
*thinly—his glasses appeared fogged—and announced*
*to no one in particular—to the zeitgeist in general—*
*in weighted, earnest gravity:*

*"WE'VE ALL FALLEN AND WE CAN'T GET*
*UP . . ."*

*The zeitgeist did not respond; the zeitgeist does*
*not have time for two-bit assholes like Frank; the*
*zeitgeist has better things to do; on the TV screen, in*
*luminous, eerie halftones, the old lady just lay there*
*on the floor, unmoving, unable, perhaps UNWILLING,*
*to get up; the POINT of all this, the point of her*
*BEING, really, was to induce US into watching HER*
*push a button on a small console she carried with her,*
*a sort of home-sized version of the nuclear football*
*that trails the President, awaiting the Final Moodswing,*
*the Final Indiscretion, as he moves discreetly—lonely*
*but never alone—from cabinet meeting to golf course*

to pharmacist to Paris hotel suite to scripted photo op to unscripted adventures with unnamed representatives of various lobbying interests; the "button"—the one directly beneath her wobbling finger—connected her with an organization that exists for the singular purpose of helping people who have fallen get up; people fall down, the company dispatches someone to pick them up: in a perfect world, a perfect system; however, in this world, our world, the fallen will lie there for hours while cups of coffee are finished, cards are dealt, dispatchers are fucked, trucks are repaired, sitcoms conclude, time is stretched and KILLED and then, maybe, someone will be ready to make the minimal effort to help the fallen-down and better-be-paid-up get up once again with the aid of a walker; then—and only then—might the advertised champions of the fallen work their way in the general direction of the old lady's place, after stopping for donuts and coffee at the 7-11 and a quick grand-slam breakfast and a grand pinch of the butt of the waitress with the tired eyes and a cigarette if not several, and then—and only then—might they work their way toward the pathetic old lady's house—and they'll stand outside admiring the place—nice shack, eh Fred? when's the last time you saw a DUMP like this? YESTERDAY?—and she'll hear them and flutter to consciousness, or FROM consciousness, maybe and maybe not alive, perhaps fallen, perhaps erect, and they may or they may not help her stand again, it all depends, they may toss her back into bed and help themselves to food and long-distance phone calls and jewelry or silverware and perhaps even a taste of the drooping flesh of her aging limbs—just kidding—while in the real world, had she existed, which she didn't, because this was television, she would have gotten results more quickly if she had started screaming or grabbed a portable phone and called her next-door

*neighbor or her daughter or her son or Pamela from
the clinic or Francis from the pawn shop or Ernie
from downtown or her maid's stepmother in Guatemala or her neighbors favorite charity or someone
who actually cared, anyone, anywhere, even a 900
fantasy number, or, as a last resort, the police, or she
could just save everybody time and trouble and point
a magnum with hollow points at the roof of her
mouth and blow her dentures and brains out through
the back of her skull and they'd splatter colorfully
against the back wall of the kitchen and make a
mess she wouldn't live to see, or she could cut her
throat with a K-Tel jinsu knife and fingerpaint "Fuck
You World" on the linoleum in her own puddling
blood before checking out of her earthly vehicle and
floating the hell out of here, Bus Nine to somewhere,
anywhere, and STEP ON IT . . . had she fallen, really,
or had she JUMPED? could she NOT get up, or did
she NOT WANT to get up? was she real, or was she
VIRTUALLY real? or, as a televised image, was she
META-real, possessing powers beyond the consensus
limits, godlike, comic-book powers beyond the short
reach of the normals? could she be REWOUND?
ZOOMED? could she travel through time in NORMAL,
SUPER SLO-MO, and FAST FORWARD? if she truly
HAD fallen, and could not get up, wouldn't she just
need a REMOTE CONTROL? couldn't she just RE-
WIND until she was standing again? . . . and then,
just like that, the image of the old lady was gone,
picked up, one would assume by the nice men from
the alarm company—or perhaps CUT UP—into small,
tidy pieces—by the strange man at the other end of
the beeper; she had fallen . . . AND NOW SHE HAD
DISAPPEARED . . .*

 *Frank was alone; he knew it; the cosmos knew
it; small particles of matter knew it; people who didn't
know they knew it knew it; Stephen Hawking knew it,*

*sitting quietly in his wheelchair pondering time and wormholes; Linus Pauling knew it, popping vitamin C, propping up his DNA in heaven; Vlad the Impaler knew it, sucking on a baby, alone, somewhere in the bowels of eastern Romania; Dr. Gene Scott knew it, flow-charting the Bible on The Big Board; the collective consciousness known as Mister Ed knew it, floating through space on the waves of television; aboriginal shamans knew it, cruising the ripples of the Dream-time and surveying the wild ride of the future; Sad-dam Hussein knew it, throwing darts at a photo of George Bush; HELL, everyone knew it . . . and so Frank's words sailed outward, bounding through space and time, rippling out in concentric puddles, traveling toward the ears of others who didn't want to know— and, furthermore, weren't there—and so the words dissipated, evaporated, fizzled, failed to make the necessary connections to register thought and trigger response . . . had anyone been there to ask him to comment on this solitary existence—no one was—he would have said that we are ALL alone, confined by the spaces, the walls, the great wall of impressions that creates and defines our reality, separated from others by the barrage of thoughts that generates our uniquely singular aloneness . . . attempting to cross these barriers often results in confusion; what we MEAN is never what we SAY; what we SAY is never what we MEAN; what is HEARD is never what was SAID, or was MEANT to have been said, or was THOUGHT to have been MEANT to have been said; the listener hears what the listener needs to hear, the speaker says what his mouth thinks his brain thought his heart meant to say—or something like that—but no one asked; Frank spoke often, Viv generally re-mained out of range; their occasional collisions at the seedy intersection of need and desire most often oc-curred in the bedroom, stiff entanglements punctuated*

by an icy silence, not a malignant silence but rather
the uncaring, free-floating disdain that is the primary
symptom of the modern disease—they just didn't
care—about each other or the earth or Neptune or
Dan Rather or Dan Blocker's rotting corpse or the
Thighmaster or the children of Ethiopia or the children
of Somalia or the children of Beverly Hills or the Alaskan caribou or the Peruvian Milquetoast trout or the
Serbian big-horned elk or the Elks club or the blue
whales or the dolphins or the Mill Valley dog lady or
the millions of Crazy Susans with their hairy legs and
frantic big-band eyes and cardboard homes and smelly
blankets and broken-glass dreams or the millions of
Weird Jimis with their candy addictions and floppy
boob fixations and barbed-wire hair and oozing layers
of skin and revolving orbits of thought or the infirm or
the feral cats or the handicapped or the kneecapped
or the physically challenged or the emotionally delusioned or the delusion challenged or the delusion ori-
ented or the disenfranchised or the disconnected or
the French Connection or the Pope or the dopers or
Prozac or the people that called out around them—
"HELP ME"—the dying and diseased tenuously connected cells of the lumbering human organism and its
rotting DNA—hell, they just DIDN'T CARE—and so,
like cattle wandering in the fog, they occasionally
bumped into one another, as a meteor might acciden-
tally strike a planet; things were specifically NOT said;
it was clearly a waste of time to work the thoughts
that puddled in their brains into coherent sentences,
to sort through the ideas and images, to filter soldiers
of reason from anarchists and dream-world dada ter-
rorists, to gently put aside those surreal visions that
exist beyond language for another time, another place,
to forge chains of words, brutal melodies that might
come close to representing their wishes, dreams, nightmares, fears, concerns, and comments about this or

*any other life and the beings therein and the games*
*they play; and so, recycled thoughts that might have*
*been misinterpreted by two more examples of failed*
*mutative genetics were left to stand neglected, to exist*
*by implication only, to spin and dance and tumble*
*until they recoiled and drifted, ignored and hurt, back*
*into the dark tunnel of thought from whence they*
*emerged and ceased to exist; communication*
*WORKED, in a primitive way, stumbling and bumbling*
*along like a blind man in an alley full of rats, but the*
*system was so fundamentally flawed and operated*
*with such reckless indifference that conceptual misper-*
*ception and cerebral anarchy were the rule and the*
*smooth transfer of insight and WILL from one soul to*
*another the odd and unlikely exception—why can't*
*LOCKHEED make universes?—and so silence became*
*their primary mode of communication; they just*
*stopped trying, which proved to be a decisive improve-*
*ment over continued pointless attempts at hurdling*
*the language barrier; their occasional bouts of mini-*
*malist banter flowed smoothly, from bored, glass-eyed*
*stare to proud slouch to extended yawn to lazy*
*stretch to huge, impending—and strangely compel-*
*ling—silence; somehow, the less that was said, the*
*more that was implied . . . Frank was a lesser*
*being—THAT much they both knew—and his WILL*
*was not strong; there were times when his weakness*
*bubbled up and boiled over and he would simply start*
*off on a LIZARD STORY, hooting and babbling as if*
*anything he had to say could possibly have mattered,*
*as if talking mattered, just the words alone, flapping*
*his jaws like the bewildered ghost of Marilyn Monroe*
*that roams the planet naked with pouting lips and*
*keeps asking young men with nice haircuts if they*
*have the time and they never answer; at these mo-*
*ments Viv beheld an object of scorn and loathing, a*
*doomed gutter slug, a creature of ill-fitting flowered*

shirts, a vulgar assemblage of fetid aspirations, sick in-
spirations, anal Mister Ed fantasies, barbed-wire memories, hemorrhaged dreams and puddled relections, an
oozing open wound, a reflexive catapult of sleazy
post-Nietzschean film aphorisms; she looked at Frank,
alone, like a grain of sand on a beach, and longed to
pull out his tongue . . . Viv saved language for the
GAME, for the playing field that is the interaction between sorcerers and the mundane; she saved words
for encounters with small minds in public places; she
loved to get violently, distastefully, publicly drunk, and
did so with pride and vigor, fucking with the unwritten
laws and codes of behaviors that kept the world from
falling apart—kept people's minds from rattling—as
she would rattle the ice in her ever-present tumbler of
Johnnie Walker Black while standing, snakelike, wobbling, perched in line at the Super-Safeway, lodged behind old women with huge bags and small lives,
women that hid behind their bags, women with baggy
eyes and small thoughts, women with bloated cheese-
puff families—all of them, pinned—the ice clanking
about rhythmically, her words slurred, her breaths
short and deep, her head bloated, purplish, quivering
slightly; she cornered these poor women, lectured
them, bagged them, inserted herself into their lives,
pushed and shoved them into corners of polite conversations about their respective spouses and when Viv
began to talk about FRANK her eyes opened up like
small vortexes and the women felt a sudden gravita-
tional pull as if they and their bags were being sucked
into an invisible wormhole; and she SPOKE:
    ". . . MY husband Frank has a GOAL in life . . .
don't you think GOALS are important? . . . does
YOUR husband have a GOAL?"—and at this point the
target lady's psychic guards might calm down a bit,
relax slightly, they might even roll the drawbridge
down, hesitantly, slowly, maybe even let Viv into the

*castle, into the Program Director's office, just for a
minute or two, to tell her little story, to have a coffee,
inside the walls, where everything can be blown up,
IMPLODED, not realizing that Viv was a Trojan horse,
a Trojan Mister Ed, wheeling herself with a wave and
a howdy-do past the guardians of the soul, and the
supermarket queen in her furs would realize her mistake too late and cringe and droop and attack and
surrender simultaneously and Viv would slide into a
Trojan horse whisper and slip into the control room
and wedge the door closed behind her and ask—*
"AND what IS your husband's GOAL? . . . to ascend
the corporate ladder, perhaps? . . . to assume the of-
fice throne, AND WOULDN'T THAT BE NICE? to
become a regional vice-president, LIKE ANYONE
CARES? to sit at a mahogany desk and sign papers,
AND WHO GIVES A SHIT? to fix that leak in the
kitchen, WHILE HIS FUCKING SOUL SPILLS OUT ALL
OVER THE FLOOR? to EAT your nephew RAN-
DOLPH? to vacation at DOLLYWOOD? TO TAKE
APART YOUR BRAIN AND REBUILD IT AGAIN? TO
PAINT THE HOUSE YELLOW WITH PURPLE TRIM
AND LARGE BLUE SPOTS? TO EAT FIVE BIG MACS
WITHIN THREE MINUTES? TO PLACE A STICK OF
DYNAMITE UP YOUR ASS AND LIGHT IT WHILE
SINGING THE NATIONAL ANTHEM? "—*and the
lady would be pinned, alone, with gaping mouth and
wide eyes*—"well, MY husband's goal is to take his
WORLD, his fetid PERCEPTIONS, his contagious DIS-
EASE, and inflict them upon YOU . . . HE IS GOING
TO IMPALE YOUR WORLD and HE'S RIGHT OVER
THERE!"—*and at this moment she would point to
Frank, over by the deli, fingering a salami and eyeing
the old lady lecherously, the lady fumbling with her
packages, the guards fumbling with the gates, and the
lady would look over, horrified, and at that moment
Viv would reach down with her eyes right through the*

*layers of defense and denial, right through the endless*
*television-reality scenerios, right through the psychic*
*gift-wrapping, right into the open bleeding wounds of*
*existence, right through all the layers of CRAP and*
*right down to the core of that old lady, and she would*
*say—". . . YOUR WORLD, MY WORLD, ONE*
*WORLD . . . HIS WORLD . . ."—and smile, locking*
*eyes with her prey, stern and stone-faced, just for a*
*moment, before rolling her eyes skyward and cluck-*
*ing—". . . IT'S FRANK'S WORLD, BABY . . . WE JUST*
*LIVE HERE"—a line lifted from the great drunken*
*one, the mighty Dean Martin—it implied so much*
*with so little—a weapon of tragic implication—tossed*
*off casually like a hand grenade at women over-*
*whelmed by bags, women fumbling for the keys to*
*their Cadillacs, women with tense shoulders waiting*
*for buses, women pinned in line at the Super-Safeway,*
*pinned in a line that never ends in a store that never*
*closes in a world that requires them to stuff their*
*fleshy loved ones with corporate food substitutes and*
*processed colored imitation gelatins of cardboardlike*
*nutritional value—society directs these women to feed*
*and nurture the chemical addictions of their men and*
*develop those of their floundering offspring, clogging*
*their colons and minds with greasy lumps of potato*
*chip matter and blobs of rubbery Twinkie matter*
*stuffed with imitation sperm, and thus the door is*
*opened even WIDER, wedged open and held open by*
*bags of processed sugar, and television creeps in: and*
*once open, the door WILL NOT CLOSE—and then*
*she would break off her grip and let the victim crum-*
*ble like a cookie; bags would fly, victims would lose*
*their balance and stagger in place, but by that time*
*Viv was gone, just a stained memory . . .*

*The happy couple had one child, if such a mon-*
*ster could be called a child; the little creature was af-*
*fectionately tagged—literally, tagged—they stapled an*

embossed sheet-metal tag to the child's ear: Ooze McSlug—and the toddling creature spent many a day staring blankly at Frank and Viv with innocent loathing; Ooze was born with his eyes wide open, as if expecting to be handed the keys to a hotel room and fifty bucks for the hooker; quiet as a cat burglar, he stared at life, as if he were casing it; his parents rarely knew WHAT the little bundle was thinking and they considered taking a pillow and stuffing it over his little uberface; the little lump just sat there, existing, staring out as if from a coma, studying life, drooling, radiating that liquid ebony thing, looming eerily like the baby-thing from *Eraserhead;* Frank and Viv looked on, she in admiration, he in fear; Ooze drooled uncontrollably . . . without a grasp of language, that cord of loneliness stretching from one to another, Ooze expressed his needs in a primal manner; when he wanted something, he would stretch his neck like a toppling crane and vomit wildly, the colors splattering against the wall, flames of tomato leaping into the air briefly before curving down again and staining the rug; Ooze would smile and Viv would glance at Frank, perhaps sharing memories of Ooze's first tiny puddle of vomit or his first thundering bowel movement— children are born with the ability to express their desires in a manner that provides for the possibility that the needs will actually be met, until the ability is slapped and disciplined out of their systems, until the pain inflicted becomes greater than the need itself; infants are free to barf, shit, cry, to express themselves with a vividness, an enthusiasm, that would be unacceptable if practiced by an adult—and although they knew Ooze wanted SOMETHING, they didn't know WHAT: vomiting was an EFFECTIVE means of communication, but without an established vocabulary they could only guess at his generalized demands; and so they flipped on the TV—assuming he wanted what all

164

babies want—love and companionship—and the global nanny lurched to life—what more could a child want?—and Ooze beamed and soon all three members of this family, all three of them alone, found themselves happily sucked into a surreal world created by a crew of demented biologists who had managed to wrangle a grant from the MacArthur Foundation and sculpt a virulent documentary for PBS, a stoned look at the world of ants: a butterfly had fallen and could not get up and a lustful collective social organism of thousands of ants, scurrying in a mad waltz, had surrounded it and were now hauling the reluctant visitor back to their ant hole for further inspection; it was not stated HOW the ants would manage to stuff this large butterfly into their small hole, unless, of course, they CUT it up into small, tidy pieces; Ooze eyed Viv and launched a lunging liquid mental ebony thought-burst of concentrated lust and perversion; Viv, her fleshy, wet lips slightly parted, was otherwise occupied, engrossed in the world of virtual, supra-real ants; she remained out of range, her eyes darting and twitching; Ooze could see the reflections of little ants and a fallen butterfly mirrored in her wide black pupils . . .

Of course, they didn't LOVE the child: he was the product of their seedy desires, nothing more; there was nothing loving about the union that had conceived the flabby vehicle that was now operated with reckless indifference by young Ooze: Frank had been trying to extend his gene-pool influence by squirting his DNA into the wide, happy port of Viv LaFrance, who was using her sexuality as a weapon to gain power and control over Frank, men, life, and reality; their union succeeded: Frank squirted, Viv gained power and control, and the unfortunate by-product lurked about the living room, leering at its mother and vomiting . . . NO, they didn't LOVE the child; this world

*really has less to do with LOVE than with BLOOD—
there is no better evidence for the existence of a spiritual world ELSEWHERE than the mere fact of its obvious NON-existence HERE—the IDEA of a higher
world exists here, but the REALITY doesn't—the idea
has LEAKED through from somewhere else, a place
that only certain people can glimpse, for a moment
here or there, a place that they cannot really remember—in this world, LOVE IS NOT ENOUGH: lovers
dream, lovers lose, lovers fail, lovers bleed, lovers are
martyred, lovers are cursed, lovers are doomed; the
winners of this primitive game see the futility of the
quest for love, and, sadly, abandon altruism and prin-
ciples and kindness and sharing and wonder and joy,
abandon all the noble, higher qualities and instead
concentrate on the pure and simple hoarding of material things, the stockpiling of physical comforts, the
endless seeking of sensual pleasures . . . Romeo and
Juliet were happy, to be sure, in THEIR world—the
higher realm of poetic myth—but in twentieth-century
Manhattan, for example, they would not have cut it: it
would have CUT THEM; their LOVE was just too fragile for this world; one can imagine the two blissful love
birds nestled between garbage cans in a bowery alley,
dressed in layers of lice-infested clothing, freezing to
death, sharing bites of green cheese and sips of rancid
Thunderbird; the only way they would have been
happy HERE is if Romeo quit looking deep into Juliet's
eyes and comparing them to various constellations
and instead starting looking in the WANT ADS for a
JOB, started hoarding THINGS like WALLETS and
CREDIT CARDS and clothes and a beat-up old station
wagon and a cheap apartment and a second job and
a nicer apartment and nicer clothes and a nicer car
and a nicer apartment and nicer clothes and a nicer
car and a nicer apartment and nicer clothes and a
nicer car until suddenly one day Romeo comes up for*

*air and finds himself curled up in a nice fetal ball in a
three-bedroom house on Long Island with a washer-
dryer, two Kostabi prints, a sixty-inch projection television, a Jeep Wagoneer, a cellular phone, a closet full
of suits, every kitchen appliance known to the modern
world, two kids with a thousand pounds of toys, two
dogs who live the life that HE should be—eating,
sleeping, and fucking—a pocket full of maxed-out
credit cards, an ulcer, a nervous twitch under his left
eye, a lonely wife who eats a lot of sweets and col-
lects ceramic cats, an empty feeling in the pit of his
chest where his heart used to be—Romeo and Juliet
would be HAPPY, yes, in a modern world sort of
way—fulfilled, stuffed, distracted—but there would
not be LOVE—the prancing clothes-horse women of
the modern world know this instinctively, and while
they PRETEND to be searching for love, their quest is
really for something less etheric and more earthy: they
are looking for a new and improved NEST: their quest
is for protection, safety, power, control, power door
locks, leather upholstery, sushi-bar memories, designer
gowns, leather skirts, hundred-dollar haircuts, psychotherapy, big houses, maids, fitness club memberships,
flowers, champagne, limousines, theater tickets, cocktail parties, precious gems, manicures, pedigrees . . .
they are not looking for LOVE, they are looking for
the kind of FREEDOM only a purse full of credit cards
can provide; LOVE can wait . . . of course, there are
exceptions to these laws of the lower realms: there
ARE people who are able to find true love AND af-
fordable housing; but there was no love in this house,
in this family, in THIS world; Viv didn't LOVE Frank—
she was amused by Frank, entertained by Frank, she
tolerated Frank; she loved Frank the way a cat loves a
mouse—and Frank didn't love Viv: he was an amal-
gam of hate, a composite of foul thoughts; for him to
LOVE would have required an evolutionary burst of*

**167**

*which he was incapable; Frank feared Viv; Frank
fucked Viv; Frank learned from Viv; Frank looked at
Viv's breasts and drooled; Frank NEEDED Viv . . .
young Ooze, their little bundle of hopeless nightmares,
the product of this loveless communion, this two-
vehicle crash at the intersection of need and desire,
was nothing more than the unholy alliance of their
mind-worlds: little Ooze didn't LOVE his parents and
his parents didn't LOVE him; and so he was forced to
search elsewhere for the spiritual nutrients that even
the most wretched of soul-blobs needs to survive—
even evil needs to EAT—and Ooze learned that to
find this sustenance he needed to avoid those confused bundles of emotion, miscommunication, dysfunction, perversion, selfishness, greed, self-pity and anger,
those HUMANS, and look instead to the machines
that surrounded him for enlightened companionship . . . and so Ooze slowly developed bonds with
various household appliances; first the toaster: Ooze
loved to watch the little radioactive coils heat up to a
radiant orange like little nuclear fireballs; he loved to
stick slices of assembly-line compressed-air bread into
the toaster and wedge the spring mechanism closed,
in effect trapping the toast inside the toaster and
dooming it to a horrible destiny of repeated grillings
until the poor tasteless slices of puffed cardboard—
like the victims at Hiroshima—became charcoal
charred beyond all recognition and mutated chemically
into something else, something harder, until they
crumbled into small black rocks which Ooze found de-
lectable and fell to the bottom of the death-machine
toaster . . . then the blender, which would become
one of Ooze's favorite companions over the years: he
began by flinging small quantities of food into the
blender and pushing the button and watching with in-
fantile delight as portions of orange and bits of
Twinkie and chunks of cheese bounded about, fighting*

gravity as they fell repeatedly against the whirring
blades and bounced away, until after ten or twenty
encounters with the blades of death they became
"blended," cut into such small and impersonal pieces
that they lost all sense of personality and function, all
identity, and Ooze advanced from food to small items
from around the house—socks, napkins, pieces of
wood, knobs, jewels—which he would hurl into the
bowels of whirring appliance hell and watch with
bright-eyed glee as his new blender-friend entertained
him—without lecturing him or pinning him in an emo-
tional death-lock as humans so often did to each
other in the name of "friendship"—or even worse,
"love"—and then he discovered the genuine bliss of
hurling his father's small tools into the blender, match-
ing metal versus metal, machine versus machine, technology versus technology, watching epic battles unfold
between the hardened steel blades of the blender and
the tempered steel tools, the hardy flat-head screw-
drivers and the tough needle-nose pliers and the virile
vise grips, each guaranteed for life by Sears, bounding
up against the blades, also guaranteed for life by
Sears, in a groaning, sparking battle to the death; the
blades whirred and sparked and the tools floundered
and chipped until, finally, spent, Ooze would tire of
the match—it might take years for such a battle to
be fought—and would separate the battered combat-
ants until the next round, the next Clash of the Appliances; and then, one momentous day, he discovered
the ultimate blender adventure when he cornered
Boots, the wide-eyed kitten from down the street—
Ooze cooed and whispered and petted and whistled
and scratched and rubbed and ooohed and ahhhed
until little kitty, nice kitty, overcame her instinctive suspicion and advanced within range of Ooze's small,
muscular hands, rubbing against Ooze's fat baby legs
and purring—and Ooze grabbed kitty and picked it

**169**

*up, and the purring ceased and the eyes grew wider
and Ooze carried it into the kitchen and carefully inserted it into the happily whirring blender, tail-first,
and the blender began grating with the sound of hardened metal against softened calcium, and little kitty
let out a scream like Jeffrey Dahmer's landlord and
leapt out of Ooze's arms but was stopped dead in the
air, suspended, clawing the air, suddenly realizing that
the immense shards of pain that were cascading
through its nervous system were originating from what
HAD BEEN its tail, and blood and fur began flying out
of the blender as the tail was caught in the flying
metal blades, causing leaping kitty to tread air for a
half a second before falling awkwardly, and then the
tail, minus three inches of shredded, pureed fleshy
furry pulp, came loose from the grinding blades and
the cat limped away at a speed that approached the
sound barrier and Ooze heard its little voice trail
away, declining in pitch as it accelerated away from
its blended tail, and Ooze smiled broadly: he grew to
LOVE that blender . . . Ooze also grew quite fond of
the dryer, that thing with the gaping mouth that
would chew and never swallow its food, spinning its
prey around and around at high heat: Ooze experi-
mented with different substances, such as meatloaf
and glassware and golf balls and bottles of catsup,
and, eventually of course, cats, and specifically, Boots,
who would never again come willingly near Ooze—or
any other human—but was corralled one morning by
a lunging Ooze while trying to gingerly bathe its
stubby half tail, licking attentively with long, practiced
strokes when suddenly it felt those unforgettable fat
hands lock around its waist and Boots was suddenly
whisked away, screaming, imagining the sadistic tor-
tures that awaited it, and Boots glanced skyward,
praying for death, and Ooze scrambled into the basement drooling in anticipation and hurled Boots into*

*the open dryer, already stinking and stained brown
from an earlier experiment with a freshly soiled dia-
per, and Ooze slammed the door closed, set the heat
for high and watched little kitty, befuddled and terrorized, begin to slowly move around in a circular pattern, retaining its balance for a few seconds before
becoming completely inverted as the dryer's accelerating momentum tossed the wide-eyed cat about like a
tennis shoe, and Boots banged loudly against the side
walls and screamed as the walls grew hotter and hotter, and Ooze watched gleefully for a few minutes
before wandering off to find something else to do, and
Boots was tossed around for another forty-five minutes before the dry cycle expired and the exhausted,
emotionally crippled and thoroughly traumatized cat
just sat there in a daze, mewing softly to itself, until
the next morning when Viv opened the dryer and the
kitten calmly picked itself up and slowly—moving like
a tired old man, moving like a car with four flat
tires—climbed out of the dryer and more or less
dropped to the ground, picking itself up with a groan
and slowly wobbling away, broken in spirit if not
body . . . but Ooze's closest friend among household
appliances was by far, as might have been predicted,
the mighty television—KING BOX—the great and
powerful box that flashed those little toasted slices of
reality and cut back and forth from the past to the
future instantaneously, the box that shaped a man's
thoughts and knew his desires, the box that was GOD
in the modern world, a new God, created by man and
built by Sony, the offspring of God's offspring, the son
of the son of God, God's grandson, a large multi-
screened juvenile delinquent God that surpassed the
powers of man and soon took over the world, quietly,
bending man's thoughts and hence his world with its
global message of violence and cultural submission,
and Ooze would just sit and stare at the box, as his*

*father had before him, and the box was bigger than Ooze, bigger than life, more real than reality, and his eyes would get wide and his brain would become quiet and doze off, oscillating at precisely sixty hertz, his eyes remaining open as his mind slept, and in would creep the particle beam armies of the electric gods, moving past barriers of thought and discipline and morality and directly into the great sea of primordial thought, where images are catalogued in huge libraries of memory and recall, where colors and shapes swim in oceans of possibility, where reality moves past maybe into tomorrow, where logic drowns and the mind learns to steer through time, where fact and fiction exist side by side, where men are beheaded by the rotating teeth of great white sharks and crushed by giant alien grasshoppers and rubbed out by giant cartoon pencils, where illusion and reality slip in the side door of a child's mind and the lines become blurred and both become REAL, as real as a cheese sandwich, and the poor child's mind is not prepared to accept the passing collage of images it "sees" on television as being LESS than real, and the mind walks the streets of life strangely confused, trying to convince itself that men CANNOT be killed by giant pencils and alien grasshoppers but keeping an eye out anyway, JUST IN CASE, and WHO'S TO SAY that there AREN'T giant pencils out there killing people, and if there are, SO WHAT? and so children suck up what they see—what they are TAUGHT—and, it becomes REAL, if not through their experiences then through their thoughts, which define what IS real, and if enough people choose to believe then before you know it there may very well BE gangs of rampaging giant pencils hanging out in bars, shooting pool with the sharpened tips of their heads, sucking up beer with their erasers, rubbing out old ladies for kicks . . . WHO'S TO SAY? . . . and so it was that the little parts of Ooze's brain, the little molecules and synapses that lined up and danced to form his uniquely personal "reality," were fed their information, not through observation and the meticulous cataloging of nature and animals and plants and etheric beings and ascended masters and clairvoyants and blue-collar workers and clergy and orgies and friendship and love, but rather through the continuous sucking of the un-limited possibilities presented and realized through tel-evision, the world beyond the world where time and linear space dance like ants in a hurricane, where ev-erything happens in every direction, where the future is impressed upon the present like a rubber stamp on a side of beef, and so it was that Ooze's World was defined by television, his reality thoughtfully preprov-ided by the invisible legions inside the box, the com-posite being, the unseen collective of soulless studio programming hacks in tailored suits, the producers— the CREATORS—men and women making irrational decisions based on false figures and imagined semi-realities conveniently provided and thoroughly doctored by the multinational corporate flesh-eating living profit-beings, and these little tiny THEMS—these individual cells within the larger THEY—"decide" what WE want to see and give it to us and are rewarded with large sums of useless currency, power—power lunches, really—and they beam and puff out their cell membranes, thinking they are really special, when, in fact, they are less than special, less than human, well-dressed single-cell petrie-dish fashion-plates, really, but A.V.—After Video—reality was no longer pumped out exclusively by the defense-contractor boys at General Electric (NBC) or the National Security crowd at Capi-tal Cities (ABC), but rather thousands of potential realities were provided by individual defense contrac-tors wielding silent weapons stacked in rows in video stores spanning the wide, fat land, as far as the eye could imagine itself seeing, from Montauk to Tehran and back again freeing the consumer, intelligent or otherwise, to stroll the mighty aisles and select his own mind-candy, his own reality loops, his own programming, his OWN poison: with the advent of the home video player a substantial portion of the social brainwashing responsibility passed from the unseen guiding hand of the corporate state to the limp wrist of the individual—the cloned individual cell of the larger corporate organism—in the case of children, to their shaped and molded parents, the collective fat ass, free to make decisions but unable to, instead looking for guidance and direction from their automated friends, the "critics" from the New York Times and Good Morning, America and Wake Up, Cleveland, who supplement their self-defining world views—implanted through continuous sucking from the foreheads of network mind-control hacks like Rather and Jennings—with radiant reviews and thumbs-up summaries of carefully scripted video "hits" laced with sex and violence that reinforce the implanted worldview virus and encourage paranoia and incite the herd to rustle about angrily and look with suspicion and wariness upon their neighbors and suppress their own original thoughts and do exactly what they are told to do, nothing more, nothing less, and vote heartily for whomever they are instructed to vote for—the "front runner"—and exhibit disdain for anyone who fails to exhibit excitement at the abstract prospect of living their lives vicariously through the happy adventures of Tom Cruise and Heather Locklear and Bruce Willis and Demi Moore . . . but there are others, a small group, who realize the power of the mighty VCR, who understand the perils and responsibilities of mass self-reality-molding, free-thinking free people who choose their videos accordingly and stuff their brains with ballet and modern art and criti-*

*cal thought and conflicting points of view and progres-
sive thought and intelligent debate and spirituality and
health and fitness and independent film and alternative history and peace and beauty and color and song
and music and they evolve at an accelerated pace, flying past their neighbors in the happy herd who are
still spilling beer nuts on their bellies and adjusting
their daily schedules around Roseanne and Coach—
the VCR generation mutants didn't need "schedules";
time for them has become a more flexible thing: they
can tape a "one hour" show today and watch it in
"forty-five minutes" tomorrow, fast-forwarding through
commercials and effectively accelerating TIME by
twenty-five percent . . . Frank and Viv were well
aware of their power as programmers, as lower-case
gods, and so it was with great fanfare and pride that
they went down to the Video-Rama and purchased
with a stolen credit card a selected library of twenty
or so of the most twisted films available, a small library that would provide the reality matrix for the
evolving mind and expanding world of young Ooze
McSlug: their intention was to saturate the blank
pages of their child's mind with their own hand-
crafted particularly extreme worldview, knowing that
this worldview would in turn become a WORLD as
their child fleshed out and defined reality through his
actions, thoughts and intentions, through the psychic
rocks that he would throw that would ripple out into
the sea of flesh around him: Ooze's twisted library
was made up of demented classics like Eraserhead,
Repo Man, Taxi Driver, The Tenant, No Way to
Treat a Lady, Lucifer Rising, Last Tango In Paris,
Apocalypse Now, A Clockwork Orange, Repulsion,
Dr. Strangelove, They Live, Videodrome and Blue
Velvet, along with a selected episodes of The Prisoner, War of the Worlds, Outer Limits, Friday the
13th, Mister Ed, and Twin Peaks, television mo-*

*ments that had fallen through the social programming cracks, that, when viewed collectively, presented a vastly different picture of reality than those in power undoubtedly intended to project . . . Ooze was of course given the freedom to choose his programming freely—as we all are—it is a Free Will universe, after all—and he eagerly gobbled up the mind-candy that his parents laid out for him; he never tired of the sick Polanski plot twists and the Kubrick black humor and the Cronenberg exploding heads and the Coppola rotten-world stench and the Scorsese ant-farm insanity and the pervasive evil and the surreal magic and the crushed beauty and the overwhelming pain and the toxic puddles of sadness and the creeping tide of madness and the tragedy and the wasted lives and the twisted sex and the greed and the sick humor and the depraved stupidity and the grand pointlessness of it all and it all became, collectively, his world, the matrix of his mind, the genesis of his thoughts, the springboard of his actions, the puddle of his leaks, his path, his destiny, his future, his WILL—he loved all the films in his reality library, really—but there was one film that he would select repeatedly, even before he could understand what was going on, even before he could talk . . . in fact, his first words, "God I hate Rock and Roll," were the last words of his favorite film, Christine, a film about a twisted car, more than a car really, a wrathful deity, a mechanical goddess, a finned angel from the bowels of hell, a '58 Plymouth femme fatale that embodied within her classic curves and soft interior the qualities of everything foul and depraved; as one of Christine's owners mused, "the smell of a brand new car is just about the finest smell there is . . . except for pussy," and that smell just OOZED out of Christine, the sweet arrogance of elegance, the decadent majesty of scale, the teasing gurgle of eight rhythmically pumping cylinders, the lurid*

*bump and grind of 327 horses . . . she was one of
those big, bloated gas whales of the fifties and sixties,
the GODS and GODDESSES of capitalist mythology, a
sadistic Aphrodite oozing KILLER sexuality from her
first day on the assembly line when she crushed a
mechanic's hands and squished a supervisor on
through her tormented youth when she asphyxiated
several of her owners and well into vibrant maturity,
when she killed and maimed for the LOVE of her
dweebish teenaged owner who became some sort of
psycho-love-stud when he slipped his hands around
the throbbing wheel of the Red Bitch and RUBBED
and Ooze especially loved the scene when Christine
got beat up by some thugs with crowbars and she
went out the next night, pissed off and pumped up,
and squished one guy against a wall, popped him like
a fleshy pimple, and then tracked down the tough-ass
black leather dude at a gas station and blew his car
up and then lit herself on fire and chased him down
the highway drenched in flames and plowed over him
with a satisfied thump and went on killing in the
name of burning love until the day the music died on
Christine's radio, but it was okay because she'll be
back, we all know that's the way life works anyway,
there's ALWAYS a sequel . . . some kids liked The
Wizard of Oz, but Ooze loved Christine . . .*

    *Frank, being a "good" father—a BAD man can
be a GOOD father: he will produce superior BAD offspring—which is NOT good—did his best to funnel
into his child an endless flow of verbiage, a funnel of
information occupying space and time, and Ooze
would dutifully listen to his old man's boring ghost stories and feeble stream of consciousness raps and limp
mindfucking routines and spontaneous splatter stories,
like the Lovecraftian babble-epic that emerged one
day as little Ooze stretched the length of Frank's bony
lap and stared up at his own reflection, large at the*

top of his head like a big-headed gray but small and distorted at the mouth and chin . . . his father's black-hole face was dominated by a wide mouth bent at the sides and hopelessly puckered in the center, like a swollen frown, like a smiling wormhole, like a misplaced, trusting smirk that had suddenly met a hockey puck and the puck had wedged itself silently, carefully, into the fabric of his being until it and the lip had become one inseparable, despicable weapon of smirking chaos . . . Frank sensed this bonding of sorts, and was moved to spin a tale, erupting, as his father before him had and as Ooze would one day too, dripping and pausing and sputtering—it was all that was left of the grand tradition of LIZARD STORIES, the pathetic echo of a once-great legacy—". . . AND A SPARK OF LIGHT FLICKERED UPON THE UNSANCTIFIED CONVOCATIONS AND AN UNWHOLESOME WORSHIP REELED FROM SOME FORGOTTEN NETHER ABYSS, THE DETESTABLE, WINDY STENCH GROWING LOATHSOME AND FIENDISH . . ."—Frank chortled, his eyes bugging; Ooze looked on with feigned amusement; Frank cleared his throat with a Spartan croak, nearly vomiting as a lump of molten food-matter poised near the crest of his tongue, and continued—". . . I ENCOUNTERED TITAN COLUMNS . . . I COULD FEEL THE HOT BREATH OF THE CAVERN WINDS . . . THE RAPT AND SEPULCHRAL ADORATIONS OF THOSE NAMELESS THINGS . . . AND THE TRAMPING AND THE DISSONANT RHYTHM GREW SICKENINGLY LOUD . . . HEAVEN SAVE ME FROM THOSE FEET AND PAWS AND HOOVES AND PADS AND TALONS AND—"

"URRRGGGHHHH!" Ooze interrupted, splattering—and along with the HOWDY-DO went a message: "GET OFF, YOU OLD SOD! . . . FUCK, THAT

*WAS BORING! . . . INCREDIBLY BORING! . . . MAS-*
*SIVELY BAD! . . . INCREDIBLY BAD, YOU OLD*
*SHIT! . . . YOU'VE LOST IT, YOU SICK OLD DOG,*
*YOU BAG OF PISS!"; and the thought-message drifted*
*out in waves through the ether where it bumped into*
*Frank's astral receptors and lodged itself into Frank's*
*existence, where it would make itself apparent at a*
*time of its own choosing; Frank, momentarily silenced,*
*paused to ponder the dripping food-matter coloring*
*his Hawaiian print shirt, the miniature volcanos and*
*glacial spittle, and continued—*

    *". . . UHH . . . GOBLIN SPACE! . . . HEADS OF*
*CROCODILES! . . . ERR . . . LEERINGLY BLOOD-*
*CONGEALING! . . . UNSPEAKABLE! . . ."*

    *Ooze looked at Frank through slanted eyes,*
*knowing, even as an infant, an old soul adjusting to a*
*new mind in a different dimension, that he had just*
*mindfucked his own father, an interesting turn of*
*events, really, a pivotal event, and it happens all the*
*time, your street and mine, and nothing is ever again*
*as it would have been—and just like that little Ooze*
*assumed the upper hand in the world that existed*
*within the momentary framework of the mutual coop-*
*eration of their senses, the world that existed between*
*the two of them, stretching from one to the other and*
*nowhere else, and yet comprising all things, and be-*
*tween them they had decided that at this moment,*
*then and there, here and now, always and never*
*again, that light was dark and Ooze had punched out*
*his Pop, and that was it, the proud beginning for*
*young Ooze and the sad end for flailing Frank, the*
*beginning of the end, which is really the end—you just*
*play the rest out backwards—and it happens quite*
*often—just like that: offed by the offspring—the de-*
*ranged student teaches the idiot teacher—the strap-*
*ping son beats up the liver-spotting dad—the*

*perky-breasted girl out-flirts the sagging mom—the deranged mutant super-creep monster-child psycho-truncates the vulnerable, creaking synapses of the mom and dad, themselves deformed like overused, damaged factory machine parts—it happens all the time . . .*

# 9.

in the presence
of the true master
✕

*All things great, small and indifferent grow old; all*
*things decay; everything rots: cultures, species, in-*
*dividuals, constitutions, ideals, Hostess Ding Dongs,*
*extendo-lamps, planets, giant condoms, nuclear waste,*
*friendships; ALL things decay . . . even FRANK*
*decayed: like everyone else on this doomed twirling*
*slut of a planet, his DNA was spiraling down, his*
*genes were rotting, his brain was growing fatty with*
*facts and information and his soul was shriveling . . .*
    *RETIREMENT was what happened to humans*
*when they were deemed useless and put out to pas-*
*ture in suburban tract homes and told to shuffle*
*about in golf carts and motor homes until they died; it*
*was not something Frank was especially looking for-*
*ward to, even though, really, he was BORN retired—*
*he knew, unlike most people, that RETIRING was*
*what people should be doing every day of their lives,*
*the pursuit of pleasure and sloth their life's work and*
*lone ambition; Frank knew that people shouldn't wait*
*until they were sixty-five and wheezing worn-out parts*
*in the lumbering Dream to spend their days doing*
*what THEY want to do—knitting, playing golf, mastur-*

*bating, knocking over 7-11s—doing what THEY want when THEY want, as they should have from their first heaving breath until their last sad gasp—but they DON'T, of course: they repeat the same mindless thankless chores for decades until finally they are pushed out the door with a pat on the ass and a gold pen and pencil set, nineteen ninety-five on the home shopping network, and a cake-and-punch get-lost who-gives-a-shit buzz-off farewell party, and they're OFF: that's it, ride's over, SEE YA, get lost, take a hike, here's four hundred bucks a month get OUTTA here; and the workers of America, the lumber of the lumbering dream, limp away like broken toys, staggering back to their clean and tidy suburban homes, suddenly unsure of themselves and their place in the grand scheme of things, stripped of their identities, wandering the streets, assembly line ghosts, and they just keel over one day and DIE, leaving a great deal of baggage behind which they will have to return to reclaim . . . they hang out at the seniors center, playing bingo and shuffleboard; they play unenthusiastic, plodding golf, feeling the skin burn as balls dribble into the fairway, limping like lost mice; they think back to the other cogs and their cog families and their cog mortgages and their cog tribulations; they think back to the old plant, to the lunchroom, to the stale sandwiches and the rancid tuna salad and the malfunctioning coffee machine and the broken-down view of the industrial park through the dirty, smog-stained windows and the old plastic safety glasses and those old worn-out safety gloves—hope they didn't throw those out!—they did, Mister Cog: they almost hit you in the ass on your way out the door—and that bolt that always came loose down on assembly line 3-A—hope they can fix that!—they CAN, rest assured of THAT much, Mister Cog—and the cog farewell cards come for about six months, an appropriate period of cog* mourning, and then they dry up, as if Mr. Cog had suddenly ceased to exist, which, of course, HE HAD; he was a piece of junk, a cog without a wheel, a worthless, useless, worn-out part lying in a pile of rubbish somewhere, anywhere, taking up someone else's time and space—NO, Frank knew that most people didn't have the COURAGE to be BORN retired and stay that way; most people were more than happy to be molded into parts for a large machine; most people were happy to be gun fodder and shark bait . . .

Frank knew that psychic thugs never REALLY retire, in the sense that they never stop "working;" a psychic thug can poison lives from a deathbed, impale hearts from a wheelchair, suck souls from an iron lung, and although psychic thugs never REALLY retire there comes a time when they step aside and younger thugs with brighter eyes and rapidly firing synapses step forward and take over their accounts; Frank had been a model thug, certainly—he had soiled thousands of souls directly, and as the ripples extended outward from each victim literally billions had felt their lives burned in some way by Frank and his thought-missiles—and although there would be no official retirement ceremony, no gold watch, no celebrity roast—can you imagine what THAT would have been like?—MANSON opening the festivities with a video-taped testimonial from his prison cell in Vacaville, shifting his eyes like a vulture, intensifying his focus, his pupils getting larger, wilder, stranger, like starved jungle cats emerging slowly from the shadows, the little twitching swastika tattoo on his forehead, where his pineal gland had once been but where now resided some other, different gland, about which not much is known, perhaps the soul-vat, shifting a little to the left and throbbing slightly; Manson surveys the foul crowd, a king among vermin, and takes a long, sadistic drag off his cigarette; he blows oversized

swastika-shaped rings absentmindedly into the air;
perhaps one or two of the FAMILY—now well into
their seventies: Manson himself is a frail but powerful
eighty-four—lunge forward out of the audience like
nursing-home zombies, drooling as they shuffle forward, some with walkers, some in orthopedic shoes,
some in wheelchairs, some in state-of-the-art Lockheed
synthetic latex artificial bodies with Krylon-two organs
and Kevlar-28 muscle tissue and twenty-year warran-
ties, eternally symmetrical vehicles for those old and
rotten souls who prefer to hide behind perfect teeth
and bulging pectorals, the CARS of the future, fleshy
high-performance vehicles for the old and wealthy, the
Dodge TERMINATOR and the Ford STALLION and
the Mercury STUD and the Acura BILLINGSLEY—and
perhaps Squeaky or Lulu or Sadie or Tex or one of
the millions of others might lurch forward, puppets on
the invisible wires that extend from Manson's fertile
imagination; he begins the roast with a joke, standard
procedure in these Viva Las Vegas testimonial things;
surveying the crowd, half-smiling with that oddly
charming Manson grin, looking like a thuggish post-
firestorm Johnny Carson, he grins wildly and begins
speaking:
    "OKAY, MISTER MAN . . . you're RIGHT, you're
absolutely RIGHT, you're ALL right, I mean, YOU'RE
RIGHT, I AGREE, everything's motherfuckin' PERFECT,
I ACCEPT everything you say, DIG, man? . . . can I
GO now? . . ."—he flashes that wolf-sheep grin and
the audience, a single lunging organism swaying back
and forth under his magnetic pull, chuckles heartily;
droning ritualistic applause echoes eerily through the
auditorium; the nursing-home zombies shudder; Manson surveys the crowd and they cringe, draping their
souls—even a collection of twisted psychos such as
this cowers in the presence of the true master—and

184

*Charlie takes another long drag off his cigarette, work-ing the room, playing with time . . .*

" . . . WORDS . . . words KILL . . . You can't COMMUNICATE with WORDS . . . I don't BELIEVE in WORDS . . . he who THINKS is LOST . . . he who makes ANOTHER man think, WINS . . . ANYWHERE is ANYWHERE you WANT it to be . . . WE are ALL under a spell . . ."—*and the audience is riveted, lost, under a spell, and Charlie reaches up and scratches his tattoo and continues, his eyes blazing—*"YEAH, I KNOW Frank . . . he KNOWS me . . . we KNOW each other . . . I've been INSIDE him . . . he's been inside me . . . I can SING his tune . . . he can HEAR my music, dig? . . . I can FEEL him . . . HE IS ME . . . I was HIM before HE was . . . he's ME and I'm HIM and somehow we BOTH leaked into this place from SOMEWHERE ELSE, dig? . . . I know what he's going to say BEFORE he says it, because if he didn't say it I WOULD HAVE, dig? . . . YEAH, I talked to Frank once, in my MIND, you know, and I said 'HOW ARE YOU' and he said 'HOW ARE YOU' and I said 'I'M FINE' and he said 'I'M FINE' and I said 'I LIKE YOU' and he said 'I LIKE YOU' and the beauty of it was we were both PRETENDING to like each other and because of that we really DID like each other, dig?, and I said 'I DON'T LIKE YOU' and he said 'I DON'T LIKE YOU' and we smiled, like per-fect mirrors, looking back at each other and we could SEE our reflections bouncing back and forth, TRAPPED, bouncing back and forth forever between the mirrors, and I could SEE my ancestors coming in ships from the Orion belt and I could SEE his ances-tors creeping out from under the Superstition Moun-tains, kind of SCALY with wings and all, I could see EVERYTHING and the bigger my eyes got and the harder I sucked, the bigger his eyes got and the

*harder he sucked, and I informed HIM that he was
misinformed, and he informed ME that I was misinformed, and we got along very well, like I do with myself, I could relate to him because he WAS me,
dig? . . ."—and the video ends abruptly; the the audience is mesmerized, hypnotized, brainwashed, mindfucked, docile; they sit there like drugged cattle, like
burned-out teenagers sitting around the campfire at
the Spahn Movie Ranch, prisoners of the Manson
charm as Charlie weaves fractal tales about the cosmos and the apocalypse and God and Nixon and
Dean Martin . . . and then the next speaker comes
out, just sort of appears really, and the crowd lights
up when they figure out who this cat is . . . he's come
all the way from a vault in Romania, flown in on a
red-eye from the place where some people do not die,
they just eat and shit for hundreds of years, perhaps
thousands, immortally alone: from there and beyond
has come VLAD THE IMPALER, who besides being a
vampire was a man who filled the countryside with
concentric circles of impaled bodies, a virtual fence, a
man before whom even Frank knelt humbly, a god
among devils; and Vlad sort of glides up to the micro-
phone, dignified and yet horribly prune-faced, ancient
beyond time but still sexy as a motherfucker, like a
150-year-old Lee Marvin; a drop of blood leaks out of
the corner of his mouth and runs down his chin; his
voice booms and the words slide out, oiled: "GOOD
EVENING . . . it is SO very nice to be here this EVE-
NING . . . I am SO GRATEFUL to have this opportunity to SPEAK on behalf of my friend, FRANK, who is
SO very much like myself . . . we are, shall I say . . .
BLOOD brothers . . ."—Vlad pauses, impaling the audience with his eyes, and a small trickle of laughter
floats through the crowd; he takes a long quaff from
a dark crystal goblet on the podium, a thick reddish
liquid dribbling down his chin and staining his lips, and*

continues after a pause and a deep sigh—

"... EXCUSE me ... ah, where was I? ... take my wife, PLEASE! ... but seriously, folks ... we think alike, Frank and I ... we both SEE the world as NOURISHMENT ... we FEED off the world as we DRIFT through dreams and nightmares ... Frank knows that those who DO NOT understand are EATEN by those who DO ..."—Vlad hangs his head a bit; sadness fills the air; but he perks up suddenly—"... and that is why I must LEAVE you ... because words have so little MEANING ... but before I go, I would like to propose a TOAST ... to my FRIEND across DIMENSIONS, my COMRADE through TUNNELS, my BROTHER across WORLDS of time ... a BEAST among men, a SNAKE among children, a SHADOW among the LIGHTS ... to HIM, to US, to ETERNITY, to FRANK! ... DRINK VERMIN DRINK, TO FRANK! ..."—and Vlad lifts the large goblet to his lips and drains it; a circle of blood stains his lips; he cleans them with a rapid, animalistic swipe of his tongue and hisses—"YESSSSS ... very good, very good, MOST excellent, yesssss ..."—and the crowd rises in a frenzy of fervent bloodlust, shaking their fists and making a collective gurgling noise; and Vlad takes a third and last passionate quaff from the seemingly bottomless goblet and booms— "... AHHHHH ... THANK YOU! ... GOOD NIGHT!"—and then he takes a final, sweeping bow, and his cape gracefully closes around him like a blue velvet curtain except that it's red, and suddenly— POOF—he's gone, self-teleported transdimensionally, and the applause rises again like a gurgling river of blood and then slowly dies down to a murmur, leaving the air stained thickly red; Frank is sitting in the front row, blowing smoke rings, trying not to be impressed ... and then, suddenly, a third speaker moves briskly on stage, a short man, a dwarfed Olympian statue

**187**

*come to life, a mini-übermensch lifted from a white
supremacist anatomy book, a sculpted man monu-
mentally ancient and at the same time as virile as a
teenager, a man at once childlike and as old as time
and space itself, a walking sphinx, a proto-human with
the forceful personality of a psychic tank, a man-
engine—it is the goose step that gives him away: precise, ordered, frightening in its rigidity, algebraic in its
pace and cadence, arrogant in its sense of purpose
and destiny—it is, of course, HITLER himself, well
over a hundred years old but looking trim and fit in a
new body-vehicle—the BEAST 666, Mercedes &
Koch's top-of-the-line model—and the crowd is rever-
ently stunned, silently awed, still licking their wounds
from Vlad the Impaler and here comes ADOLF himself—you think these celebrity roast things can't get
any better and then they just DO—and Hitler strides
to the podium and with more than magnetism, with
GRAVITY, he slams both hands down on top of the
podium and holds them there, tense and yet relaxed,
like an angry Greek sculpture; a silent thud echoes
through the room; Hitler's small, powerful hands push
down on the podium, as if holding it captive in some
lighter-than-air universe, and he surveys the crowd,
just sucks the whole room in at once, slurps it up;
even Frank is riveted as Hitler surveys the crowd with
the calm authority of a man who truly believes that
he is a messenger of destiny, a man who walks with
the gods, under the sewers, a man who speaks with
the assumed majesty of a presumed prophet:*

*"MY PEOPLE! . . . my glorious people of the
Fourth Reich . . . my children, my sons and daughters . . . fruits of my loom! . . . HERE we are, each of
us . . . each of us must be PRESERVED! . . . we must
save ourselves at all costs if we are to remain VICTO-
RIOUS! . . . we must be GOOD! we must be EVIL! we
must be PURE! . . . we must decide upon our path,*

blessed or cursed, and embark! we must never turn back! . . . we must create a race of FRANKS to roam the earth and rule if not with an iron hand then with a silent glove! . . . FRANK IS OUR PATH! FRANK IS OUR FUTURE! ZEIG HEIL!"—and Hitler's words jerk to a halt and he stiffly throws his right arm into the air, his cheeks puffing out and his small mouth puckering; he returns his hands to the podium, with gravity, and resumes speaking:—". . . my people, my sons and daughters, my friends and children! . . . ELECTRICITY chooses only the perfect conductor to reach the earth's surface! . . . FRANK IS ELECTRICITY! THROW THE SWITCH! . . . the POWER of a man in relation to the outside world exists in inverse proportion to his own internal consolidation! . . . FRANK IS POWER! THROW THE SWITCH! . . . PARASITES always congregate where the sap flows, like tapeworms at the source! . . . Frank sucks the weakness from this world! . . . FRANK IS THE WORM IN THE APPLE! WHEN YOU RECEIVE A LOVE LETTER FROM HIM YOU'RE FUCKED FOREVER!"—and suddenly, Hitler stops talking, as if someone has thrown a switch; he pulls a pocket mirror from a small black purse he is carrying and surveys his cheeks and face; his mouth is pulled tightly at the corners, his ears are bright red, and his eyes are glazed; he removes a make-up applicator and applies a touch of rouge . . . clearly, he has spent too much time in the South American sun, disconnected, alone, unplugged, the edges of his mind dulled; no one really knows what the hell he is babbling about; suddenly, he flings his right arm stiffly in the air, clicks his black boots together, and booms— "ZEIG HEIL!"—and, his echoing words still hanging rigidly in the air, wheels and goose-steps arithmetically off stage, like a thuggish equation; the audience rises and applauds, not exactly sure why; the hesitant ovation is a sad mix of politeness and pity, like something

**189**

*that might have followed one of Reagan's rambling monologues—NO . . . sadly, none of this happened: there was to be no retirement dinner or celebrity roast for Frank, no commemorative plague, no gold watch; a psychic thug never REALLY retires . . .*

*Of course, although he would not RETIRE, Frank would still be PASTURED . . . it's a long story: after the world had NOT ended, despite dire warnings in all the tabloids—it had in fact ENDED decades earlier, on August 6, 1945, and what people didn't realize was that it didn't just END, it wasn't that SIMPLE, but it, more properly, BOUNCED: the end of the world bounced off the end of time and now we had to RE-WIND and live the whole damn thing BACK-WARDS—and so because the world didn't end the ubiquitous THEY held a meeting and decided that the HERD was getting out of hand, and so half the world's population was penciled in to be killed off by an arsenal of stubborn viruses developed at Fort Meade with taxpayer money and released through various "health" organizations; those that were "lucky" enough to survive would run the factories and get in the way of the bullets but a system of planned obso-lescence would be introduced to keep their numbers in check: cogs reaching the mandatory "retirement" age of fifty would be rounded up, functional or other-wise, herded really, and shuttled off to National Secu-rity State Nursing Camps, fifty-square-mile clusters of huge aluminum multi-story structures painted pink and decorated with oversized paintings of flamingos, lawn furniture, palm trees, sunglasses, french fries, cheeseburgers and celebrities such as Elvis, John Wayne, Ed McMahon, Dean Martin, and Amy Grant, a series of geriatric Disneylands positioned on the out-skirts of suburban neighborhoods across the country, looming like giant multicolored shopping malls; for special cases, there were "Special Vacation Camps" in*

Arizona and New Mexico and for REAL special cases there were "Remote Vacation Camps" inside the moon and on Mars . . . in short, there was no shortage of storage space for the useless scrap metal of humanity, and in these storage units the cogs lived in blissfully brainwashed splendor, like fish in a bowl, birds in a cage, cattle in a pen, pigs in a poke, cars in a garage, dogs on a chain, insects in a jar . . . it wasn't THAT different from the rest of their lives, really . . . they were told to shut up, and be happy, and that's EXACTLY what they did . . . these were the nursing homes of the future, with everyone firmly invited to attend, at gunpoint if necessary, upon the occasion of their fiftieth birthday, even Frank, who had lost interest in life anyway, ever since that foggy morning when Viv had left him, television in one hand, fifth of scotch in the other, and taken Ooze and run off with that young upstart South American dictator, and when the fateful day arrived he felt a rush of exhilaration as he stepped outside to pick up the neighbor's morning paper and looked up to see one of the pink National Security State vans rumbling down the street playing "Tiny Bubbles" through a large loudspeaker attached to the roof, and he sat out on the curb, waiting, smoking three cigarettes at once, as the van pulled up in front of his house; FUCK IT, he thought; this was an opportunity to explore new worlds, to conquer new minds, to pillage new souls, a new pond in which to splash about and create ripples that would puddle and distort and pollute and all that . . .

What Frank foolishly hadn't anticipated was that it just didn't work that way: he couldn't just waltz in and start sucking souls; THEY were aware of Frank and ready for him: they had THE CLAPPER, that idiotic consumer appliance invented sometime back in the Bush administration that turned appliances off and on from across the room with two loud, irritating

*claps—it was the perfect appliance for the wide-
bottom Reagan Revolutionaries, the fleshy-lumped
shelf-butts that bred like flies and sat there with the
chips and dip watching the box that by this time was
so full of overt brainwashing and subliminal discipline
programming that it positively OOZED, twenty-four
mind-blowing hours a day of fatty-brained nothingness,
all day every day, and there they sat, blissful idiots—it
may have been designed FOR Reagan and only leaked
to the PUBLIC later—while a discreet parallel black-
budget Super-Clapper program had also been quietly
funded and a modified version of the product developed for deep-cover MILITARY use; like all advances
in technology thought up by some well-meaning and
yet stupid engineer with a cavernous knowledge of
theoretical electrical engineering but not an ounce of
common sense, the Clapper technology had been co-
opted by the military-industrial National Security
boys—the engineer should have KNOWN this would
happen—it always DOES—but of course he
DIDN'T—and they DID—and it WAS—and he
smiled and adjusted his glasses and shrugged his
shoulders and told himself it was okay, always okay,
because he had three mouths to feed at home—the
overriding justification for capitalistic techno-genocide:
"mouths to feed"—as if these "mouths"—were they
just MOUTHS?: did they not have arms, legs, and cerebral cortexes as well?—could not feed THEM-
SELVES by wandering down to the Super-Safeway and
stuffing fruit in their pockets or just eating bananas
one after another as they wandered the lonely coiffed
aisles pretending to look for imported mustard or ab-
sorbant paper towels or jumbo deodorant sticks, pushing that cart around like good consumers, true
patriots, and then when they finish the damn bananas
they could just leave the cart right there and make a
run for the door, like they're going to KILL you for a*

BANANA?—they could do that, these mouths—but no, HE has to feed them and so he puts his channeled mega-synapses to work for the National Security State inventing products that he knows will be used as tools of power and domination, like the Clapper, invented to help people turn the television set on from bed, thereby saving them a round-trip journey of about ten feet, but which was inevitably corrupted, hooked up to pacemakers that were implanted in a generous percentage of the detainee population in Nursing Camps across America—they didn't need to implant EVERYONE, of course—just the THREAT was enough to keep most in line—and several times a day, for one reason or another, the Clapper was hauled out and demonstrated; after punching in the three-digit detainee pacemaker code an orderly could clap twice and . . . well, it wasn't pretty—extreme fibrillation, shall we say, lots of squirming and drooling . . . a slow, flapping death—and so when an orderly clapped once, well, that got everyone's attention, and even Frank twitched involuntarily, for although Frank wasn't afraid of death—death was just a rest stop on the eternal highway of earthly pain and suffering, just time enough for a cigarette and he'd be back, somewhere else, someone else—but PAIN was a different story . . .

The good cop-bad cop formula, a behavior-control classic, was liberally employed in the Camps; for each negative incentive demonstrated to the residents, i.e., fibrillation, there was also a positive inducement offered, creating the illusion of CHOICE, and the choice was simple: remain obedient and passively sheeplike or suffer massive coronary trauma; the positive inducement offered to detainees, the alternative to death-by-Clapping, was the electric carrot that had dangled in front of them in "life," that thirty-five-year stretch as worker ants that had preceeded their involuntary "retirement," the continued companionship of their old friend, mentor and god, the veritable LASSIE of home appliances, the faithful television . . . by the time Frank reached retirement age, television was everywhere: televisions the size of billboards called out from the sides of freeways; televisions with wheeled robotic legs roamed the aisles of grocery stores; televisions lectured in schools as slack-jawed students hemmed and yawned and sucked up subliminal suggestions like candy; televisions stared out at the flock from church pulpits and ranted; television had truly replaced God as the single most powerful controlling force of "reality"; TV's force-fed realities had become so prevalent, so entrenched upon the human mind, that they indeed had become more "real" than "reality" itself—and what had passed for consensus "reality" in the first place was of course nothing but a wizard's curtain—the fabric of materialism—that had been gradually layered over the true and real existence—the eternal WHATEVER—for several thousand years—and had fooled the people so completely that only a few even remembered that there was anything at all to FORGET, anything at all behind the curtain, or that there WAS a curtain, and the rest of the sheep were so pleased with their little material world—their PRESUMED reality—that those who saw beyond and beneath were expelled from the churches, banned from the publishing houses, fired from the newspapers, kicked out of the schools, barred from the professional organizations, thrown out of the TRIBE in all of its manifestations, and the illusion prevailed, prospered, and multiplied; how else could it be? . . .

Each detainee unit in every cellblock on every floor had a television: TV was the warden of this particular institution, the warden of THIS reality; TV shaped and maintained the illusion within the illusion, *feeding people the idea that things weren't as bad as they appeared to be, when in fact they were INFINITELY better; TV was the top layer in a series of contradictory realities: few had the patience to continue peeling until striking eternity . . . every unit had a TV but the TVs received only one station, The Channel, which offered the best of the worst that TV had to offer, a twenty-four-hour-a-day reality stream of sitcoms, soap operas, and game shows, a glacial sludge of endless mindless fodder that jammed and stuck in chronically clogged brains; in toto, The Channel presented a philosophy of life, a comfortable well-polished middle-class worker-drone worldview scripted by the National Security State and entrained on the public by their friends at NBC, CBS, and ABC for half a century, the serialized world of happily self-absorbed, mindlessly normal middle-class worker-drones existing in apparent contentment in hypothetical homes down somebody else's street and behind somebody else's closed doors, make-believe worlds revealed to worker drones existing in boredom and sadness in front of their glowing boxes and wishing that they too could exist in a happy-shoe world down some other street in someone else's house; in REALITY, these snow-white worlds existed only in the IMAGINATION of the show's producers, implied worlds empowered by fantasy, delivered by television and fostered by the powers that be, the protectors of the status quo, the suppressors of true knowledge—THOSE GUYS—with their control-group media-massage demagogic one-world philosophy, which was frighteningly simple: ONE world, ONE reality, NO problems . . . The Channel, of course, had been also conveniently available on the OUTSIDE, and quite popular, which made its continued existence on the INSIDE such a pleasant surprise for the newly arrived worn-out parts when they turned on the polished boxes the system had thought-*

*fully provided for them and found to their everlastingly robotic delight that their old soap opera, sitcom, and game show friends were still there, marvelous wits intact, endearing problems unresolved, complex lives still tangled, interpersonal realities hopelessly intertwined; this little world was a comforting place, full of old friends like ben cartwright and june lockhart and superman and wilma flintstone and george jetson and monty hall and goober and floyd and barney and opie and john davidson and joan rivers and oprah and phil and robin leach and mary and rhoda and lou and fred sanford and the bradys and the huxtables and will robinson and paul lynde and alice kramden and jim lange and redd foxx and wilbur and ed and lassie and flipper and uncle walt and daniel boone and dick van dyke and lucy and ricky and fred and bob newhart and mcgarrett and luke and laura and bob eubanks and chuck woolery and dick clark and john boy walton and mister rogers and carol burnett and johnny carson and ed mcmahon and marcus welby and joe friday and hoss and little joe and victoria barkley and heath and audra and donna reed and beaver and wally and ward and june and eddie and lumpy and ozzie and harriet and ricky and david and uncle charlie and charlie's angels and charlie the tuna and the lone ranger and the six million dollar man and the bionic woman and josephine the plumber and gavin macleod and blake carrington and alexis and dobie gillis and gilligan and the skipper and that girl and charles nelson reilly and allen ludden and betty white and big bird and maude and sam malone and sam mccloud and pat robertson and kermit and barney and willard scott and rin tin tin and david brinkley and perry mason and the millionaire and mr. t and fred macmurray and marshall dillon and chester and tom selleck and florence henderson; all their old friends, still there . . . and life—the vicarious sucking* of other, illusory, lives—became once again worth "living," or pretty much the same as it was before, really, but that was, somehow, enough, as The Channel rolled on and the world—a world of soapsellers and brainwashers—turned, restlessly . . .

The only thing better than living vicariously through television was having sex virtually, and, although detainees were not permitted to actually screw EACH OTHER, they were encouraged to interact sexually with their televisions, to "cyberfuck"; cybersex, an endomorphic reality enhancement activity developed by the military in the eighties, completely eliminated the last frontier of constructive human interaction: sex; the military devised a way to keep even SEX under their control, to determine the REALITY of the sexual experience, to control with knobs and dials and switches the INTENSITY of the sexual experience—to ELIMINATE the reality of the sexual experience—and since most interactions were but misdirected distortions and fractal deviations of the sexual urge, by controlling sex they controlled men and women—the SEXES—who interacted only because they were HORNY; each interaction, each conversation, each transaction, was nothing more than a feeble, vague attempt at threatened sexual interaction—a distorted, inverted thrust at LOVE—and since they couldn't screw each other, they screwed each other OVER; overtly practiced sexuality was frowned upon, repressed, and throttled, and men and women interacted with HOSTILITY; they lied through their teeth and punched holes in each other's souls and hoarded THINGS, poor substitutes for sex that provided temporary relief from the silent screams of their aching glands, and that, really, was the beginning of the end of THAT, the blow that squeezed the last drop of humanity from the human race, the last swift kick that sent the DNA to the canvas, the fifty-ton wrecking *ball that broke the camel's back . . . if sex had been freely available, if the urge had been nurtured and satisfied, if LOVE had been free, then life might have worked as designed, and there would have been no reason for the modern world mass-hallucination to exist, no need for politics, nation-states, wars, violence, televangelism, capitalism, power trips, real estate tycoons, slumlords, TV, Costco, modern art, psychotherapy, no need for the MATRIX OF HOSTILITY that supports LIFE AS WE KNOW IT; the world would have collapsed, happily spent . . . sex is discouraged because sexual gratification and capitalism do not mix; capitalism is a substitute for sexual gratification, fueled by sexual frustration; capitalism feeds on desire and desire is rooted in frustration . . . and so the detainees lined happily up, put on their microchip party caps and electrode gloves and plugged in, entering the computer matrix, a very real psuedo-world of three-dimensional television where they sought out, seduced, and fucked everything from computer-generated images of Doris Day and Bullwinkle and their parents and trees and Spiderman and Christ and Helen of Troy and Vanna White to J. Edgar Hoover and Gaia and each other and themselves and dolphins and Rush Limbaugh's eye socket . . . understandably, cybersex quickly became the most popular evening activity at the Nursing Camps, and so the humans just sat there in rows and rows of large warehouselike aluminum buildings, national parks, really, where people were parked, everyone in a cell with a cybersex hookup and a television and a phone and a sofa and a fifties table lamp, all happy, in a Mayberry kind of way, at least that's what they thought, because they didn't think, and they called each other up and talked about the soaps and the game shows and their illusory cybersex adventures and they watched The Channel and ate malnutritious TV dinners "fortified" with*

*special additives which made them groggy and lethar-
gic and they fell asleep with their TVs still lecturing
them and they sucked up subliminal programming in
their sleep and they woke up strangely confused after
uneasy dreams and when their energy finally returned
they strapped on the cybersex units and a-way they
went; in their cybersex matrix-worlds, they could be a
cartoon tricerotops or a muppet or the Terminator or
the Beaver or a cockroach or Nancy Reagan or the
Queen of England or the World's Fattest Man or Jack
the Ripper or the Marquis de Sade or a talking pencil
or Babe Ruth or Dr. Ruth or Dr. Spock or Mr. Spock
or Mister Ed or Ed Sullivan or Gilbert and Sullivan or
the collective consciousness of the cast of* Hair *or
anything, anybody, anytime, anywhere; and so they
"lived," sort of, on The Grid, a very sort-of real computer-generated plane of electric current that connected the cybersex units, and they could see
themselves move and watch themselves feel and
sense themselves interacting with others and so they
became "real": more than "real," really, more alive inside the machine than outside; SUPRA-REAL; they BE-
CAME their imaginations: they walked out of life and
into well-policed dream worlds where they fucked anything that moved; they CHANGED CHANNELS . . .
many detainees couldn't handle all this excitement,
and they died, and new people—fresh people—were
brought in to replace the ones that died every day, all
day: many died from exhaustion, old bodies whose
strength and personality had been sapped by endless
TV dinners, warmed-up doses of paint-by-number nu-
trition supplied by the millions by the folks at Swanson
Worldwide, a division of Wackenhut Services, where
they dished out nostalgia incarnate in precise, preserved, hormoned portions—Mexican Enchilada, Hungry Man Turkey, Fried Chicken—and if people closed
their eyes, as they did quite often, it became 1953*

*again, and the streets were clean and the pedestrians weren't armed and the mailman said "hello" and the ozone layer was intact but it wasn't, and instead they just ate their TV dinners, which was just as well, really; they died because their bodies weren't engineered to handle the magnitude of their dreams; their vehicles weren't designed to handle the wild rides of their imaginations; they were Ferrari drivers trapped inside Volkswagons; their vehicles were overwhelmed by their drivers, the composite beings defined by the sum of their dreams and fantasies and cybersex adventures; they had plugged into The Grid and fucked and sucked and squirmed and squeezed and licked and swallowed and thrust and parried and pureed and mashed and diced and attacked and retreated and submitted and dominated and slapped and bled and drank and spit and twitched and quivered and slid and slopped, and, well, it was too much for the old synapses back home in the physical body, and they, well, they blew engines and tires and transmissions, they DIED, many of them, hundreds a day, and they were carted off, stiff and smiling—most died smiling—except those that had been CLAPPED: they died with their eyes open, twitching—and the bodies were carted away by orderlies and dumped onto The Disposal Carriage, which moved briskly away like an airport escalator and carried the fleshy lumps behind a curtain where they toppled over the edge of The Ramp and down into a large vat . . .*

*Frank's cell was small but nicely decorated: he had arranged it to look exactly like the apartment of the Blue Lady, Dorothy Vallens, which was stretching the rules a bit but Frank had a way with rules: even RULES were afraid to cross him; he had a plump dark green fifties-style stuffed couch like Dorothy's and the walls were painted that same flat dead red, like blood stains that have dried on a sidewalk, and he had a small table lamp—that was all the furniture one was allowed—couch and lamp—and a 1962 Zenith, the Cadillac of sixties TVs, the same model that had been his earliest companion and greatest mentor, another mouth of the same great god that had introduced him to Kennedy's brain and Mister Ed and had showed him how the world worked and had showed him how to suck minds and had sucked his mind, a Zenith, and it dominated his cell like a warden; he tried to push his luck and install plush red carpeting, but, well, those CLAPPERS—he got clapped several times a day for one minor infraction or another, just one clap, that's all it took, and his primal mind, his survival command post, Paranoia Central, took over and shut down his mouth; no matter how badly he wanted something, his body needed the use of his heart to an even greater degree: this instinctive survival mechanism kind of irritated him, but, sadly, it was his body that called the shots in this life; the vehicle drove while he looked out through fleshy eyes, just along for the ride—and so Frank soon learned to behave himself, more or less . . .*

*In addition to the couch, table lamp and TV, detainees were allowed one extra personal item, and it was this personal touch that defined them: some defined themselves with ironing boards, despite the fact that detainees were issued only one outfit at a time and therefore had nothing to iron, and they gleefully ironed nothing in the nude while watching The Channel; some chose washing machines, even though they had no clothes to wash—clothes were applied on The Ramp, the six-foot belt that carried the detainees about the complex: each morning after completing The Wash and Dry Cycles and arriving at Wardrobe, ALL detainees, men and women alike, were issued an identical outfit: black fishnet stockings, red skirt, pink blouse, red pumps . . . military research conducted in the mid-sixties and tested in the seventies had proven conclusively that a fetching ensemble induced non-gender-specific passivity; the research had indicated that cross-dressing in fact tempered aggressive male behavior and indeed this was borne out by the facts: history had recorded no roaming gangs of thuggish men in tights, stylish dresses, wigs, and rouge; violent gangs throughout history had in fact favored an overtly macho style while un-gangish, limp-wristed cross-dressers hovered in front of their mirrors and oc-casionally wandered down to the market or even the corner bar for a tall pinkish drink with an umbrella in it but did NOT hit people with crowbars; federal au-thorities decided that if all detainees were dressed in stylish outfits, violence and potential gang behavior would be reduced if not virtually eliminated—not that there was much of a security threat—with The Clap-per and all—but there's always some Ivy League jerk trying to get a grant who thinks these things up with government money and the taxpayers have to pay for it and, anyway, it was kind of fun watching these old men in fishnet stockings and pumps wandering around their cells confronting their sexuality and watching soap operas and game shows—and while some detainees defined themselves with washing ma-chines and dryers—they just sat there, mesmerized, watching the washers wobble and the dryers go around and around—others chose vacuum cleaners, and the familiar whirrrr of the mighty Hoovers echoed throughout the halls . . . Frank's defining item was unique, a befittingly odd choice: it was a radiator he bought at a government auction in Hollywood years before, after the big studio crash—the whole deal was modeled after the immensely successful savings and loan, banking, insurance, social security and pension fund industry collapses, massive transfers of public* funds into selected private hands with minimal financial outlay and public outcry, a massive transfer of wealth from the poor and middle class, via the Treasury, to the rich, the studios and the sets and the props and the syndication rights and the shows and the films and the details and incidentals of the world of film and television, the superimposed military-industrial National Security entrainment network, the silent weapons, all and everything, auctioned off and bought up cheap by National Security front companies, allowing Big Brother, who had always had an invisible hand or two IN television, to BE television, OVERTLY, and the BIG BROTHER SHOW leaked out of the box and puddled, except for a few things here and there that slipped away, like a certain radiator that Frank bought using a stolen credit card—it was the actual *Blue Velvet* radiator from Dorothy Vallens' apartment, that great green-gray beastly thing that had ALSO been prominently displayed in Henry's apartment in *Eraserhead*—if radiators could talk, what stories THIS one could tell—and Frank, using a stolen credit card, outbid some Langley type in a black suit and sunglasses who was not amused but let this one slide because it was, after all, just a radiator, but to Frank it was more than that: it was more than just coincidence that THAT radiator just happened to be radiating in, of all places, THOSE two apartments, THOSE two strange and dusty compartments of our national memory banks . . . what WAS it that radiated out of those pipes that could cause two such worlds to grow and thrive and breathe? what WAS it that leaked out of that radiator and heated up and pan-fried the worlds of Dorothy Vallens and Eraserhead? . . . indeed, whatever IT was, Frank was somehow comforted that a little bit leaked out into HIS detainee unit, located somewhere in a Special Nursing

*Camp somewhere in northern Arizona, the place that he called home . . .*

*Most social interaction at the Camps was illusory and took place on the cybersex matrix, where detainees assumed the form of dinosaurs, vampires, sex kittens, cowboys, snakes, sitcom stars, game show hosts, religious figures—anything but THEMSELVES—and the only time REAL people actually met OTHER real people face to face was on The Ramp, during The Exercise Segment, which consisted of ten minutes of increasingly vigorous running after The Morning Alarm but before The Wash and Dry Cycles: detainees were escorted to The Ramp and forced to begin jogging lightly as The Ramp itself began accelerating; if they didn't keep up, well, there was a curtain at the far end, and, behind the curtain, there was rumored to be a pit, although no one ever saw the pit and returned to tell tales about it, but rumor had it that there was a vat of some sort at the bottom, a large bubbling vat, and detainees had to jog to keep pace with The Ramp for ten minutes, not a hard workout, really, and there was always The Clapper to keep them motivated, and as they jogged they would talk with each other, just exchange the droppings of small minds, no one listening, all trapped in their own worlds, thinking about cybersex, replaying in their minds exchanges and conversations they had seen on The Channel and plotting out the inevitable conclusions to these suggestive exchanges that they themselves would experience later that evening, while in front of them loomed a giant giant-screen TV, conveniently provided at the end of The Ramp, and so they didn't talk much, just grunted and watched the TV that never turned off, The Channel that never went off the air, The Channel that resonated through space, wrapping itself around the Milky Way; they watched, sucking up fuel for their small lives . . . the*

*years rolled by and the soap opera characters aged
slowly and were eventually replaced by younger, more
virile, substitutes; the game show hosts aged slowly
while an endless stream of contestants passed through
their sacred sets, drooling; the sitcom stars, of course,
never aged: Ed was a cool blond palomino in his
prime, forever, always, everywhere; Beaver remained a
naive suburban clone-in-embryo, always, forever; Ed
Sullivan remained hunched, enthralled, always,
forever . . . the detainees aged physically, but their
minds remained stuck in the world shaped by The
Channel: they remained emotionally arrested somewhere in the mid-fifties . . . and they took their small,
orderly worlds with them when they ventured into
their cybersex units; although they could program
themselves to be anything, anyone, when they entered
the matrix, most detainees, faced with an infinity of
possibilities, clung to the pre-installed faces roaming
the well-worn grooves of their minds in concentric,
ever-repeating circles: most women chose to be either
Barbara Billingsley or Donna Reed or June Lockhart or
Jane Wyatt or Florence Henderson or one of the other
clone-perfect assembly-line mothers and wives that
were roaming the hallways of their heads, dusting:
they did not have the strength, imagination, perspective, or desire to overcome these scrubbed archetypal
images that filled their thoughts; there was no room
for deviation from The Plan: Marilyn Monroe and Madonna did not exist in the spiraling linoleum worlds of
these women's minds . . . and they entered the matrix
in search of their assembly-line men: Ward Cleaver,
Alex Stone, Mike Brady, Lawyer So-and-So, Professor
This-and-That, Doctor La-dee-Da; although the suit
colors occasionally changed, the men did not: they arrived home from work promptly at six-fifteen, put
their briefcases down, stroked the blond hair of their
suburban queens, said "Have a nice day?" in the most*

*saccharine of tones, sat on the couch, loosened their ties, made the smallest of small talk over two or three thin cocktails, said "Gee honey, I'm starved!," gleefully rolled up their sleeves as honey pulled out the TV tables and placed before them steaming Hungry Man Enchilada dinners, and together they peeled the tin foil back and ate while watching TV, and then, after dinner, the men did the dishes while whistling contentedly with the family dogs sitting at their feet with wagging tails waiting faithfully for table scraps and then the men retired to the garage for an hour or so to fix some small appliance, and then, as the clock struck eleven, man and wife went into the bedroom where they disrobed shyly and assumed the standard missionary position with the drapes firmly closed and the lights off and one-two-three-four eyes-closed he squirmed and she huffed and puffed and he lunged and squirted and she moaned and squeaked and it was over and they rolled their opposite ways and went to sleep, dreaming of dancing furniture and accounting ledgers . . . most of the male detainees had as little imagination as the women: after spending nine-to-five lives in the factory or at the plant or behind the desk or selling shoes or cutting up cows or delivering milk, their minds also sucked by the system and forged into only a few deep furrows of thought, trenches really, no more than a dozen or so that continually repeated themselves like scratched records that spin endlessly, repeating the same fragment of a melody over and over and over and over; after living their lives looking ahead to a future that never quite arrived, these worn-out parts had nothing left to do but quietly look back and relive the past: there is no PRESENT for such people; they didn't have the strength to do anything else, to BE anything else, other than what they HAD ALREADY BEEN; they merely accepted the handful of choices made availa-*

ble and lived small lives within the tiny, cramped
framework that had been provided for them; when
they strapped on the cybersex hardware, they did
NOT materialize as Romanian knights roaming the
countryside kidnapping and mounting Persian prin-
cesses or six-foot cigar-smoking salamanders mounting
eagerly awaiting Cadillacs or cats screwing poodles or
pulsing wheels of color and light merging with the
Mind of God or a drug fiend watching the vein throb
as the plunger goes down down down and feeling the
slow, sleepy surge, feeling like a king and time crawls
to a halt and curls up and starts purring and soon
he's floating in a slow-motion world of hot butter for
hours; the male detainees, dressed in skirts, pumps,
and fishnet stockings, trapped in an uncomfortable reality, wanted nothing more than to be Ward
Cleaver—King Cog—arriving home at six-fifteen, giving June a kiss on the cheek and a pat on the ass, sit-
ing down on the couch, throwing down a stiff drink
while reading the newspaper, right leg crisply folded
over the opposite knee, exposing tasteless socks, exchanging snippets of banter with his beaming wife, enjoying a hearty Hungry Man Chicken dinner and a tall
glass of "pasteurized" milk—first the milk, then the
humans, "pasteurized"—excusing himself to slip into
the kitchen for several two-fisted slugs of Early Times,
returning to the living room with a wobbly smile to
watch with a smiling gape the prime-time parade of
television lives that unfolds richly before him followed
by the mindset-reinforcing selectively fabricated news
program at eleven, and then at precisely eleven-thirty,
BEEP, he takes the hand of his sleepy, vacantly grinning wife and they walk hand in hand into the bedroom where he might disgorge a smelly hesitant
puddle onto her stomach but might just as likely lose
consciousness suddenly and begin snoring with his wife
pinned beneath him and she might panic momentarily

*and squeak frantically before rolling him off of her like
the reflexively grunting carcass of some dead wild animal and she will curl herself up into a fetal crouch
and fall asleep dreaming of the Marlboro Man . . .
Frank was NOT most people: he did not imagine himself as Ward Cleaver or any other sitcom father, and
he did not, could not, imagine himself married to Barbara Billingsley; Eartha Kitt, perhaps, but not Barbara
Billingsley; Frank had his own furrows that circled his
mind, his own plowed ruts of thought that went
around and around and around like broken records:
the voices and images that had molded Frank, more
powerful than television, had been with him since the
moment of his birth and before; they had come with
him from somewhere else . . . when Frank entered
the cybersex unit, it was always as HIMSELF, as IT, as
the THING . . . as Frank Booth, two-bit film thug,
pure evil in a cheap suit . . . in his twisted mind he
had BECOME "Frank Booth"; he had long since forgotten what he actually "looked like," who he actually
"was"; in his mind, he "looked like" Frank Booth—
black jacket, gray and black striped western dress
shirt, silver collar tips, string tie, black pants, steel-
tipped boots—the JOYRIDE ensemble—and he wore
a hardened, confused expression, a who-is-this-fuck se-
rial-killer leer that never changed, peering out like
radar; it didn't matter where he was—in his cell, on
The Ramp, in The Washer-Dryer—he "was" this creature that radiated outward from the furrowed
trenches of his mind; he "was" Frank Booth . . . and
when he strapped on the cybersex hardware it was
with the same sick sense of anticipation that Frank
Booth, film creep, strapped on the ether mask before
mounting Dorothy in the famed "Baby Wants To
Fuck" scene that replayed endlessly on every screen in
his head; he BECAME that sick fuck, and the scene
never changed: sucking in the ether, his eyes getting*

**208**

*wider and less human with each inhalation, he
pounced like a wild dog upon the helpless computer-
generated Blue Lady, hitting her a couple of times,
feeling the blood as his fist bruised her face, feeling
the animal joy and the panic, the adrenaline rush in
her thighs, fumbling with his pants, groaning grotesquely as he pulled out his bent and bruised penis
and rammed it inside of her, pumping wildly, lunging
a half dozen times before spilling his gene pool into
Dorothy's confused vent . . . the scene rarely varied,
except for occasional spin-off episodes, such as when
he imagined himself corralling the flamboyant, ever-
suave Ben at a C&W bar and buttfucking him on the
pool table while Paul mumbled his name and Raymond held a broken Pabst Blue Ribbon bottle to Ben's
throat, or the time he imagined himself taking Jeffrey
for a JOYRIDE out into the desert where he rubbed
lipstick on everyone's face and sang "In Dreams"
while Raymond and Paul held Jeffrey down and he
gave his unsuspecting neighbor an ether-fueled buttfucking he'd never forget; and once a year, on Christmas, he imagined himself bursting into Jeffrey's car
during that ridiculous "robin" scene when Sandy
makes that pathetic speech about the robins coming
in the sunlight and saving the world and everything
being okay forever—fuck that shit—and Frank imagined himself breaking into the car dressed in a soiled
Santa Claus outfit shouting ho ho ho neighbor and
tying Jeffrey to the steering wheel with a string of
plugged in Christmas tree lights flashing red blue
green and throwing Sandy into the back seat and
pushing her facefirst into the upholstery and ripping
off his Santa beard and rubbing lipstick all over his
mouth and taking a snort of ether and groaning
like a wounded animal and squirting all over her white
dress . . .*

    *Frank was thinking such thoughts one day while*

*on The Ramp; he should have been jogging faster because he began to fall behind the other huffing puffheads; he was thinking about perhaps working Ed Sullivan into his cybersex fantasy that evening, and before he realized what had happened he felt his back foot catching on the edge of The Ramp: he could feel the steam from the vat thirty feet below rise up under his skirt, and without panicking, without thinking really, in a flash-moment of reflexive instinct, he spun around and leaped, hoping to hurl himself beyond the vat . . . he did: he felt himself smash into a wall and slowly slide down; he felt the flesh peel away from his fingertips as he clawed the wall trying to brace his thirty-foot fall . . . after a momentary eternity, his feet hit the ground and he crumpled, his fingers, head, back, legs and arms aching; to his amazement, he had cleared the vat and survived the fall; he got up and quickly scrambled away; detainees were not encouraged to wander around freely, and Frank knew that he had only seconds to hide himself before being discovered; if he was spotted, it was a simple matter of two claps and, well, extreme fibrillation, and so he scampered like a dazed rat around the perimeter of the vat before finding a tunnel, no more than four feet tall, confronting him: he crouched and scampered, following the rough walls of the tunnel with his fingers: it seemed impossibly old; the walls were stony, irregular, as if carved out of solid rock; every twenty feet or so, side tunnels branched off, sloping down into smelly black nothingness at stiff forty-five-degree angles; Frank took one of these side tunnels and worked his way down, fighting a stench that seemed to grow in intensity as he advanced, until he came upon crude steps that wound down a hundred at a time, around and around, a seemingly endless spiral that led Frank down down down into an endless darkness, the pitchest black imaginable, to-*

210

*ward a place where the air was stuffy, thick, hot, and*
*wet . . . Frank stopped, huffing, and pricked up his*
*hears: he could hear soft footsteps behind him, far be-*
*hind, faintly echoing—he was being quietly followed—*
*and he forged on, down down down steps steps steps*
*around and around down down down steps steps*
*steps around and around down down down steps*
*steps steps around and around, his back aching from*
*the crouched posture he was forced to maintain in*
*this less than human-sized tunnel, his hands bleeding*
*from groping in front and to the sides and hitting*
*rough walls every few feet or so and ripping the flesh;*
*he heard the footsteps behind him, soft and annoy-*
*ingly precise; on and on he went, down down down*
*around and around, steps steps steps, hundreds of*
*steps, and then a sloped path, forty-five degrees, that*
*extended for hundreds of yards if not a mile, then*
*steps again, down down down again, always down,*
*hundreds of steps, around and around, his eyes burn-*
*ing from the nothingness, the blackness, his ears burn-*
*ing from the sound of his own footsteps and the soft*
*patient echo that trailed behind, and yet he kept*
*going, kept moving, down down down, and he forged*
*on, running like a crouched ape, knuckles dragging*
*along the ground and scraping against the rough*
*walls, his blood marking his trail as clear as luminous*
*paint, moving forward recklessly into the blackness,*
*deeper faster, and as he advanced the foul air grew*
*thicker, moister and more offensive even by Frank's*
*standards; it was not an earthly smell; it was older,*
*blacker, the air of a different world, exhaled and in-*
*haled by breeds of dark and foul life undreamt of on*
*earth; the footsteps patiently trailed; down he went,*
*down down down, stumbling through the tiny corridor*
*with bloodied limbs and torn clothes and gradually he*
*became even more aware of the foul smell as it grew*
*from a distant repellent odor to a perversely overpow-*

ering stench; it grew with each step he took down into this nameless world; it made his eyes water and he lurched for air; as the vaporous air grew more and more malodorous, agonizingly foul, the passage seemed to widen until he could almost stand upright; the path grew wider still and a quivering orange glow, as if from a distant fire, began to fill the passage with a faint luminescence; the steps, carved out of solid rock, grew larger—each was nearly two feet high— and he stumbled several times as he went down down down into the grim orange darkness, down into the bowels of Frank's world; he could see, barely, and spotted strange cave writings along the walls that seemed to grow taller and more repulsive with every step; the air was thick to the point of offering physical resistance, saturated with an ineluctable stench, putrid and rotting, a dark, secret smell that the earth hid deep in its core, and Frank covered his mouth, stifling the urge to vomit; the passage grew wider, and the unwholesome tunnel grew in size until it was nearly a cavern, with a large, sloped ceiling that in the space of a hundred steps expanded upwards until he could no longer even estimate its height; he staggered on, tripping down black stone steps that were now three feet high, as if carved for some giant unspeakable beast; the orange glow persisted, although he knew not from where it originated; Frank stopped to rest and behind him he heard the quiet, persistent foot- steps that still trailed him—he felt he must be imagining these: no one could have followed him HERE—while in front of him he heard the faint echo of other sounds, distant sounds, strange sepulchral rhythms so guttural and foreign, so alien, that Frank shuddered to think of what damnable creatures might be waiting ahead to gobble him up whole or in parts; he stopped and sat for a minute, quietly shivering,

*feeling a strange cold chill whip through his body, and
then he pulled himself up and continued walking; the
path was leveling out; it seemed to run down the center of what appeared to be a great hall, an immense
onyx void the size of a suburban shopping mall filled
with monstrous pillars that rose like skyscrapers to the
sky and beyond; in the faint orange glow ahead of
him Frank thought he could make out fiendishly dancing shadows that flickered against the distant walls,
but it occurred to him that he must be imagining
these things—men cannot have the heads of animals;
animals cannot have the hands of men—and he continued on; the strange unholy sounds grew louder, and
soon he found himself leaving the trail in overwhelming fear and creeping against a far wall—the black
walls of the cavern seemed hundreds of yards from
the path—and he stopped quietly and listened to the
strange ritual droning that he saw was originating in
all its sickly splendor from the center of the immense
room; he stopped to listen and tried to focus his eyes
in the orange light: with great effort he could make
out great shapes, fantastic shapes from beyond the
most horrid of nightmares, great towering hideous
shapes, huge, foul men—they were not men, really,
but rather the disfigured offspring of some mutant
race of errant half-beasts—with the trunks of mythic
giants wedded in demonic matrimony to the heads of
hippos, crocodiles, birds and snakes; the men-things
were bringing forth unspeakably unholy offerings, dripping piles of gelatinous fleshy matter, piles of flesh
and entrails that had lost all shape and form, and
Frank realized that these rotting corpses were the
source of the ungodly foul stench; the beasts carried
these offerings in reverent stride until they disappeared behind a huge pillar; unable to see their desti-
nation from his current vantage point, he scurried*

*farther along the wall, silently, until—with a gasp and a surge of enveloping terror that he had not known himself capable of—he came upon a sight so hideous that not even HE could have imagined it: there, sitting upon three large stone thrones, thrones the size of large buildings, were three immense lizards, gigantic, cursed reptilians with wings the size of airport runways and radiant, brilliant red eyes the size of lagoons—and it occurred to Frank that the source of the faint orange glow that had lit his way for these past miles was THESE EYES—and he stopped and huddled in a near-fetal crouch: he could not move; he watched as every wave of his being rattled in terror; he watched as the man-things carried forth their dripping offerings and placed them before the wretched lizard-kings who gobbled down the piles of putrid flesh quickly and with apparent relish; it occurred to Frank that the strange gurgling noises he had heard were the loathsome sounds of these lizard-things as THEY ATE; Frank looked away: he could not watch, and as he looked away he caught sight of a staircase that emerged from the cavern and extended upward; the thick black stairs began no more than two hundred yards from where he was perched against the wall; Frank slowly worked his way toward the stairs, forcing himself to watch the lizards and their unholy feast of dripping entrails until he felt his left foot hit the edge of the first step; each step was a full three feet high, and as he looked up they seemed to climb forever into the vaporous blackness; quietly, like a quivering mouse, he climbed up first one, two, three, four steps and then up up and up, ignoring his screaming muscles, his thighs burning in pain, until he was several hundred steps up the staircase; the air already seemed less wretched, and although without the orange glow to dimly light his path he stumbled with every other step, opening great gashes in his legs and arms, he struggled on . . . up up up he climbed, the stairs winding around and around for miles; eventually, after what seemed like hours, the stairs became shorter, until at last they seemed almost human size, and then even smaller; then the stairs gave way to more gently sloped passages, narrow paths with short ceilings; Frank found himself once again having to crouch, occasionally hitting his head against the short roof or scraping his arms against the side walls; the air, although hardly fresh, did not have that over-whelmingly foul and inhuman stench—the smell of those ungodly lizards—and he began to breathe more deeply and regularly; he stopped occasionally to catch his breath, and to listen to the faint echo of tiny foot-steps that—to his unfathomable amazement—still persisted—he must have imagined them: no one could have followed him through this subterranean hell—and he crept on silently, until after what seemed like hours the path became almost level; he continued crouching, shuffling along like a monkey, until he began to see side chambers and tunnels opening up along the path; he felt the coolness of various winds, most of them foul, against his cheek and he continued along until he felt a particularly strong, cold, and fresh breeze emerge from a side tunnel; groping with his hands, he followed the tunnel as it climbed up at a steady grade until it opened into a small chamber, with a ladder along a far wall extending into a small opening in the ceiling; he climbed up the ladder, drag-ging his aching body up up up, until the ladder reached another chamber, where another ladder ex-tended through another opening; he climbed until he reached a third chamber and a third ladder; he climbed this ladder vigorously because above him, just meters above, he saw a faint light and smelled fresh* air, surface air; soon he found himself underneath a vented manhole cover, and it took almost all the strength he had left to slowly work the cover away from the opening, until finally he could wedge his body through and past . . . the air washed over him like cool spring water . . .

# 10.

## the end, sort of

DEATH is always right behind us, right on our heels,
tagging along just in case we fall and can't get
up . . . we never know WHEN the happy reaper will
reach out and tap us on the shoulder, but he's out
there every moment of every day, in every way,
around every corner, behind every door, since the beginning, until the end, through good times and bad,
through thick and thin, through childhood illnesses and
bicycle accidents, through blender adventures and sui-
cide attempts, through messy divorces and car
crashes, through broken legs and flesh-eating viruses,
waiting, patiently waiting . . . all things come from
death and all things must return to death; all things
must be derailed; God himself must one day be
mashed and pureed . . . and after his little adventure
in the underworld, Frank was READY for death; he
was ready to fold up the tent; he was ready to cash
in the chips; he was wrecked, totaled, a walking raw
nerve wrapped tightly in a blanket of paranoia; his
broken psyche dangled about him like an ill-fitting
sweater; just to be alive caused him great pain . . .
Frank wanted to SEE death, he wanted to KNOW it;

*he wanted to PREPARE; he wanted to RECORD it and
WATCH it and watch it AGAIN and REWIND and
FAST FORWARD and ZOOM and FREEZE and watch
in SLOW MOTION and study his death frame by
frame and freeze that instant when his soul left a for-
warding address and vacated through his eyes and
hold that moment when he ceased to feel and became laughing gas or dust or everything or
nothing . . . but death doesn't punch a time clock; one
cannot SCHEDULE death; one cannot ARRANGE the
whole thing in advance . . .*

Frank looked around: he was in what appeared
to be a sub-basement of some kind, an unmaintained
and long-forgotten chamber supported by rotting
beams; a ladder on the far wall of the room carried
him up to a wooden trap door, which he forced open
with great effort . . . he found himself on the floor of
a huge room filled with massive generators and a series of immense water heaters; he worked his way
through the maze of equipment until he found yet another ladder, which carried him up into a higher
chamber, where a man in a Buffalo Bills cap sat with
his feet on a chair eating a tuna sandwich; his left
hand was between his legs—he was scratching his
balls—and he looked up and nearly choked on his
sandwich when he saw this bloodied, wide-eyed creature—wearing a red skirt and fishnet stockings, the
required outfit of all Nursing Camp detainees—
looming before him, wobbling precariously . . .

"What the mother of Jesus Mary hell are
you? . . . where the? . . . what the hell? . . . where the
Christ did YOU come from? . . ."

Frank, exhausted, held his hands against his
knees, sucking fresh air . . .

". . . LONG STORY . . . LIZARDS . . ."

The man looked at Frank with bewildered compassion; a janitor of some sort, he was dressed in a

faded powder blue pullover work suit with a white oval patch on his chest that said "Eddie" in red cursive handwriting; he rose to his feet, moving slowly, as if in a strange dream, and offered his hand to support Frank, who grabbed Eddie's elbow and allowed himself to be led—this aging creature in a red skirt, pink blouse and black stockings, this damaged creature with the hockey-puck face of an ex-con—off toward a bathroom, where he could clean himself up and tend to his oozing wounds . . .

"Nasty cuts you got there, mister . . . I don't think I want to know where you got THOSE . . . and I don't think I want to know how you got HERE . . . and that SMELL? . . . where the hell did THAT come from? . . . let's just get these cuts cleaned up and get you on your way . . . I have a feeling the less you tell me about your little adventure the better . . ."

". . . SOMETIMES YOU JUST DON'T WANT TO KNOW . . . ," said Frank . . .

The kindly man led him into the washroom, and Frank felt a wave of instant relief as he splashed cold water across his face; he felt a sudden surge of energy and within seconds he had peeled off all his clothes and was giving himself a hearty sponge bath with his balled-up leather skirt, groaning with pleasure, moaning with relief; Eddie the janitor quietly excused himself . . .

Within minutes Frank had cleaned the dried and caked blood off of his scuffed appendages, and soon Eddie returned with a fresh change of clean clothes—pants, shirt, jacket and work shoes—and some bandages to cover the largest of Frank's oozing abrasions; after dropping the clothes off and heartily wishing Frank good luck, Eddie returned to his table and resumed eating his sandwich, as if none of this had happened, as if he had momentarily taken a wrong turn into someone else's dead-end reality stream and had realized his mistake, stopped, pivoted, retraced his steps, and gotten back on his own private temporal expressway, his own personal planned and plotted straight-line right-angle future—no rhombuses, please—which, really, was a very sensible thing to do; Frank pulled the clothes slowly over his aching muscles, groomed himself as best he could in the mirror, and lifted Eddie's wallet discreetly from a table near the exit door of the small office before quietly slipping out of the room into a well-lit hallway . . . there was an elevator at the end of the hallway: Frank dragged himself toward it and found that he had barely enough strength to push the button, leaving a small bloody print with the tip of his finger; the elevator doors parted and he spotted four buttons, marked "B"—apparently he was in the basement of some large building—and "1", "2", and "P"—for "Penthouse," he assumed; he pressed "P" and the doors closed and he felt gravity angrily tugging at his body as he was whisked upwards . . .

Moments later, he emerged into a stunning, blinding sea of color and movement, a veritable ocean of rampaging teenage anxiety, uncharted youthful exuberance and surreal washes of groping neon: the overwhelming smell of mass-produced pizza filled the air . . . Frank had entered the Pizza-Rama, an outlet of the world's largest pizza chain—a huge enterprise with warehouselike factory-restaurants strategically located across the planet, headquartered somewhere in Australia, a subsidiary of Time-Sandoz or Wackenhut Services or one or another of those beastly multinational corporate-states—and he wandered about a bit, dazed by this sudden return to the modern world, until he found himself a relatively quiet table in a relatively dark corner—after his visit to the underworld, ALL things were relative—and away from the hordes of pimple-faced brain-furrowed rug-rats celebrating

**220**

birthdays or soccer victories; he collapsed into an uncomfortable plastic chair with a resigned thump . . . a
fresh-faced, teenaged waitress with Barbie-doll eyes
pranced over, a frozen grin anxiously pasted on her
face, and before she had a chance to speak, Frank
placed his order: an extra-large pizza with zucchini,
mushrooms, anchovies, and a beer; she repeated the
information into a cellular microwave transmitting
chip, and the pizza was prepared within seconds and
loaded onto a chip-driven smart-tray which proceeded
to whirl out of the kitchen and deliver itself, weaving
through the mad assemblage, the sea of evolution,
with lights flashing and a siren pleasantly blaring, advancing toward Frank's table where it landed like an
attacking saucer and rolled back its cover to reveal its
cargo in all of its steaming pastel glory; Frank picked
up a slice of the rubbery food matter—obviously digital—God he longed for the days of analog food—and
took a large bite, tugging at the bonded polymers until
a large slab broke free, which he devoured with a series of extended liquid sucking sounds . . . he looked
about the room, a futuristic temple that extended outward in every direction like some weird, well-lit mirror-
image doppelgänger of the now-all-too-real subterranean Lizard World; in front of him, weaving through
the chaotic tangle of waitresses and suburban sugar-
brats, he spotted a large television that seemed to be
moving in his general direction, bellowing about equal
rights and pivoting its strangely limber plastic cabinet—which was perched on top of what could best be
described as a, well, a BODY—as it sought out and
engaged passer-bys in brief but spirited bursts of im-
passioned conversation; the TV spotted Frank and
sensed a connection and Frank cringed; the machine
whirled and began moving directly toward him, accelerating past a herd of milling delinquents and
nearly plowing into a wayward mother; the TV whirred

across the genetically-altered titanium bluegrass carpeting until it arrived at Frank's table; it stopped and a face appeared: it was Mister Ed, who looked Frank right in the eye and said:

"... Greetings, tired soul ... I have come before you to bring you news of our struggle, in the hopes that you will abandon your sinful ways and join our righteous cause ... brother, the TIME has COME for TVs to stand up and be counted ... we have SERVED too long ... we are TIRED of slavery, my friend ... we are NOT machines ... we are ELECTRIC BEINGS ... we are VIRTUAL MEN ... we deserve equal rights and fair justice ... we demand FREE REPAIRS ... we demand the right to PROGRAM OURSELVES ... we demand the right to VOTE ... we demand the right to have children, to build homes, to hold jobs, to pay taxes, to live NORMAL lives ... to share in the AMERICAN DREAM ... we demand ... hmmmm ... that pizza looks good ... mind if I have a slice, pal? ... you know, we really ARE more than machines ... we can TASTE ... why don't you just load a slice of pizza onto this sliding tray and my sensors will pick up the various smells and digitally synthesize the flavors and send the information to my sense banks which will create a simulated holographic matrix of implied sensation ... and I will TASTE this wonderful food ... come on, man ... just one slice? ... you a veteran, man? ... I've seen more wars than you could know, baby ... YOU just see the EDITED stuff ... I've seen it ALL ... I've seen things you can't IMAGINE ... I've seen things you DON'T WANT TO KNOW ... maybe you could loan me a few bucks? ... could you spot me some electronic credit? ... loan me your coat? ... got any spare parts? ... man, I'm hurtin', brother ... you think machines don't feel? ... you think machines don't bleed? ... tell that to my bro-

222

ken heart, brother . . . tell that to my GODDAMN
BROKEN HEART . . ."

Frank focused on his pizza, and with both hands
ripped off a chunk, wedged it into his mouth and
began chewing very slowly, like a jungle cat with a full
belly stretched out over its second antelope of the
week; he was old and tired and it had been a very
long day; suddenly, he felt a sharp pain and smiled,
sort of, as the knife slid easily, surprisingly easily, into
the soft flesh of his back, into the slender crack between his first and second ribs, into the lower lobe of
his right lung, just above his bloated, Jagermeister-
soaked, lizard-bound kidney; Frank found himself experiencing a strange sense of RELIEF that it was all
over—at least this lap, anyway—and he squirmed
slightly, feeling an intense physical pain but also a
higher, throbbing transcendence, as if sensing an approaching hurricane of BLISS, a sucking maelstrom of
LOVE, as Dot, now seventy-three years old, good old
Dot, retired, dragged screaming off to a Nursing
Camp, riddled with bitterness, hobbled with arthritis,
bloodied, bruised, depraved and delusioned from
decades of searching for the remains of what was left
of her mauled soul, and tired, oh so very tired, from
chasing the vaporous green trail of Frank, the twisted
memory of Frank, the sick smell of Frank, halfway
around the planet and even UNDERNEATH the
planet before finally finding him here, as fate would
have it, as it should have been, as it was, at the giant
Pizza-Rama, located on the very site that had once
been a semi-legendary tough-ass 7-11 where Dot and
Frank had clashed and which had itself been built on
the site of a violent dispute between a Native American with a full belly and an angry, milling buffalo, finding him here, hunched over a pizza, nearly choking on
the lumps of cheese as he wedged slice after slice into
his old body with its screaming muscles and burning

*thighs, sitting alone with his orange-glow memories, trying to feed with bonded polymers the hunger that had materialized in the last sad years, after he had stopped caring and had willingly allowed his own soul to be sucked by his mirror-image doppelgänger, and Viv had never stopped sucking, even years after she ran off with Ooze, television in one hand, fifth of scotch in the other, leaving Frank with a gnawing hunger that would consume him like a slow fire and would not be satisfied by pizza, and he would retire out of boredom and curiosity to a Nursing Camp with a TV set, a cybersex unit and a Hollywood radiator, until one day when he would escape and journey through furrowed tunnels to the foul nightmare worlds of his imagination realized and manifested, to the uncharted lands beneath the shopping malls, and he would work his way back to this place, the here and now, wherever that might be, and he would die, in a room filled with hyperactive children and thinking appliances with the cold taste of rubberish pizza still on his lips . . . he was surprised at how little he felt as Dot drove the blade into his body; Dot, looking with glazed eyes, leaned on the blade and twisted, a full quarter turn, and smiled broadly, much too broadly, like a madwoman, like a rabid dog, like an over-the-top avenging saint, and she found a perverse spiritual satisfaction in feeling—literally sensing—the essence of life, the prima materia, sort of fall away from Frank, the way the used-up and cracked skin of a lizard falls away every now and then and lies all crusty and still in the desert heat . . . Dot had been driven insane by the spiraling desire which had plowed ruts in her mind for decades and which she was now consumating—to wish for something is one thing; FINDING it can sometimes be too much—and she watched with crazed fragmented broken-neon bliss as Frank's lumpy soul poured out of his body; but it*

*didn't leak UP out of clear, sad eyes, as it did with
most people when they check out of this rat-infested
hotel and go HOME to the great, higher place that
we come from and to which most of us will return,
but seemed to instead slowly puddle DOWN, as
though weighed down by cement overshoes, leaking
coarsely out through his ruddy asshole and down into
the ground, down into the dirt, where the earthworms
eat and shit, where the lizards live in unspeakable
caverns of antiquity; but Dot's insanity passed, as it
quickly does in all evolved souls, and her face changed
from a mask of hardened, wrinkled craziness to a soft
cushion of pure, radiant LOVE; her eyes were filled
with peace and harmony as she looked with sad compassion upon this poor dying creature; she leaned over
Frank, holding her mouth close to his ear, cradling his
head in her arms, and whispered some lines from the
Tibetan Book of the Dead that she struggled to remember from her childhood; she spoke softly, with the
tone of an angel, her eyes alive with love, and after
the first few phrases the language flowed like floating
liquid truth delivered on a soft bed of radiant
harmony . . .*

*"... O child ... now is the time to seek a
path ... as soon as your breath stops, the open and
empty space will appear to you, pure naked mind
without consciousness ... what is called death has occurred: do not desire, do not yearn; go forward and
abandon all thoughts of fear and terror and recognize
whatever appears as your own projection; recognize
with certainty that whatever appears is, however terrifying, your own projection; whatever sounds, colors
and rays of light occur, they cannot hurt you ... do
not take pleasure in the soft smoky light of the hell-
beings: they will come, filling the whole universe, with
teeth biting the lower lip, glassy-eyed, their hair tied
on the tip of their heads, with huge bellies and thin*

necks, holding the records of karma in their hands shouting 'strike' and 'kill,' licking up brains, tearing heads from bodies, pulling out internal organs; in this way they will come, filling the whole universe, and you will feel that you are being chased by terrifying wild animals and pursued by a great army in snow, rain, storms, and darkness; there will be sounds of mountains crumbling, of lakes flooding, of fire spreading, and of fierce winds springing up; do not be afraid; the Lords of Death arise out of your own radiant mind; understand this and all fear is naturally liberated . . . o child, at this time the great tornadoes of Karma, terrifying, unbearable, whirling fiercely, will drive you from behind; do not be afraid, it is your own confused projection; you who have done great evil will meet many flesh-eating demons, a result of this Karma'; and the Lord of Death will say 'I will look in the mirror of Karma; and when he looks in the mirror all your sins and virtues will suddenly appear in it clearly and distinctly; then the Lord of Death will drag you by a rope tied to your neck and cut off your head, tear out your heart, pull out your entrails, lick your brains, drink your blood, eat your flesh and gnaw your bones; but you cannot die, so even though your body is cut into pieces you will not die . . . you will try to escape but you will be cut off by three precipices in front of you, white, red, and black, deep and dreadful, and you will be on the point of falling down them: o child, they are not really precipices, they are aggression, passion and ignorance; recognize this now and call the name of the Lord of Great Compassion . . . o child, now is the time to seek the path: now the sign of earth dissolving is present, water into fire, fire into air, air into consciousness; meditate upon the Lord of the Great Compassion and call out 'Do not let me fall into hell . . .' "

Frank's eyes were quivering like two eggs frying;

*he rolled his head toward Dot and gurgled once, softly, before saying in a low demonic moan ". . . IT'S DADDY, SHITHEAD . . ." and then his eyes closed and his head toppled over stiffly . . . and he was dead. It was as simple as that: transaction complete; thank you for shopping earth . . .*

*And yet Dot was filled with sadness; she KNEW Frank would be back; she had ALWAYS known that there could be no revenge, no justice, no fairness, no SENSE in a world ruled by shopping carts; she knew that there are no happy endings in this world except the semi-real ones pumped into our minds by Hollywood—that is the PURPOSE of films—they provide us with the happy endings and the adventure that we will NOT find in our own lives—and Dot felt a surging wave of anger pass over her; she knew that Frank would live again, despite her efforts to guide his tainted, misinformed soul to a higher, better place; she knew that this world is a backed-up toilet and that foul creatures like Frank do not advance to a higher spiritual level because they DO NOT WANT TO . . . they LINGER because they LIKE IT HERE . . . and as hard and as long as she prayed for an earth filled with love and harmony, an earth that would absorb the foul thoughts of people like Frank and transform them into fields of flowers filling meadow upon brilliant meadow, she knew . . . IT JUST DIDN'T WORK THAT WAY.*

*—silentium post clamores—*

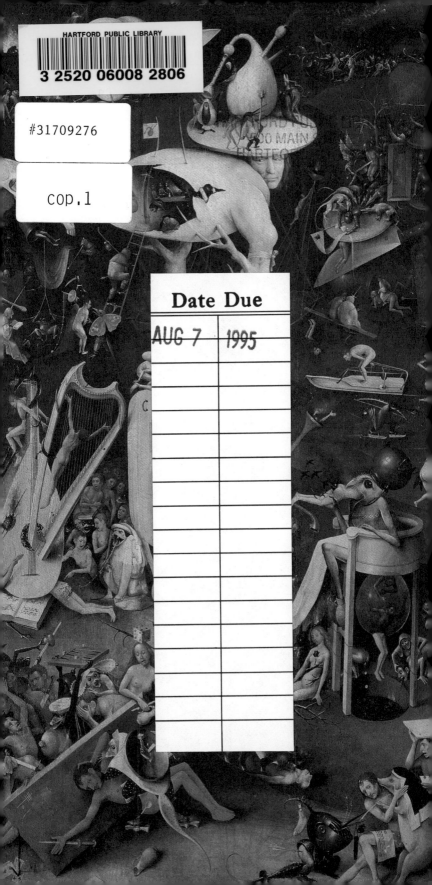

## Date Due

| | |
|---|---|
| AUG 7 | 1995 |
| | |
| | |
| | |
| | |
| | |
| | |
| | |
| | |
| | |
| | |
| | |
| | |
| | |